A BIG FAT MESS

I began to wonder whether I'd made a colossal mistake by plunking down my severance pay as a down payment on this program. What kind of looney tunes place is this?

"Is torture by food *du jour* included in our 2K a week?" I whispered to Evelyn.

She shrugged. "He's just showing us that we have to change our eating ways," she said. "Dr. Hoffman says we fatties have to totally reprogram our brains."

Reprogram sounded like a cult term. Hopefully they didn't serve Diet Kool-Aid in the dining room. Cult or no, I was stuck with this place now. Durham's Channel Twelve was expecting me to produce my weight loss series here. Maybe I could turn the whole assignment into an exposé. That'd be a much more interesting story than watching my thighs disappear. . . .

"MORE FUN THAN AN EXPLODING WHOOPIE PIE! When plus-size and out-of-work news producer Kate Gallagher heads for Durham, North Carolina, the 'Diet Capital of the World,' to take up residence at a diet clinic, she finds more than low-cal meals and fellow dieters. Instead, the plucky heroine is introduced to a dead diet doctor with a love for S and M, dueling diet clinics, and more suspects than she can shake a carrot stick at, not to mention a charming detective who finds Kate delightfully delicious."

—Sue Ann Jaffarian, author of *Too Big to Miss* and *The Curse of the Holy Pail*

DYING TO BE THIN

A Fat City Mystery

Kathryn Lilley

AN OBSIDIAN MYSTERY

OBSIDIAN

Published by New American Library, a division of
Penguin Group (USA) Inc., 375 Hudson Street,
New York, New York 10014, USA

Penguin Group (Canada), 90 Eglinton Avenue East, Suite 700, Toronto,
Ontario M4P 2Y3, Canada (a division of Pearson Penguin Canada Inc.)
Penguin Books Ltd., 80 Strand, London WC2R 0RL, England
Penguin Ireland, 25 St. Stephen's Green, Dublin 2,
Ireland (a division of Penguin Books Ltd.)
Penguin Group (Australia), 250 Camberwell Road, Camberwell, Victoria 3124,
Australia (a division of Pearson Australia Group Pty. Ltd.)
Penguin Books India Pvt. Ltd., 11 Community Centre, Panchsheel Park,
New Delhi - 110 017, India
Penguin Group (NZ), 67 Apollo Drive, Rosedale, North Shore 0745,
Auckland, New Zealand (a division of Pearson New Zealand Ltd.)
Penguin Books (South Africa) (Pty.) Ltd., 24 Sturdee Avenue,
Rosebank, Johannesburg 2196, South Africa

Penguin Books Ltd., Registered Offices:
80 Strand, London WC2R 0RL, England

First published by Obsidian, an imprint of New American Library,
a division of Penguin Group (USA) Inc.

First Printing, October 2007
10 9 8 7 6 5 4 3 2 1

Acknowledgments

I would like to thank some of the people who helped me bring Kate's story along:

- For her early guidance and advice, Lyn Stimer, who helped me get a running start on shaping the story.
- My fellow writers and beta readers, who were very generous with their feedback: Elizabeth Ralser, Mary Farrell, Lynn Schwartz, Warren Deasy, and Trudy Sonia.
- Nancy Gottesman, the diet and fitness writer, for her help with diet and exercise tips.
- My agent, Kim Lionetti, and my editor, Kristen Weber, for all their hard work.

And finally, a word about the story's location. While the settings and characters in this story are entirely fictional, Durham, North Carolina, is a real city that has actual weight loss clinics. Years ago, I arrived in Durham weighing more that two hundred pounds, having been told I needed to lose weight in order to land an on-camera job in TV news. I'm forever grateful to the supportive community I got to know in Durham, including fellow dieters, dedicated doctors, and staff. My experiences there sparked my imagination in ways that helped breathe life into Kate's story.

Chapter 1

Don't Make Whoopee Before You Start

When starting a new eating program, avoid the temptation to go crazy with your favorite foods. On average, a prediet binge fest adds an extra pound to the weight you'll have to lose. But if you succumb to temptation, don't berate yourself. That extra pound will come off quickly.

—From *The Little Book of Fat-busters* by Mimi Morgan

Two p.m. On the road to Durham.

I didn't know it yet, but the Whoopie Pie was ready to explode.

The creamy gob of chocolate cake had been sitting next to me on the passenger seat of my TR6 for hours now, all the way from Boston, Massachusetts, to Durham, North Carolina. I'm crazy for Whoopie Pies, but so far I hadn't laid a finger on this one. See, the minute I got to Durham I was starting a Diet, a residential weight loss program (read: "fat farm"). I'd brought the Whoopie Pie along for the ride as a Challenge. Sort of like Willpower versus the Pie, *mano a mano.*

But then . . . well, just before we hit Durham, the Whoopie Pie started singing my name. "Kate Gallagher." Before long it was belting out a veritable fortissimo about how I really *deserved* a final treat before

I started the diet. And suddenly, all I could think about was doing evil deeds involving fudge cake and whipped cream.

I grabbed the Whoopie Pie and stuffed it in my mouth.

Heated almost to a boil from sitting on the sunny car seat, the cream-filled puff burst apart. It went off like a sugar grenade, spewing blobs of custard all over my face. Even the windshield caught some of the white shrapnel.

Serves you right, I thought, wiping frosting from my eyebrow. Zero self-control is precisely what had started me down the road to Durham in the first place.

In the War on Fat, Durham is the nuclear option. The city is home to half a dozen residential weight loss programs, including my destination, the Hoffman Clinic. And I was headed there not a moment too soon. Over the past few years, stress eating and late-night vending machine raids had packed an extra fifty-odd pounds around my hips and thighs. The stress part of the equation was from my job back in Boston, where I work as a news producer. Check that—where I *used* to work as a news producer. That job had ended exactly two weeks ago on a Friday, when I got laid off in the latest round of cost cutting at Channel Nine, my former employer. By some evil coincidence, Mack, my boyfriend, decided to dump me the same week. During our breakup lunch, I'd dragged it out of Mack that he was replacing me with the new TelePrompTer girl (who, by another evil coincidence, was a size two). It was a week that would live in infamy.

The only thing I had to show for a three-year slice of my life was an underwhelming wad of severance pay and an award I'd won the year before. It was a silver baton, the Dupont Award for Journalism Excellence from Columbia University. My name and title were inscribed on it—*Kate Gallagher, Special Assign-*

ments Producer. But that award and five bucks would buy me a latte vente in the current job market. Investigative producer jobs like mine were getting hard to find. And at fifty pounds up and counting, a new boyfriend was probably going to be hard to find, too.

My cell phone rang with the polymorphic chords of "Ms. New Booty," the customized ring tone I'd set up in honor of my trip.

"I hear chewing. Are you eating?" It was my best friend, Brian Sullivan.

"Certainly not," I said indignantly, forcing down the rest of the Whoopie Pie.

"So what if you are?" he laughed. "I'm halfway through a large goat-cheese pizza, myself."

That's the only annoying thing about Brian: He's always eating, but stays boot camp trim due to a metabolism that's supercharged by his six-foot-five frame. We'd grown up roaming the streets of South Boston together. Nowadays, Brian is a demolitions expert with the Boston Police Department, under the command of my father, Captain James Gallagher. Brian's gay, but only his family and close friends know it.

"So why don't you just hang a U-ey with that Green Machine and come back home?" Brian said, referring to my TR6 by its nickname. "You don't need to go to a fat farm, you and your Miss America cheekbones. Half the guys on the squad have asked me how they can get into your pants."

I paused just long enough to appreciate the bit about half Brian's squad wanting to bone me.

"That has nothing to do with it," I said. "The fact is that at thirty percent body fat, I'm obese."

I glanced down. My butt in its black skirt overflowed the bucket seat of my tiny vintage TR6. It was becoming a tight squeeze. Never mind fitting into your jeans—when you can't fit into your car anymore, things have gotten totally out of hand. At the rate I was going, my next vehicle would have to be something in an extra large, like an SUV.

"All I'm saying is, you certainly don't need to lose weight before looking for something else. Or some*one* else," Brian went on. "And don't you dare settle for another jerk like Mack. You wasted an entire year on him, remember? You need to learn how to party with your Inner Player. Just go for it."

"Who are you, Dr. Phil all of a sudden?" I protested.

"No. But still."

I hadn't confessed to anyone, not even to Brian, the real reason for my journey to the land of fat farms. Being laid off from my job had been an ugly wake-up call. It made me realize I'd had enough of life as an underpaid, unsung news producer. The night I was axed, I'd made a solemn vow that my next job would be in front of the camera. It was a simple accommodation to the harsh reality of local TV news. Only the reporters and anchors have any real clout, or real salaries. And I've often been told I have the "face" for TV: *über* pronounced cheekbones, plus Technicolor highlights like blue eyes and cascading auburn hair. But below the neck . . . aye, there was the rub.

As a news professional, I know that you practically have to be anorexic to land your first on-camera job, because the camera adds ten pounds (that's not a myth—it really *does* add ten pounds). Sure, later on you can gain weight. But not on that first job. All the women new hires were superskinny like my friend Mimi Morgan, the midday anchorwoman. It could be absolutely infuriating to clothes shop with Mimi, because she'd complain that size fours were "cut way too big these days." But Mimi had once lost a bunch of weight to get *her* first on-camera job, and she was a master dieter who knew all the tricks. As a parting gift for my trip to Durham, she printed out all of her personal diet and exercise tips, and had them spiral-bound into a tome called *The Little Book of Fatbusters*.

I'd need all the advice I could get. It was now or never time for me to blast off fifty pounds of Whoopie Pie, fast. As soon as I digested the one currently in my stomach, that is.

Brian's sigh came loud and clear across the phone. "All right, I give up," he said. "I can see you're determined to starve in the Steel Magnolia state. But watch yourself down there."

I knew what Brian was referring to. The night before, he and a few friends had sent me off in traditional Irish style—by playing drinking games at Molly's, our favorite South End pub. At one point, we'd all bumped mugs in a drunken toast. The plastic steins had bounced off each other, sloshing beer all over the table.

Looking like he'd seen a ghost, Brian had pounced on the spillage with a napkin.

"When you spill your beer while making a toast, you invite the Devil to the table," he'd announced solemnly. (Brian's always spotting bad luck omens in everyday things, especially after a couple of rounds of Guinness.)

But we were stone sober now. Plus, I was driving with the TR6's convertible top down, and the sky around me was a brilliant blue. All of which made it easy to dismiss my friend's antiquated notions about the Devil.

"You're always predicting doom and gloom, Brian, but nothing ever comes of it," I said into the phone.

"And I want to keep it that way. Remember, I work on the bomb squad."

"Well, you don't have to worry about me down here," I reassured him, then said good-bye and clicked off.

But the truth was, even I was a tad superstitious. You probably can't help it when you're raised in the heart of the Shamrock.

I adjusted the rearview mirror to see what was coming up behind me on the road. If there were such a thing as the Devil, I hoped he wouldn't find me in North Carolina.

Chapter 2

The Many Benies of Exercise

Research indicates that dieters who exercise regularly lose more weight, keep it off longer, and have a greater sense of well-being than sedentary people. As an added bonus, regular exercisers feel more confident about having sex, and enjoy the physical act of sex more. (And if <u>that's</u> not an incentive to hop on the treadmill, what is?)

—From *The Little Book of Fat-busters* by Mimi Morgan

Just off the interstate exit, a green road sign marked the Durham city limit:

WELCOME TO DURHAM, NORTH CAROLINA
DIET CAPITAL OF THE WORLD

The sign struck me as more than slightly embarrassing. It was as if the city fathers were announcing, "Welcome, fatsos!" Swigging down the last dregs of a Diet Coke, I wondered what kind of place billed itself as a citadel of dieting. Would it have a city ordinance banning fast food? Double-wide public toilet seats?

There was certainly no law against fast food, I quickly discovered as I cruised the main drag of downtown Durham. Totally the opposite, in fact. I'd never seen a place so thick with eateries. Dairy Queen, Hardee's, Waffle House—they were jammed in cheek to jowl, lining block after city block. On every corner not taken up by a restaurant, I spotted plus-sized clothing shops: Lane Bryant, Zaftig Zelda's, even one called Fatty Cathy's. (*Who'd walk in* that *door?* I wondered.) And everywhere I looked, there were heavy people. Walking with headphones, shopping, and most conspicuously, eating. Durham appeared to be a watering hole for the obese. From the look of things, that road sign should have said Fat City, U.S.A., not Diet Capital of the World.

"Well folks, here I am, your newest citizen," I observed to no one in particular.

My destination, the Hoffman Clinic, prescribed a strict fruit-based regimen. The diet had originally been created in a hospital to treat patients who were severely ill with diabetes, but it had turned out to have an unintended side effect—extreme weight loss. The clinic had first become popular when a famous Hollywood star whose weight had ballooned checked herself in and shed forty pounds in just six weeks. She'd gone from national joke to international bombshell, practically overnight. I was hoping for similar magic—at two thousand dollars a week, I had just enough cash in my account to cover six weeks on the program. I was planning to supplement those funds with a part-time job at the local TV station in Durham.

The Hoffman Clinic loomed into view as I rounded the final corner onto Palmetto Street. Set back from the road on top of a slight knoll, the clinic was a tall Queen Anne–style house that was wrapped like a sausage snack in a wide porch. A relatively modern wing splayed out from the older, central structure, making the whole layout seem off-kilter.

I turned onto the gravel driveway. Out of nowhere

a bright yellow Camaro blew past me going the other way. I had to jerk the steering wheel hard right to avoid a collision, and almost wound up in the ditch.

I craned my neck around to glare at the driver. It was a young dark-haired boy. He kept going, never so much as glancing back in the rearview mirror.

The Camaro swerved onto the paved road that ran along the side of the clinic. It screeched rubber and took off down the street, leaving a plume of gravel dust in its wake.

After recovering my breath, I straightened out the wheel and looked for a parking space. I squeezed my tiny TR6 next to a black Navigator that looked as though it ate sports cars like mine for lunch.

It was oppressively hot as I advanced up the concrete walkway toward the front portico, dragging my two-ton duffel bag behind me (*Why hadn't I gotten one of those rolly things?* I thought, too late). I picked out the silhouettes of half a dozen large shapes arrayed on a collection of rockers and porch swings. Gradually, I realized that those shapes were the outlines of people. *Big* people.

"BABY FRUIT?" A man's voice boomed in my direction.

I looked around, confused. "Uh . . . you talkin' to me?"

"Fresh meat!" The man yelled, this time apparently to the other people on the porch. "Newbie arrival!" He heaved himself up from his rocker. Lurching with a kind of Frankenstein gait, he made his way down a ramp that ran alongside the steps to the porch. He was extremely tall, and his width matched his height. I'd never seen such a big man. He advanced toward me, his hand out.

For a wild second, I wondered if the man would try to devour me.

"Jack Delaware," he said, shaking my hand. "I'm

four hundred pounds, but I've already lost seventy-five."

"Kate Gallagher. Thanks, um . . ."

I was at a loss for words, a rare event for me. I wondered if I should announce my weight, too—maybe that was part of the dieter's protocol, like declaring you're a drunk at AA.

"You look a little nervous," Jack said, as if he'd read my mind about the being devoured thing. He had kind eyes above an unexpectedly boyish smile. "Don't worry, we don't bite gorgeous redheads. Not unless we're really hungry, that is."

"Thank God," I laughed, surveying the half-dozen or so people who were draped about the wide front porch. All appeared to be well over three hundred pounds. Style-wise (or lack thereof), the women favored heavy gold jewelry layered over voluminous caftans. More like tents. I could see running shoes peeping out from underneath their brightly colored yardage. Compared to these people, I was . . . well, I was practically *thin*. It was a strangely liberating notion.

"Paige is still in there—she'll check you in." Jack jerked his thumb toward the front door. "You're lucky you missed Dr. Hoffman. He'd scare you to death with his induction."

"Induction?" I repeated, feeling a bit like the slow student in class. Induction sounded like a military term.

Jack put his hands over his fanny pack, which he wore facing front, the way heavy people do. The pack's belt maxed out somewhere along his stomach; it was tied the rest of the way around his girth with a rope.

"You'll find out. Welcome to the Fruit House."

I rocked back on my heels, trying to keep up with

the flow. "Fruit diet . . . equals Fruit House?" I ventured.

"Yup. Now you're an official Fruiter. Catch you later, Red." Gathering up his girth, he lumbered off toward the street.

I nodded to the people on the porch as I climbed the steps, then opened the heavy oak double doors to the clinic. My nostrils picked up a whiff of lemon. The furnishings inside were simple. A few wide-bottomed chairs, a blood pressure station, and some doctors scales—that was all. I could hear the clinking sound and chatter of people dining in the next room.

"Kate Gallagher?"

An unnervingly thin young woman rose to greet me. She was about my age, mid- to late twenties. She wore a stethoscope around her neck and had the monochromatic coloring of a starving field mouse. Her lips were slightly pursed. "I'm Paige, the physician's assistant. I stayed overtime thinking you might make it," she said, glancing at her watch. Paige managed to sound both polite and peeved in the same breath. "I'll take your blood pressure and your weight now."

"Yes, take my weight . . . please," I said.

Paige's lips retracted into a smile at my lame joke.

I conducted my usual ritual of weigh-in. Removal of shoes, followed by watch. Briefly, I debated whether to go to the bathroom to void the half pound of Diet Coke I'd just drunk. (*A pint's a pound the world around,* according to the weights and measurements ditty I'd known since childhood.) There wasn't enough time for a pit stop, though. Paige was already checking her watch again.

The scales must have been way off—they said I was 194. Even subtracting a half pound for the Diet Coke, that was ten whole pounds more than I'd thought.

"What?" I exclaimed. "No way."

Paige threw me a look of practiced sympathy. "Our scales are calibrated daily. That is your true weight, I'm afraid," she said. Probably most of the dieters underestimated their weight coming in.

"I'll introduce you to Marjory, the manager," Paige said, leading me to a small office off the weigh-in room. "She handles check-in."

Paige handed me off to a casually dressed woman who was sitting behind a desk.

"Y'all just made it!" Marjory the manager rose and greeted me with that odd but friendly way some Southerners have of addressing everyone in the plural.

Marjory was an outdoorsy-looking brunette dressed in a sleeveless denim work shirt. Every visible surface of her skin—face, shoulders, chest—was scattershot with constellations of dark brown freckles. You could have made a celestial map out of them.

"Kate Gallagher." She said my name as if retrieving it from her mental organizer. "Aren't you the one they're doing that TV story on?"

"That's right."

Before leaving for Durham, I'd contacted the news director at Durham's local TV station, WDHM Channel Twelve. I'd arranged to barter my part-time producer services in exchange for enough money to see me through the summer on the program. Much to my chagrin, the news director had suggested I start my job by producing a personal weight loss transformation story. It would be an extreme makeover, starring Yours Truly as the chubby duckling turning (hopefully) into a swan. I wasn't exactly thrilled by the prospect of displaying my thunder thighs on TV all over the Durham tri-county area. It'll be *Haha! She's fat*, I thought, reflexively running a hand down my butt to feel how far it was sticking out. But what the hell. I didn't know any of the people here from Adam. And anyway, I needed the paycheck.

"Your story should be good publicity for us," Marjory said.

The way she said it made it sound as if there'd been some bad publicity of late. That was surprising. I hadn't run across anything negative when I'd Googled the place before coming down.

Marjory thrust a stack of brochures into my hand while reaching for my duffel bag. She swung it easily over her shoulder, which made me think it was time for me to find a gym and start doing a few marine presses. "I'll walk you to your room and then back so you can get some dinner," she said. "Everyone gets lost here the first day."

It was a long trek. Every door we passed was closed, the hallways silent and deserted. As we walked, Marjory's initial effervescence faded away, and an uncomfortable silence descended.

To break the sudden pall, I apologized for running so late.

"Don't worry about it. It's just nice to see someone checking in. Too many folks going the other way lately," Marjory said, pausing in front of a door.

I'd assumed that the Hoffman Clinic was popular. It was certainly famous enough. But in fact, it had been easy to get a reservation when I'd called the week before.

"Here's your room," Marjory announced, swiping a card key. Just down the hallway, my neighbor's door was ajar. Marjory glanced at the door and cocked her head, as if she were listening for something.

"Everything okay?" I felt compelled to ask.

"Oh, yes. Fine," she said, her voice sounding artificially bright. "Your room's in a great spot. It's right near the swimming pool and the side entrance to the parking lot."

"Ah, a side entrance—the better to cheat through, my dear?" I cracked.

Marjory returned a serious look, laced with a dollop of concern. *Oh, dear.*

Inside, the room's décor screamed the seventies with a swagged ceiling lamp and avocado green shag carpeting. It was a look that should have been laid to rest thirty years ago, along with Disco Fever. The only concession to modernity was an Internet port on the desk.

As I glanced out the window that overlooked the pool, a mountain of flesh emerged from the water. The mountain peaked in a small, dark, round head. It was a man—a man who must have weighed at least five hundred pounds. Sheets of water cascaded off him as he pulled himself slowly up a set of steps and out of the pool, dumping large puddles of water onto the concrete. Astonishingly, the man was wearing an ultra-low-cut European brief. It was like watching a mana-tee model a thong.

Marjory caught my expression. "That's Norm," she said. "He's the biggest guy in the Fruit House. But he started out at seven hundred pounds, so he's already down a couple of hundred."

"Seven hundred pounds. Wow."

"Norm would be dead right now if it weren't for Dr. Hoffman," Marjory said, watching him through the window. "When he heard about Norm's condition, Dr. Hoffman arranged for him to be brought here, and funded a scholarship at his own expense."

"That's amazing," I said. "Maybe I could interview Norm as part of my transformation series."

Marjory nodded enthusiastically. "Norm's a perfect example of Dr. Hoffman's mission, which is saving people from morbid obesity," she said. Then she paused to look me up and down. "You know, you're actually on the small side for a new Fruiter."

"Maybe they'll toss me back in the water?" I suggested.

"Oh no, Dr. Hoffman would never do that," she

said, still with that earnest tone. "He considers any amount of excess fat to be the beginning of chronic disease."

"Darn."

After I parked my bag, Marjory showed me the side entrance, which was just down the hallway and opened directly to the parking lot. She explained that I'd have to use my card key to get in and out that way. Then we retraced our steps to the dining room.

I looked around, scanning the tables. A young woman with a shiny zit on her face—a nose stud, actually—was embroiled in a frowning conversation with the guy sitting next to her.

Skirting the couple's negative vibe, I moved a few chairs past them and dropped into an empty seat next to two women. Moments later, a dour-faced waitress slapped a bowl of yellow mystery gruel and a nectarine before me on the vinyl placemat. She returned seconds later with a glass of ice water that had several lemon wedges floating in it.

I felt the nectarine. It was rock hard. After staring glumly into the bowl of yellow goop for a minute, I tried a spoonful. It tasted like oatmeal spit. They'd left a few details out of the marketing brochures, like the spit and the petrified fruit.

The woman sitting nearest me threw me a sympathetic look.

"Believe it or not, it'll actually taste good after you've been here a while," she said. "I'm Evelyn Brooks. I've been here seven months and lost sixty-eight pounds." Having evidently lost enough weight to graduate from the caftan uniform, Evelyn wore a plum-colored tracksuit that precisely matched the polish on her long fingernails.

"Kate Gallagher," I said, shaking hands. "What's the stuff in the bowl? I thought they only gave you fruit here."

"It's a protein-replacement mix." Evelyn explained. "It keeps you from losing muscle on the diet."

"But we call it Piss Paste," her companion piped up. The woman's face and neck were etched with a layer of fine wrinkles. A tiny bit of red lipstick had leaked into a gouge along the top of her lips.

Evelyn gave the other woman a reproving look. "Don't discourage the Baby Fruiters, Lila," she warned.

"No, that's okay. I like the sound of 'Piss Paste,' " I said, smiling at the two women. "I was thinking 'Oat-meal Spit,' myself."

I tried not to stare at Lila. She looked like a stick figure wearing the skin of a much larger person. Soft folds of skin, drained of fat, hung from her arms and neck. She appeared to be in her sixties but could have been younger.

"Have you been at the clinic long?" I asked Lila hesitantly. Too long, from the look of things.

"Nine months—I hit my goal two weeks ago," Lila announced with visible pride. "They're working me back up to regular food. I'm scared, though. I don't know what would happen if I bumped into a Milk Dud right now." Lila grabbed a fistful of flesh under her upper arm and waggled it back and forth. "Next stop's plastic surgery," she said. "When I leave here, I'm getting a total body lift."

I was almost afraid to ask. "What's a body lift?"

"That's where they cut you across the middle and pull the top half down and the bottom half up," Lila explained. To demonstrate, she lifted her jersey top, grabbed the skin at her waist, and pulled forward about a foot of excess skin. The flesh was riddled with pink and white stretch marks.

"See, talk about pinching an inch—I can pinch a yard," Lila said, folding the skin between her fingers. "They're gonna cut this all off."

"Oh," I gasped, trying not to look appalled.

The idea of having plastic surgery to repair damage self-inflicted by eating made me squirm. I hoped I'd caught my own fat and skin in time. At least I didn't have stretch marks, thank God.

"It's a new technique, but only for drastic cases. I didn't exercise at all as I was losing," Lila added in a rueful tone. "Now I'm paying for it."

"That's why you have to keep moving here, Kate," Evelyn interjected. "Why don't you join our walking group tomorrow morning? It's a great way to learn the ropes. Some of us exercise all day to keep from thinking about food." She made a circling gesture, as if stirring a pot of candy. "We call ourselves the Sunrise Walkers."

"Sounds great," I said, trying to pump some energy into my reply. To my dog-beat-tired self the idea of a sunrise walk sounded about as appealing as a sunrise round of teeth cleaning. But I needed to set up some interviews for my weight loss story to show what life was like at the clinic. I could start with the Sunrise Walkers.

"But you don't really mean sunrise, do you?" I asked.

"Yup. We meet on the front porch at five a.m." Evelyn nodded.

"*Five* a.m.?" Ugh. "Sounds great."

Maybe by tomorrow morning I will have shaken off the road weariness and be ready for exercise. Like maybe pigs could fly.

As if by a secret signal, the dining room fell silent. Evelyn and Lila exchanged a look.

"Sounds like Dr. Hoffman is back," Evelyn said.

Pocketing my nectarine, I followed the two women across the lobby and outside to the porch, where the twilight was rapidly fading to black.

Chapter 3

Avoid Emo Eating

Stress, fatigue, and strong emotions can all lead to unplanned eating episodes. Ask yourself the HALT question (Am I Hungry, Angry, Lonely, or Tired?). If you're not truly hungry, drop the food and back away from it—slowly—with your hands in the air.

—From *The Little Book of Fat-busters* by Mimi Morgan

Perched on the edge of a rocker surrounded by a rapt circle of listeners, a fifty-something man was holding court. Tilting forward on the rocker as he addressed the group, he wore a doctor's coat over white bucks.

"That's the head of the clinic, Dr. Hoffman," Evelyn whispered in my ear. "He's like a god around here."

The "god" was brandishing something dark and oblong in the air, waving it about like a baton. I leaned in for a closer look, then did a double take. It was an ice-cream sandwich—Neapolitan. He wiped out the chocolate end in a single bite.

The surrounding dieters, openmouthed and silent, seemed hypnotized by the spectacle of the diet doctor eating the ice cream. Between mouthfuls, Hoffman was delivering a lecture.

"I can eat sweets like this all day because I have a fast metabolism," Hoffman said. "But not you. And why is that, you ask?"

Hoffman had an intense way of drawing out his words, as if he were a general admonishing his flabby troops.

"It is because all of you here are cursed with slow metabolisms," he said. "You can never eat sweets like this again. To be successful you must accept this fact."

As a finale, he polished off the rest of the ice-cream sandwich. His light blue eyes, enormous behind rimless glasses, swept the circle of onlookers.

I wanted to laugh out loud at the scene, except that it seemed kind of cruel for a diet doctor to be chowing down in front of a bunch of his starving patients. Everyone had glazed-over looks in their eyes. Except one. Norm, the manatee man I'd seen in the pool before dinner, was now standing on the perimeter of the group. His face had turned red, and he looked upset.

Maybe it was Norm's face, plus the fact that the place was seedier than the brochures had shown, and that I'd had no trouble getting a reservation. But I began to wonder whether I'd made a colossal mistake by plunking down my severance pay as a down payment on this program. What kind of looney tunes place was this?

"Is torture by food *du jour* included in our 2K a week?" I whispered to Evelyn.

She shrugged. "He's just showing us that we have to change our eating ways," she said. "Dr. Hoffman says we fatties have to totally reprogram our brains."

Reprogram sounded like a cult term. Hopefully they didn't serve Diet Kool-Aid in the dining room. Cult or no, I was stuck with this place now. Durham's Channel Twelve was expecting me to produce my weight loss series here. Maybe I could turn the whole assignment into an exposé. That'd be a much more interesting story than watching my thighs disappear.

Norm stepped forward, the porch floorboards groaning under his weight. He whispered something into Hoffman's ear. The doctor shook his head and waved him off with a defensive energy, as if he were swatting away a bee.

With a violent shoulder motion, Norm broke away from the group. He strode down the steps and away from the clinic.

"Weak fool," I heard Hoffman mutter.

I couldn't believe everyone else was putting up with this nonsense—why didn't they *do* something? Like . . . like, stage a revolt! I visualized a mob of fat people storming the gates of the diet clinic. They'd brandish Maui Brownie waffle cones instead of torches, and smash the windows with nectarine rocks.

This place was starting to do something to my brain. It was time to retreat to my room and think it all over. I edged away from the circle, heading back toward the lobby.

Something firm seized my wrist, holding me back. Swiveling my head, I was confronted by an intense blue gaze.

"You." Hoffman's eyes bored into mine. "You are new?"

"Yes, I am new," I replied, mirroring his stilted phrasing.

Hoffman kept a grip on my wrist. I felt as if those probing eyes could x-ray my stomach and spot the remains of the Whoopie Pie digesting there.

"It's good that you have come now," he said. "It's too late for some of these cheating fools, but you have a chance to become a truly thin person. You have caught it in time."

It had to be my weight. Hoffman was saying it

wasn't too late for me, body-wise. I felt my negative thoughts about him being washed away by a sudden sense of relief. It felt like being given a pass by the Diet Pope.

"You must follow my program exactly, and walk three miles a day," he commanded.

"Roger that," I said. *Roger that?* I sounded like an escapee from an old flying ace movie.

Hoffman's expression changed. For a second, he looked amused.

"You have intelligent eyes and good facial bone structure," he said, scanning me up and down. "I believe you will do well. Be at weigh-in tomorrow at seven a.m. sharp."

I nodded, not trusting myself to speak for fear of saying something even more ridiculous, like "ten-four."

Hoffman kept his eyes screwed on mine for another long second, then released my wrist so abruptly that my hand thumped against my side. I'd obviously been dismissed.

Evelyn caught up with me in the lobby. Her expression was electric.

"Ooh Kate, what did Dr. Hoffman say to you?"

"Um, that he thinks I'll do okay on the program."

"See?" She gave my forearm a big squeeze. "You're here two seconds and he's already praised you. Normally Dr. Hoffman doesn't even *speak* to new people until they've been here a week," she added. "I bet you'll be a superstar."

"Superstar?"

"Those are the people who breeze through the program and lose all their weight quickly. For people like me, it's more of a struggle," Evelyn said, grimacing ruefully. "The superstars are Dr. Hoffman's special pets."

"Will I shrink into a purse dog?"

Evelyn laughed. "No, but I love that idea," she said. "I can already tell we're going to be friends."

After promising again to meet Evelyn the next day for our predawn walk, I retraced my steps to my room. My neighbor's door, which had been open earlier, was now shut. A DO NOT DISTURB card dangled from the knob.

The second my door was closed, I grabbed a big T-shirt from the suitcase, washed up, and unfolded my travel alarm clock. A complimentary copy of Hoffman's book *Follow! Follow! The Hoffman Diet* lay on the bedside table. By nature I'm quite the diet book junkie, but right then I was too beat to even open it.

I needed to rest. The drive, the horrible dinner, and the odd encounter on the porch with the diet doctor had taken their toll. I threw myself down on the bed. But once I stretched out, sleepiness vanished, so I plugged my laptop into the Internet port on the desk and sent an IM to my friend Mimi back in Boston. I didn't plan to tell her, however, that I'd already blown her "Thou shalt not make whoopee before the diet" edict.

Mimi, this whole thing is a BIG mistake. Piss Paste served here, crazies roam. Only 1 saving grace. I'm thinner than most.

I didn't expect to hear back that night, because Mimi's usually out on a date. But miraculously, she wrote right back.

Katie my love, see tip about negative thoughts. Speaking of negative, I got dinged today for saying it's a doggy-dog world on the air. Who knew it should be dog-eat-dog?

I laughed out loud. In the goofball world of TV news, Mimi was one of the goofiest balls. And that's exactly why I loved her so much. I wrote back:

No D8?

Mimi sent her reply:

Had 2 ditch boring dude. I want u 2 cheer up. Check out gift I hid in your bag.

Gift? Thnx . . . Brb . . . , I wrote.

I rummaged through my suitcase and dug out a gift bag, which Mimi had hidden underneath my spandex hip smoothers. Inside I found a round candle with a crumbly brown surface, and a lighter shaped like a hula girl.

The card read:

Light this in case of emergency. Happy Early Birthday! Love, Mimi.

Oh. My. God. I'd totally suppressed the fact that I had a birthday coming up in a few days. . . . I'd be twenty-six. Yippee-yi-yay.

Ceremoniously, I lit the candle and placed it on the side table next to the bed, then closed my eyes. Thirty seconds later, the smell of warm, gooey chocolate enveloped the room, causing my stomach to growl. My eyes snapped open again.

"Cookie dough?" I picked up the candle and examined it—the label said "Cookie Crunch."

I wrote Mimi again:

Considering eating wax.

When I didn't hear back from Mimi right away, I clicked on the TV to Channel Twelve. A reporter was standing in front of a fire truck, wrapping up a field report. I winced as he muffed his throw to the anchor. The production values were uneven, typical for a smaller market station. Hopefully they'd have a half-decent videographer who could help me get through the weight loss story I was supposed to produce. The way my luck was going, though, I'd probably get some intern who wouldn't know a black balance from a barn door.

I wasn't aware of having fallen asleep when a sound jolted me awake. It was just past one a.m. A woman's voice penetrated through the wall from the room next door. She was yelling something in a series of staccato bursts, alternating with gaps of silence and responses that vibrated in a lower, male register.

Oh great, they're having a bitch fest next door, I thought as I rubbed my cheek against the pillowcase, trying to get back to sleep.

The argument escalated quickly. There were several more shout-volleys back and forth, louder each time. Then something banged against the wall. Hard. Whatever was going on next door sounded like it was turning physical.

Fully awake by now, I tossed back the sheet and crossed the room to the bureau. I mashed an ear to the wall, trying to make out the words. There was another noise from the woman, which sounded like a scream.

"Hey, are you guys okay over there?" I ratcheted up my volume while scrunching my face in an anticipatory flinch. The last thing I wanted to do was insert myself into a couple's spat, but I had to make sure no one was getting hurt.

"Mind your own fucking business," the woman's muffled reply came back through the wall.

Well! That was clear enough. The woman sounded pissed—good. If she was swearing at me, she must be okay.

A minute of dead silence went by; then a door slammed with enough force to rattle the wall. Someone, probably the man, was going to have to find another place to sleep that night.

"Whatever, guys. Just don't wake me up two hours from now with your friggin' make-up sex," I muttered, crawling back into bed.

What a creepy, horrible place. Maybe we *had* invited in the Devil back at Molly's Bar when we'd spilled that beer. This whole day had certainly felt like the beginning of a journey to hell.

*   *   *

I almost chucked the alarm clock across the room when it went off at four thirty the next morning. I struggled to my feet, my head already pounding from a wicked case of sugar withdrawal, which is reportedly as bad as heroin withdrawal. I would have sold my soul for a White Mocha from Starbucks right about then. With a coffee cake chaser, thank you very much.

I pulled my "thin" shorts out of the suitcase and tried them on to see if by any miracle they fit yet.

"Ugh," I said, stripping them back off and heaving them across the room. Then I brushed my teeth and threw on a pair of ancient Wellesley College sweats in preparation for joining Evelyn and her Sunrise Walkers. It seemed to be the only sane plan of action—at four thirty a.m. in a guest room in Durham, when you're crashing from a twenty-five-year sugar habit, there is literally nothing to do but move your body.

Heading outside through the side entrance, I paused under a light next to the parking lot. The predawn air felt moist and chilly, totally unlike the brutish heat I'd battled all the way during the drive down from Boston yesterday. I was grateful that I'd grabbed my green Boston Celtics windbreaker before stepping out the door. I sniffed the air. A shift in the overnight winds had brought in a whiff of tobacco leaves drying in the fields beyond the city.

As my feet hit the pavement, my ears caught the pebbly crunch of wheels turning on gravel. I paused under a lamppost and looked around.

In the white-gray morning mist I could just make out the round taillights of a vehicle leaving the parking lot. The two brake light orbs brightened for a second as the driver slowed down. Then the driver killed the lights and gunned the engine, spitting gravel on the way out.

That seemed odd. Why would someone be leaving the clinic this early? I thought back to the spat I'd heard in the middle of the night. Maybe the guy had slept in his car. Or maybe it was a jail break, and someone was making a run for it to the nearest Krispy Kreme.

I headed toward the front of the building to wait for Evelyn and her Sunrise Walkers. Using my key chain's little LED flashlight, I picked my way along the winding walkway. The front of the clinic stood silent and deserted underneath the pale pink shafts of the oncoming sunrise.

"Kate, wait up!" I heard a voice call out behind me.

Evelyn came jogging up. She wore a yellow tracksuit with the jacket tied around her shoulders. A matching headband held back a waterfall of hair. "Everyone's always late," she said. "Let's wait on the porch for them."

I climbed the steps just ahead of Evelyn, heading toward a big metal couch on gliders. Then I stopped cold.

In the faint light, I could just make out the pale outline of a figure. It looked like a man in crumpled white clothing, asleep.

I sucked in a breath. The guy was way too thin to be a dieter, and something about the way he was lying looked wrong, somehow. His white-haired head was turned away from us, one arm trailing limply off the side of the glider.

In my peripheral vision, I saw Evelyn's hand fly up to cover her mouth.

"Hey, are you okay?" Reaching forward, I gingerly poked at the man's bony shoulder. I felt something ice cold and wet and drew back my hand. It was vomit.

The smell of the vomit sent me spooling about, disgusted—the guy must have passed out drunk. I accidentally jarred the glider, which caused the man's head to flop toward me.

It was Hoffman.

There was something bizarre about his face. I blinked rapidly to clear my vision. Something was sticking out from two blackened holes where his eyes should be. Something long and made of metal.

Behind my left ear, I heard Evelyn scream.

But I couldn't take my eyes off Hoffman. Someone had driven a pair of fondue forks into his eyes.

One blood-streaked fork through each eye.

Chapter 4

Dealing With the Unexpected

Life throws us curveballs. Like the time I missed lunch because I had to do a live shot, and was starving by the time I arrived at my favorite restaurant—Anthony's Pier 4—for a dinner date. I practically swan-dived into the popover basket, and wound up gaining two pounds overnight.

When events go awry, don't use it as an excuse to go off the deep end with food. (But I hereby declare an exception for Anthony's popovers. They're totally worth it.)

—From *The Little Book of Fat-busters* by Mimi Morgan

For a split second I froze, unable to draw a breath. Evelyn's screams barely registered over a rushing sound. Slowly, I realized that the deafening noise was my own pulse pounding in my ears.

Two fondue forks protruded like ghastly bull's-eyes from the centers of the blackened orbs that had once been Hoffman's eyes. I leaned down to get a closer look. Each fork ended in a little fruit-shaped ceramic handle, the left a cherry and the right a banana—a ghoulishly absurd touch. Someone had skewered the diet doctor through the eyes and left his body on the couch like some kind of freaky appetizer. The odor of Hoffman's vomit stuck in my nostrils, sending my throat into spasms. *Morning exercise with the Sunrise Walkers. Bad, bad idea,* flitted through my head.

"Dr. Hoffman—oh my God oh my God . . . ," Evelyn was babbling behind me. Out of the corner of my eye I could see that her jacket had fallen off her shoulders

My teeth started to chatter the way they do whenever I'm totally terrified. I'd seen murder victims before, but never one who had been shish kebabed. It was gruesome. I flashed on the car I'd seen booking out of the parking lot a few minutes earlier—it might have been Hoffman's killer.

Neither Evelyn nor I had brought a cell phone, so I told her to run back to her room to call the police. Evelyn nodded and backed shakily down the stairs.

I immediately regretted sending her off. I suddenly felt very alone, standing next to the swaying couch glider with Hoffman's body. Clamping my jaw shut to stop my clattering teeth, I soon became aware of every tiny sound around me, down to the faint buzzing of a transformer halfway down the block.

Was Hoffman definitely dead? I had to know. Dropping to my haunches, I carefully placed first my fingers, then the heel of my hand on the doctor's neck. There was no pulse. His body was as cold and wet as the metal porch swing, as if it had been out all night and was covered with morning dew. There wasn't much blood coming from the eyes, I noticed, which meant they must have been stabbed after he died.

Hoffman's lips looked dark, almost black, I thought as I moved in for a closer look. Then, to my utter disbelief, his lips moved.

Another shockwave jolted up my neck—and then I realized it was something *on* his lips that was moving. It was black and crawling.

A mass of black ants was swarming on Hoffman's lips. An undulating, seething ribbon of insects.

A blast of disgust sent me reeling back from the body; I tipped over backward and fell flat on my ass. I struggled to my feet and made it to the front door of the clinic in two long strides. To my surprise, the brass doorknob turned easily—it was unlocked. That couldn't be right.

The door yielded with a crack. Groping my way through the lobby and dining room, I stumbled into one of the doctor's scales, nearly toppling it over. When I reached the kitchen I felt around for a light switch. I had just located the phone when I heard sirens approaching in the distance. Either Evelyn had found a phone, or else someone had heard her screams and called the police.

My throat spasms fingered their way down into my stomach, and all of a sudden I had to heave. Leaning over the kitchen sink, I spewed out the remains of last night's dinner, including undigested bits of nectarine flesh. I reached for the tap to wash the mess down the drain, then thought better of it. Would the police want everything preserved? The front door hadn't been locked, so it was possible that the kitchen was part of the crime scene. I hated to leave my retching remnants there, but it was probably best to, at this point.

As I recrossed the lobby and headed back to the front porch, blue lights pulsed through the front windows and scattered sparkles across the inside wall.

When I emerged, a cop wearing a patrolman's uniform was already on the porch, bent over Hoffman's body. His hand, which had reached for his holster as he heard the front door open, relaxed as he rapidly appraised me. I guess I didn't look like much of a threat. A police unit was parked along the street, its driver's-side door flung open.

"You found it?" he asked me. The officer's name tag said POTEET.

I nodded, thinking about how quickly death changes

us from a personal pronoun to "it," as impersonal as a lump of meat.

Poteet reached for his shoulder microphone. He requested more units and a homicide team from the dispatcher, saying he had a DB 187.

I recognized DB 187 as police code for dead body, homicide. This certainly wasn't your typical homicide, though. I was sure it wasn't every day that Durham's finest found their murder victims served up like the early bird special.

Poteet ordered me off the porch, indicating that they'd be asking me some more questions, and that I should sit at the base of the stone steps that connected the porch to the front yard.

I parked myself on the bottom step. Moments later a cruiser came barreling down the street, running with lights but no siren. The car jumped the curb and pulled up onto the grassy lawn. The cruiser's door had K-9 written on it. A cop came hard-charging out of the driver's side, but there was no sign of a dog. Maybe he had the morning off.

K-9 Cop blew past me as he took the stairs two at a time up to the porch, where he and Poteet bent their heads together for a minute. A moment later, Poteet approached me with some questions.

I ran down how Evelyn and I had found the body, how I'd sent her off to call someone, and how I'd looked for a pulse before going inside the clinic to look for a phone myself.

By now, more police units were arriving. Evelyn reappeared with Lila and a handful of other people in tow. Trading shocked and bewildered looks, they huddled near the line of police vehicles that was forming on the lawn.

K-9 Cop advanced toward them with his arms high in the air, palms and fingers splayed out. "Sorry, folks," he barked. "We're closing this area now."

When Poteet wound up his interview with me, I pointed out Evelyn to him. Evidently wanting to keep tabs on all his witnesses, Poteet parked me again, this time by a topiary bush. He told me to stand by. Standing alone next to the shrub made me feel singled out and guilty, like a garden flamingo that had been caught poaching eggs.

Poteet pulled Evelyn from the pack of onlookers. As he questioned her, Evelyn kept shivering despite the fact that the air was beginning to warm up. Her jacket, which had fallen off her shoulders up on the porch, was off-limits now. It had become part of the crime scene.

Evelyn was still being interviewed when a blond whippet of a woman wearing a doctor's uniform rounded the corner of the building and churned toward the front steps. Paige, the physician's assistant I'd met yesterday, trailed in the woman's wake.

K-9 Cop stopped the two women a few feet from the bush where I was standing.

"I'm Dr. Anita Thornburg, medical director of this clinic. What's going on here?" the woman demanded, her face taut.

I recognized the name. Anita Thornburg was the staff doctor I was supposed to meet with today to discuss my weight loss story.

"You'll have to stay back, ma'am, while we conduct our investigation," K-9 snapped. He led the two women back to the sidewalk along the street.

As the cop spoke to the two women, Paige's knees sagged and she reached toward the older woman for support. Anita Thornburg, by contrast, stood perfectly erect and still. Her white-blond hair was raked back from her face and swirled tightly into a chignon. She appeared to be in her early forties and was attractive in a Snow Queen kind of way.

Then Thornburg looked my way. She fixed on me with a long, evaluating look, as if she were wondering why I was standing off to myself. As she stared, her gaze hardened perceptibly.

What, does she think I killed Hoffman? I wondered.

Whatever she was thinking, one thing was certain—Thornburg was giving me the royal stink eye.

I ignored her and rocked back and forth on my heels, trying to puzzle out how Hoffman had been killed. Those bizarro fruit forks smacked strongly of post mortem mutilation, as if someone had wanted to garnish his body after death. Such an attack must have been fueled by revenge, or a crazed passion. But who at the clinic—if it even *was* someone at the clinic—was that vengeful, or crazy?

Thirty minutes later I was back in my room, sitting in the middle of my bed, phone in hand. I was itching to call Channel Twelve. Hoffman's murder was a story they needed to know about. The patrolman who'd dropped me off had ordered me not to discuss the murder with anyone until after the detective's interview. But maybe I could pretend I'd thought he'd meant only for me not to discuss it with other witnesses—that would be my story, anyway.

I punched the private number I had for the Channel Twelve news director.

Chuck Beatty answered on the first ring.

"Hi, this is Kate Gallagher from Boston, and—," I started.

"Gallagher! We've been looking for you. I sent a crew out to the clinic because we heard something come over the police radio." Beatty spoke in blunt news director style—no niceties, not even a "Hello." "What have you got?"

"Victor Hoffman's been murdered—the head of the

diet program," I said. "I found the body and I'm waiting for a detective. I can give you the details after
the interview."

"Victor Hoffman's dead? You found the body?
Jesus." Beatty gave a low whistle. "You positive it's
murder? Anyone else killed?"

"No one else killed that I know of, and yeah, it's
definitely murder. Someone stabbed him through the
eyes—but don't put that on the air yet. I'm on news
embargo until homicide talks to me."

"Whoa, no shit?" Beatty paused. "Hoffman's an
icon around this town. This is a big story . . . a *big*
fuckin' story. Okay, so, we've got you there on the
inside. . . ."

I could almost hear his brain machinery spinning.
Then it sounded like he took a drag on a cigarette.
That was surprising. Cigarettes had long been ban-
ished from newsrooms in Boston and most everywhere
else. But maybe not in the tobacco state.

Beatty exhaled what must have been a lungful of
smoke. "Get yourself down to the studio today when
you get free, and we'll map out something."

"Okay. I'll try to wrangle something we can use out
of the homicide detective, too." I said.

"Fantabulous. Jesus, this is hot. *Hot.* Can you give
us thirty seconds for the noon broadcast?" Beatty
didn't wait for my reply. He'd already fast-forwarded
to the production details. "We'll run your write-up
over the B-roll my morning crew just uplinked. They
got some good shots of the EMTs carrying a body out.
The cops wouldn't tell them who it was—I figured it
was some fatty who keeled over from a heart attack,
but now we know it was Hoffman. I'll send a reporter
over there to do a live shot."

Translation: Beatty wanted me to write thirty seconds of news copy that the anchor would read over
the video that the camera crew had taped of the scene

at the clinic. A reporter would do a live stand-up report outside the clinic.

"Sure thing. No problem."

"Fantabulous. Let's get you cracking right away on this."

Beatty put me on the phone with an associate producer, who took some notes and gave me directions to the station.

As soon as I hung up the phone, I got that rush of adrenaline I always feel when I'm starting work on a breaking story. I popped open my laptop in order to do some quick and dirty research on Hoffman.

A Google search brought up information about Hoffman's background: After emigrating from South Africa in the mid-1980s, Dr. Victor Otto Hoffman had founded the obesity program at Jameson University. He was famous for pioneering a "fat cleansing" diet. The diet consisted mainly of fruit, supplemented by tons of mineral water and vitamin shots (none of the articles mentioned the Piss Paste). Following the success of the Hoffman Clinic, a gaggle of imitators had opened competing dietary programs in Durham, many of them much swankier and more luxurious. But none delivered dramatic weight loss results like the Hoffman Clinic.

Most of the online information was just a rehash of what I already knew from the research I did before enrolling in the clinic, but I did find one new article that described Hoffman as a "longtime bachelor." That was typically journalistic code for gay or something unusual in the sexuality department.

I felt another surge right then, this one in the vicinity of my stomach. A hunger surge. All at once I remembered the Luna Bar I'd tossed into my duffel bag just before leaving Boston. It was my favorite kind, too, Nutz Over Chocolate. Temptation beckoned. I could *feel* the crunchy chocolate melting in my mouth.

It's amazing how quickly you can thought-shift from murder to mastication, I thought. What about Mimi's HALT question—was I actually *hungry*? Another stomach growl assured me that, yes, I really was. But I was reluctant to start down a cheating road so early in my dieting journey. I left the bar in the bag.

I was snapping shut my laptop when I heard a knock.

The man standing outside my door was tall and lightly tanned. He wore a light gray herringbone jacket, a knotted silk tie, and a crisp Oxford shirt over twill trousers. He looked like a Rhodes Scholar.

"Kate Gallagher? Detective Jonathan Reed, Durham Homicide."

Surprisingly, Reed clipped his words with a British accent. He flipped open his badge cover and held it up for me to see. "I need to get some information from you about this morning's incident."

"Anything I can do," I said, waving him inside the room. There was nowhere to sit but the unmade bed. I sat stiffly on the edge of the mattress, draping my legs in a way that I hoped would minimize thigh spread.

Reed reached inside his jacket for a pocket recorder, plus a pen and small notebook. My eye caught the dull glint of a .38 police revolver at his waist.

"I'm sorry but . . . you're British?" *How stupid did that sound?* I wondered.

"Yes, I'm here on an international exchange certification program from the Sheffield Constabulary in the UK." Reed nodded. "But otherwise, think of me as just another regular policeman here in your fair burg."

"Not *my* fair burg. I'm from Boston."

"Quite right. You're in the news business there, I understand?"

I nodded, surprised again. Reed evidently had already done his homework on me. Pretty thorough for an initial interview.

"Until recently, I was, yes," I said. "I got laid off a couple of weeks ago."

"Sorry to hear that," Reed said, pushing the record button. "Tell me everything that happened this morning, according to your best recollection."

I started by describing how I'd set off on my walk before dawn. I tried to provide as much detail as possible, remembering to add that I'd seen a car leaving the clinic's parking lot just before discovering Hoffman's body on the porch.

"I see you told the responding officer that you checked for a pulse." Reed frowned slightly, flipping through his notes. "And you also . . ." He paused.

"Hurled, yes. I left it in the sink."

"Not a problem. Most of us lose our chow the first few crime scenes."

"I think it was those ants crawling around on his mouth that got to me," I said, touching my fingers to my lips with a shudder. "I guess I kind of freaked. I ran to the door, which wasn't locked by the way, looking for a phone. How long was his body there on the porch, do you think?" I snuck in the question for the story I was planning to produce later on.

"We have to wait for the coroner's results." Reed glanced up from his notes and gave me a sharp look. *I'll ask the questions,* the look said. "What made you decide to take a walk so early this morning? You said you left your room at four forty-five a.m.?"

"I was supposed to meet a group of dieters for a walk. This was—is—my first day on the diet program."

At the mention of the word "diet," Reed eyed me with the briefest of body scans.

"What do you remember about the car you saw leaving the parking lot, just before finding the body?" he asked. "Can you describe it?"

"It was foggy and still pretty dark, so I couldn't see it clearly," I said. "It seemed like a light color. Round taillights. My impression was it was an older car."

"Older? What makes you say that?"

I thought back to how the two smeary red orbs brightened as the car paused before leaving the lot. "I know what it was," I said. "There was no third brake light when it slowed down. Haven't cars had those extra lights in back since the mid-nineties? In this country, I mean," I added hastily. "So there was no third brake light."

"Or it wasn't working." Reed nodded. He seemed to give me fresh consideration. "You have good obs for a civilian."

Good obs is squad-room jargon for having good powers of observation, I knew from my dad and Brian.

"So you just joined the program yesterday," Reed said, glancing at his notes. "Did you know Hoffman at all? Meet him?"

"Barely."

I recounted how I'd seen the doctor on the porch the night before.

"What was your impression of him?" Reed asked.

"Pretty negative, actually. He seemed like he was kind of goading some of the dieters." I described how Hoffman had been eating an ice-cream sandwich while lecturing the dieters.

"An ice-cream sandwich?" Reed asked, as if he wasn't sure he'd heard me correctly. His lips tightened in a carefully straight line.

"I know, ice cream, it sounds ridiculous," I said, a bit stiffly. "But when you think that everyone here is fasting, practically starving—it was really a mean thing to do."

"Ah, okay. How did the people around him react to that?"

"Everyone seemed intimidated. Except one."

I described how Norm the manatee man had spoken to Hoffman and then gone steaming off the porch in a huff.

"Hoffman called the guy—Norm—a 'weak fool.' But I don't think Norm heard him say it," I added hastily. I felt a pang of guilt, hoping I wasn't getting my fellow dieter into trouble over nothing. "Then, as I was heading back to my room, Hoffman caught me by my wrist and held me back for a second. He asked me if I was new and gave me some advice."

"And what was that advice?"

"Not to be a weak fool."

"I see." Reed gave a slight cough, which sounded suspiciously like a suppressed chuckle. "Do you remember hearing or seeing anything unusual happening before you found the body?" he said. "Anything that struck you as strange?"

I thought back. Last night seemed like an eternity ago.

"Just one thing. Around one a.m., a couple next door had an argument," I said, nodding toward the wall.

As I described the quarrel, Reed scribbled rapidly on his notepad.

"Could you tell anything about the voices? Recognize them?" he asked.

"No," I said, shaking my head. "I've hardly met anyone here yet, plus it was too muffled to hear anything, really. The only part that came through loud and clear was when the woman yelled at me."

That made him look up. "She yelled at you?"

"Yeah, she told me to mind my own business. I'd called out to see if they were okay."

"And did you?"

"Did I what?"

"Mind your own business after that?" Reed's lips broke their straight line, rising at the edges.

"Yes. Unless you count the ear I had pressed to the wall."

Reed laughed out loud. It was a genuine-sounding laugh.

"Did they quiet down after that?"

"Yes. First I heard a door slam; then it got quiet. I assumed it was the guy leaving, but really I don't know."

Reed shoved his notebook into his pocket, rising to leave. "I'd consider moving to a hotel, if I were you," he said. "I don't have to tell you that we have a rather bad actor on our hands in this murder."

A rather bad actor. Now there was a classic piece of British understatement.

I nodded like a dutiful child, even though I had no intention of leaving. I already had my orders from Beatty.

Reed paused with his hand on the doorknob. "So, you worked professionally as a news producer back in Boston," he said. It was a statement, not a question.

"Right. Investigative series."

"And you're not working down here at all?"

"Well, I'll be doing a little summer work for Channel Twelve." No way was I going to tell Reed that Beatty had assigned me to cover Hoffman's murder.

"Well, you'll find your TV colleagues already parked out on the front lawn, getting in everyone's way," Reed said. "They have much more information about the murder than I would have expected."

Reed wasn't smiling now. He nailed me with a strong dose of cop's eye, like I'd committed a crime. "It made me wonder whether they had an inside source," he added. *"You?"*

I lifted my shoulders with my best *Who, me?* shrug.

Reed shook his head. "I thought as much," he said, sighing. "Let's not have that again, shall we? I don't want to have to comb you out of my hair along with all the other reporters."

"It would have to be a pretty *big* comb."

A trace of Reed's former smile returned. He handed me a business card that listed both his office and cell phone number. "Think about moving to that hotel," he advised again. And then he was gone.

I dropped back down onto the bed. The session with the detective had left me shaken.

I kept replaying the way the front doorknob had turned so easily in my hand. It didn't make any sense that the front door had been unlocked at four thirty a.m. That thought led me to a disturbing idea.

What if Hoffman's murderer hadn't driven away in the car I'd seen? What if he—or she—was still inside the clinic?

Chapter 5

Delete Negative Thoughts

In every woman's head (except maybe Martha Stewart's), there's a critical voice that tries to sabotage your every move. This voice questions your ability to succeed on a new eating plan with statements such as: "You never stick with a diet. Why even try?" Or, "You'll just regain the weight you lose. You always do." And, "You know you'll never make it through the holidays without gaining."

You can counteract that negative voice with positive affirmations, such as "I will be successful in reaching my weight loss goals, one day at a time." If the voice keeps criticizing you, say "Delete" out loud. You'll be amazed at how that simple voicing of the "D" word can banish a negative thought.

—From *The Little Book of Fat-busters* by Mimi Morgan

Negative thoughts—I knew all about 'em. So the second I conjured up the idea of the murderer still lurking inside the clinic, I tried to brush it away. Certainly the police would have evacuated the building if they thought the killer was hiding somewhere inside the clinic—but how would they know whom to look for? Hoffman was probably killed by someone he knew. It could be anyone. Someone living next door to me, even.

That's why Reed told you to move out, you dumb cluck, my most negative inner voice chided me. But there was no way I could move out yet. I had an assignment to do.

I was about to get up when a loud pounding broke the silence, sending me about three feet into the air. It sounded like someone was driving straight through the door with a jackhammer.

"Red!"

It was a familiar male voice.

I slid the security chain across the door before opening it. Peering out through the crack, I must have looked like one of those frightened old ladies who live behind multiple locks with their many smelly cats.

Jack Delaware, the 450-pound man I'd met the day before, was standing in the hallway outside my door. Next to him was a young woman.

"We come seeking hot gossip, and you're the hottest thing around. Walk with us!" Jack commanded.

"Uh, okay. Just a sec."

I shut the door and paused, thinking over my options. I needed to drive to Channel Twelve to start developing a game plan for covering the murder story. But Jack's unexpected arrival would give me an opportunity to get a sense of how the dieters were reacting to Hoffman's death. We could use that information in the story.

I shimmied off my navy sweats and threw on jean shorts and a striped polo shirt. A quick fanny check in the mirror reminded me that I hadn't lost enough weight yet to handle shorts.

Delete, I told myself, trying out the tip about negative thoughts. Besides, compared to the really heavy people around here, I was as skinny as a friggin' supermodel.

Jack nodded in an intense way as I stepped into the hallway.

"This is Amber." Jack introduced me to the girl, who looked roughly my age, about twenty-five, with hair dyed in chunky blond and brown stripes.

I tried not to flinch as Amber mashed my hand in an overly hearty handshake.

"Where are we going?" I asked them.

"To the gym to get lunch," Jack said. He held open the exit door at the end of the hallway. "They're serving meals over there while the cops are here. It's the only place we can go right now, other than our rooms. Hell of a first day for you, huh?"

"You could say that," I said.

Amber fingered her necklace, which spelled out her name in pavé diamond letters. "We heard you and Evelyn found Dr. Hoffman's body on the porch. Everyone's saying he was murdered," she said, her voice sounding worried. "What happened?"

I hesitated before answering. It didn't seem wise to say too much to anyone at this point. "I don't know, exactly," I finally said. "But it was really horrible. I'm still trying to process it all." I decided to throw the questions back to them in an attempt to shift the focus. "Has anyone seen Evelyn? Is she okay?"

"Oh, Evelyn vamoosed as soon as the cops were through with her. Looking pretty shaken up, too." Jack said. "Word is she checked into the Renaissance House across town."

The Renaissance House was another diet clinic in Durham; I knew from the research I'd done before coming to Durham. It was supposed to be ultra-swanky. I hadn't even considered going there because it was twice as expensive as the Fruit House.

We wound our way through the parking lot and around the side of the clinic. In the front yard, a pair of uniformed cops guarded the entrance to the porch, which was roped off with yellow tape.

"I wonder what will happen now that Doc Hoffman's gone," Jack said, staring at the guards. "He was really the soul of this place."

Tears sprang into Amber's eyes. "Yeah," she said. "I just can't imagine the program without him."

I hesitated before replying. Last night Hoffman had struck me as a bit of a meal-time martinet. But obviously he'd inspired loyalty, too.

"I got the sense that Dr. Hoffman could be kind of rough on people," I said, thinking of the ice-cream scene on the porch.

"But don't you see? That's exactly what was so *great* about the doc," Jack said, looking at me intently. "He watched us fatties from on high, like Zeus. Sure, he'd throw his thunderbolt at you if you ate off-program. But if you followed the rules, you were the golden child."

"Yeah, he never put up with our lame excuses the way they do at those touchy feely programs across town," Amber chimed in. "Like, at the Renaissance House? People on that program don't lose nearly as much weight as they do here."

"I made the mistake of signing up at the Renaissance House once," Jack said. "I actually *gained* weight."

There was a thoughtful pause as the three of us nodded our heads over the shortcomings of the Renaissance House.

Jack broke the silence with a yelp that made Amber and me jump. "But *oh* yeah, you're right about the doc being rough on people," he said to me.

"Can you give an example of that?" I asked. In the back of my head, I was trying to come up with a motive for the murder.

"Well, see Norm over there?"

Scaling back his voice a notch, Jack nodded at Norm, who was standing off by himself near the curb.

"When Norm ate off-program, Doc Hoffman would

give him a sign that says 'Don't Feed Me' and tell him to wear it," Jack said.

"I saw Norm last night on the porch," I said. "He said something to Hoffman, and then took off down the street. He looked really angry about something."

Jack shrugged. "Well, that's Norm," he said. "He thinks because he's supersized, he should get more food than the rest of us. Last night Norm probably got riled and went off to cheat with Kentucky Fried Chicken. That's what he usually does. But Norm really loved the doc."

I wondered about that. I studied Norm's face, which was expressionless as he watched the cops working. KFC rampages wouldn't appear to rise to the level of a motivation for murder. However, if Norm or someone like him was harboring a more serious grudge against Hoffman, we could be looking at a clinic chock-full of potential suspects.

"Did anyone ever threaten the doctor, do you know?" I asked, directing that question to both of them.

Amber and Jack exchanged a look I couldn't read.

"There's this one kid, Billy Harris," Amber said after a long hesitation. "He had a pretty big fight with Dr. Hoffman yesterday just before dinner. I heard him say he'd had it with this place."

"Look, Billy's just a kid. He was ticked off," Jack said quickly.

Amber gave him a look before her eyes came back to me. "It was more than that. I heard him say he wanted to kill Dr. Hoffman. He left last night, and no one's seen him since," she said. "His car's gone, too."

"Car?" I said. "Do you know what kind of car he drives?"

"An old yellow Camaro."

A Camaro. It had to be the same one that had nearly wiped me off the road the day before. I remembered it had been driven by a dark-haired boy.

I wondered whether Detective Reed knew about Billy Harris. The fact that Billy's car was old, like the one I'd seen leaving the murder scene this morning, and that he'd threatened to kill Hoffman definitely made him a "person of interest," as we say on the news.

The thud of a sliding metal door drew my attention to the street. A news van with the Channel Twelve logo had pulled up to the curb, and a camera operator was unloading some equipment. A guy wearing a blazer got out of the passenger side and approached the cops, microphone in hand.

The arrival of the news crew jolted me like a horse hearing the bell at the starting gate. I needed to high-tail it to Channel Twelve and set up a game plan with Beatty. But first, I had one more question for Jack and Amber.

"What about any relationships Dr. Hoffman might have had? I heard he was never married?" I asked them.

Amber exchanged another glance with Jack. She checked over her shoulder. "Okay, so here's the real dirt on Dr. Hoffman . . . ," she said, leaning in. "Not many people know this, but he was all hot and heavy with this wild chick on the program. You've seen her. Bethany. She's your next-door neighbor. She's in that last room next to yours, right by the parking lot entrance."

"Yeah, and you were sitting at the same table as her in the dining room last night, too," Jack said.

"Hoffman's girlfriend lives next door to me?"

I felt a prickly sensation in my fingertips at that news. My thoughts zinged to the screaming match I'd heard the night before. Had that been the sound of my "wild chick" neighbor fighting with Hoffman, just before he was killed?

"That's right. Hoffman's girlfriend was sitting at

your table last night." Amber nodded, apparently mis-
understanding the reason for my surprised look.
"Bethany. She was sitting with Reno O'Malley, this
townie guy who hangs all over her. Why all the guys
go for her type I have *no* idea."

"For the same reason we go to amusement parks.
The crazy rides," Jack explained with a wicked grin.

"Are you sure Bethany was Hoffman's girlfriend?"
I asked him.

"Sure as sure," Jack replied. "Fruiters have spotted
him all over town driving her around in his big green
Eldorado. You can't miss the monster-mobile."

"And last weekend someone saw them going into a
club together, a place called the Razor's Edge, I
think," Amber added. "I couldn't believe it—can you
imagine Dr. Hoffman *dancing*?" she said, grinning at
Jack.

"Yeah, I can—the Willpower Watusi," Jack snorted.

"If Bethany was Hoffman's girlfriend, then what's
she doing with Reno O'Malley, do you think?" I
asked them.

Jack shrugged. "Same player, different club?" he
suggested. "The Fruit House is such a Peyton Place,
nothing would surprise me."

I remembered Bethany and Reno sitting at the dining room table the night before. The couple had
wrapped themselves in such a scowl that I'd moved
past them to sit next to Evelyn.

Bethany seemed so young—at least twenty-five
years younger than Hoffman. Could she really have
been his girlfriend? I'd need to make contact with her
and see what she had to say about the murder, and
about the fight I heard in the middle of the night.

Once we arrived at the makeshift dining room, I
picked up an orange and a to-go cup of Piss Paste.
After saying good-bye to Jack and Amber, I stopped

off at my room just long enough to change into more professional-looking attire. It was important that I look like an actual news producer when I showed up for my new gig at Channel Twelve. I pulled on a light black shell and matching flared skirt under an ivory cotton blazer, then added some black leather flats plucked from the suitcase. As a final touch I put on a pair of tiger-eye earrings my dad had given me for Christmas last year, in honor of his nickname for me, Tiger.

Back in the corridor, I paused in front of my neighbor Bethany's door. I'd told Detective Reed about hearing a fight last night, but I wondered whether he knew about a relationship between Bethany and Hoffman. I was sure he'd be interested to know that the doctor had a lover who'd been engaged in a screaming match hours before he was found dead, and that there might also be another man in the picture, this guy Reno.

What excuse could I possibly manufacture for knocking? I couldn't say I was working on a news story about the murder.

I pulled off my earrings, stashed one in a pocket, and kept the other one in my hand. Using my knuckles, I rapped lightly on the door.

No response. After a pause I knocked again, louder this time. My heart rate revved up as I heard the knob click.

Bethany opened the door. "What?" she said, releasing a puff of patchouli incense from inside the room. The *what* was as flat as an ice rink.

I remembered Bethany's metal zit from the night before. Otherwise she was quite pretty, with sculptured cheekbones and a plump but sensuous figure that was packed tightly into jeans and a T-shirt that said HOT PINK BETTY.

"Bethany?" I started. "I'm Kate Gallagher, and—"

"You with the cops?" Bethany took in my blazer and skirt with unfriendly eyes.

"No, not at all," I said, thinking it interesting that she was expecting the police. "I just started the program yesterday. And I think you were at my table in the dining room last night. I found this earring outside your door when I was on my way out for a walk this morning, and thought you might have lost it."

I opened my palm with the tiger's eye earring and held it out for her to see.

"Oh, right, I think I remember you," Bethany said slowly, then glanced down at the earring.

I tried to peer past her into the room without being too obvious about it. No one there.

Bethany shrugged. "Nope, that earring's totally not my style," she said, shifting her weight as if about to fade back into her room.

"Wait," I said, knowing I sounded too eager. "I'm new here. I just started yesterday. What's been happening around here today, anyway? They told me the head of the program was killed. Dr. Hoffman?"

I was hoping to jolt her into some kind of reaction, and Bethany didn't disappoint.

"I heard about it." She said, leaning into the doorjamb. "I just can't believe it, though. He was really cool." As she said the word *cool,* Bethany dropped her eyes.

"He was cool?" I smiled encouragingly, hoping to coax a few more syllables from her.

"Yeah, he used to bring me books on Renaissance art," Bethany said. A faint blush crept up her neck.

If he'd given her books on Renaissance art, Hoffman must have seen something of substance beneath Bethany's hoochie mama surface.

"I just can't believe someone killed him," Bethany added, blinking rapidly. "Some cop—a British dude—

came around this morning, and he was . . ." She snapped her head back and sniffed loudly, biting off the end of her sentence as if she thought she'd said too much.

That explained why she thought I was a cop. Detective Reed had already questioned her. I wondered if that meant Bethany was a suspect.

"I gotta go now." Bethany edged backward into the room, pulling the side of the door slowly with her hand as if to close it.

"Oh, okay, but I was just wondering about one thing . . . ," I said, trying to draw out the conversation a moment longer. "You know, we're actually neighbors. I live in the room next door." I indicated my door with a nod. "I'm sorry if you were upset by my calling out in the middle of the night. I just—"

"That was *you*?"

Bethany's eyes narrowed. The hint of openness she'd exhibited a moment earlier vanished. "I told you last night to mind your own business," she said, hissing the final *s*'s in *business*. "Is that why you're really here now?" Her voice rose. "Butting in again?"

Bethany's face was turning so red, I was half-afraid she'd pop a stud. "I wasn't butting in last night," I said. "I simply heard screaming and got concerned."

"Well, quit causing trouble."

"What trouble?" a deep voice boomed off to my right.

I turned my head and found myself staring into a huge, glowering face that loomed just inches away from my nose.

The glowering face belonged to Reno O'Malley, Bethany's "townie." He raised his hands toward me. It looked as if he were going to wrap them around my neck.

Delete, delete, delete.

Chapter 6

Neutralize Stress-Eating

Unpleasant people create stress, and stress can lead to overeating. When you are confronted by a negative person or situation, visualize yourself as a ship floating in a protected harbor. You are surrounded by calm water. The other person's ship is separate from yours, roiling about in choppy seas. However, in your mind, try to keep the water around <u>you</u> as smooth as glass.

You can't control the waves that are disturbing other peoples' ships—just focus on the quiet circle of water around you.

Calm, smooth, serene . . . Om-m-m-m-m . . .

—From *The Little Book of Fat-busters* by Mimi Morgan

My ship listed to portside as Reno unfurled a finger from a fist the size of a ham hock and stabbed it in the air near my chest.

"What's going on?" he demanded, looking from Bethany to me. "Who's she?"

"No one," Bethany said, putting a restraining hand on his arm. There was a little quake in her voice.

"*She* actually has a name. I'm Kate Gallagher," I said, righting myself again. "I just wanted to stop by and make sure you were both okay. Things sounded like they got out of hand last night."

"What the hell?" Reno swung his eyes back to Bethany. I could smell Jade East radiating off him. The cheap cologne created a potent methane layer, like the atmosphere on Uranus.

"It's *nothing* I said." Bethany's tone was sullen. "She's just that busybody from last night. Forget it."

Several doors down, a middle-aged woman emerged from one of the rooms. She appeared to be adjusting her fanny pack, but you could tell she was listening to us.

Reno bounced a look off the woman before returning his glare to me. "There's nothing here for you to worry about," he said from between clenched teeth. "Why don't you mind your own business and play with yourself tonight—that's what you fat women *do*, isn't it?" He brushed past me and disappeared inside the room.

After shooting me a death-ray look, Bethany shut the door.

I hurried down the rest of the hallway and into the parking lot to my car, my heart pumping in overdrive. Climbing into the TR6, I pulled out the directions to Channel Twelve that I'd taken down from the producer.

I was glad I'd made contact with Bethany. In our brief encounter, she'd revealed that Hoffman had bought her gifts, and that the police had questioned her about the murder. The way she'd blushed at my questions suggested that she and Hoffman had been involved in something more than a book club.

Then there was her simian boyfriend Reno to consider. His "fat women" jibe was still echoing in my ears. Bethany had seemed almost afraid of him. *Why do women even* speak *to guys like that?* I wondered. If women never gave jerks like Reno the time of day, his kind would eventually stop procreating, which would make the world a better place.

Evolutionary theory aside, it seemed clear that Reno and Bethany were a couple. So what about Bethany and *Hoffman*? Perhaps Bethany was seeing both men. If so, had Reno been jealous of the doctor? With her "busybody from last night" remark, Bethany had confirmed that it was Reno, and not Hoffman, who had been with her in her room last night. But perhaps Reno had killed Hoffman later, in a fit of rage. Under the right circumstances he could probably be dangerous, I thought as I shifted into second gear.

Twenty minutes later I pulled up in front of the Channel Twelve studios, which were located in a red-brick building along the I-40 bypass where it curves around the city of Durham.

Evidently reaching for a *Gone with the Wind* effect, the architect had grafted a faux Southern mansion facade onto the studio building's front side, complete with a portico and fake Corinthian columns. All it lacked were some belles sipping mint juleps. The antebellum front was incongruous underneath the layer of satellite dishes and antennae that bristled from the studio's roof.

As soon as I parked and obtained a temporary ID from the receptionist, I was greeted by the news director, Chuck Beatty.

"Gallagher! Good meeting you at last," he said. "I want to introduce you to Greg Silver—the two of you will be working together on this one. Let's walk."

Beatty was unexpectedly tall, about six foot four, with receding blond hair and aviator frame glasses. He radiated nervous energy, a trait he shared with most other TV news directors I'd known.

Trailing Beatty for a lightning-quick tour of the facility, I had to double-time my steps to match his long strides.

"Silver's trying to get an interview with Durham

PD," Beatty said. "So far all they're saying is that the Hoffman murder is under investigation. No details. Hang on a second."

Beatty popped open one of the doors, startling a young woman inside a booth who was huddled over a tape-editing machine with headphones over her ears. He paused for a nanosecond to absorb the image that was frozen on the screen.

"Remember, I want a minute *thirty* on that roaming dog story, Julia. I'm going to run it as tonight's kicker," he said. Without giving the girl time to respond or even remove her headphones, he shut the door again.

We ducked into another office at the end of the hall. The reporter I'd seen earlier that morning at the clinic was reading a newspaper. His feet were propped up on the desk.

"Silver, this is Kate Gallagher, the one I told you about from Boston," Beatty said. "She won the Columbia Dupont award for a series on graft that she produced. We'll be using her to produce the Hoffman murder story. You'll be reporting."

"The Dupont, huh?" Silver said, slowly lowering his feet off the desk. He eyed me with an up-and-down scan. "I'm honored to be working with someone so *big* time." His tone sounded sarcastic.

"That depends on how big the thing is you're comparing yourself to, haven't you found that to be true?" I said, lobbing back a full-body scan of *him*. On the word "big," I paused my eyes ever so slightly at his belt buckle. Two could play at smart ass.

"Slap down! Beatty, I think I'm in love," Silver said, grinning.

"Yeah well, keep it zipped up, Silver. We got work here to do." Beatty made a flicking away gesture with his fingers.

I wondered if Silver had adopted his name for TV. Everything about him screamed show horse, right down to his indigo linen shirt cuffs.

"Kate's gonna continue working on her assignment about the diet clinic," Beatty continued. "It'll provide her some cover while she collects information for us about Hoffman's murder. Whaddaya got so far, Kate?"

Quickly, I laid out what I'd discovered so far about Hoffman's murder, starting with my meeting with Reed, and my theory that Hoffman had a girlfriend, my next-door neighbor, Bethany.

"I already spoke with Bethany, and she let it slip that the homicide cop interviewed her. Sounded like she might be a suspect," I said.

"A girlfriend who's a suspect?" Beatty leaned forward, looking interested. "Hey, that dovetails with something juicy I heard just now from our studio engineer. He has a brother who works at the medical examiner's office. Evidently the investigators found some weird stuff at Hoffman's home where he lived over in west Durham," he said slowly. "The rumor is that it was some incredibly kinky stuff."

"Kinky stuff?" I echoed. "What do you mean?"

I glanced at Silver, who was struggling to restrain an inane-looking smile.

"Bill's brother—that's Bill Jacobs, our production engineer—didn't know exactly what the investigators found in Hoffman's home, but they asked the forensic examiner to check for any signs of trauma that might be associated with 'unusual' sexual activity," Beatty said. "Like S and M, I guess."

"S and M? Old Doc Hoffman, a sado master? This is too *good*." Silver plopped back down into his chair and tilted back, emitting a whoop. "I wonder if he liked to play on top or bottom?" he chortled, flashing a lewd grin at me.

"It's all fun and games, till someone puts an eye

out," I cracked. Then I thought back to Bethany. She had the aura of someone who might like to play rough. Maybe S and M was part of the equation. "I'd like to talk to your engineer about what he heard," I said.

"Bill's a good guy. He'll tell you everything he knows," Beatty said. "One thing you need to keep in mind, though: We keep the stuff we get from Bill on deep background, because he doesn't want to get his brother in trouble."

"Deep background" meant we could use the information, but not attribute it to a source.

"His brother works in the medical examiner's office. That would—"

"Cost you one of your best sources?" I interjected.

"You got it," Beatty shrugged.

Silver stayed behind in his office to work the phones while Beatty and I located the engineer deep in the production bowels of the station.

As we entered Jacobs's office, the stocky, pale engineer was toiling over an ENG camera that lay disassembled on his desk. He didn't look pleased at the interruption.

"I don't really know much," Jacobs said after Beatty introduced me and told him I wanted to learn more about Hoffman's murder.

Beatty opened his mouth to respond, but I leaped in first. "You said that the investigators asked the forensic examiner to look for signs of sexual trauma," I said. "Did your brother have any idea what kind of trauma that would be?"

"John told me they were supposed to be looking for ligature marks on the neck, wrists and"—the engineer reddened, adjusting his glasses—"and genitals, I guess."

"Why were the investigators looking for evidence like that? Did he know?" I pressed.

"It was because of something they found in the doctor's basement—evidently it was some kind of S and M setup. Like a sex dungeon, he said."

"What?" Beatty's eyebrows shot up behind his aviators. "You didn't tell me about the dungeon part, Jacobs."

"Well, you just seemed like you were in a hurry to rush off. Like you were busy, I guess." Jacobs didn't meet Beatty's eyes. He reached for a lens piece and took his time examining it.

I got the feeling that the quiet engineer didn't always appreciate the news director's rush-rush, Type A personality style.

"I don't know too much about sex dungeons, I'm afraid," I admitted. "Do you know what they found, exactly? Any specifics?"

"No." Jacobs shook his head. "But you know who *might* know. . . ." He paused. "There's only one store around here that sells that kind of stuff. An adult store called the Vixen's Den. It's just over the county line in Kerashaw."

"I should go check it out—maybe they'll know something about Hoffman," I said.

Jacobs grabbed a piece of paper off his desk and scribbled down directions to the Vixen's Den. "You won't find a sign outside the place. There's only a purple neon fox in the window," he said. "Not that I've ever been there, of course," he added with a sheepish grin.

Beatty snorted. "Yeah, right, Jacobs—we got the goods on you now."

A shrill beeping interrupted our conversation—it was the pager on Beatty's belt going off. He checked it, then grimaced.

"Cripes almighty, we go on the air in thirty minutes—I've gotta go get in the hot seat."

I thanked Jacobs for his information and hurried after the news director's rapidly retreating figure.

"Do me a favor and look over Silver's script tonight, would you?" Beatty said to me when I caught up with him. "He's burned us a couple of times by not sourcing his facts properly. That's one reason I want him to work with a producer."

"Okay."

Outside the newsroom door I spotted a couple of my old pals, the vending machines. I glanced at them just long enough to note that yes, they *do* have Ho Hos in North Carolina. Little Swiss-filled log rolls coated in chocolate, Ho Hos are a tubular version of Whoopic Pies. Fortunately for my diet, there wasn't time to stop.

In the newsroom, reporters sat hunched over their desks, working frantically on last-minute copy.

"Hey, Kate!" Silver came charging toward me from the opposite side of the room, clutching a page of script in his right hand. He shoved it under my nose. "I got twenty seconds of comment about Hoffman's murder from the police spokes-hole. All he would say is, it's 'under investigation.' " Silver shook his head. "The jerk wouldn't give me anything else."

"They never say anything worthwhile on the record this early on." I took his script and glanced through it.

"Wait a minute," I said.

Grabbing a pen, I flattened the script on an empty desk and drew a line through the first sentence of Silver's copy. "Why don't you lead with the police reaction, and then fill in the murder detail. It makes it seem more immediate." I scrawled a new lead across the top.

Silver stared over my shoulder at his copy. "I guess that *is* better," he finally said, with obvious reluctance.

I studied his script another minute. "And here,

where you're talking about the crime scene on the porch—there were two of us who found the body, not four. Remember my telling you that?" I said, scribbling some more on the script.

Silver looked stung. "But . . ." He opened his mouth as if to argue, then apparently thought better of it. "Okay, I guess." He snatched up the script before I could mark up anything else. Then he wheeled about and disappeared into his office.

Beatty was right about Silver. Not only did he not check his facts, he didn't even report what he'd been told correctly.

I sighed. I hated playing News Nanny to incompetent reporters. It would be easier to do the story by myself. If I ever got the chance to, that is.

My stomach collapsed into a sickening spasm. I realized I hadn't eaten lunch today. I wasn't sure which was causing my gut to roil more—the prospect of another underwhelming meal at the Hoffman clinic, or the idea that a killer might be lurking there.

But first I had to make it out of the newsroom. It would be a tricky maneuver. The exit path would take me past the snack machines again, where danger lurked.

To get prepared, I took a deep breath and lashed myself mentally to the mast, like Odysseus. Then I set sail around Vending Machine Island. And once again, I managed to survive the siren call of the Ho Hos.

Chapter 7

Keep Your Tank Fueled

When you don't eat enough food, your metabolism starts to slow down, and so does your weight loss progress. Without fuel, other body systems start to shut down, too. (For example, half the women reporters at Channel Nine are so thin they don't get their periods every month.)

Make sure you eat enough calories to keep your weight loss engine going.

—From *The Little Book of Fat-busters* by Mimi Morgan

When I made it back to the Hoffman Clinic, a few stragglers were lingering over their dinners in the gym/dining hall. A couple of waitresses were already cleaning up and stacking chairs.

Paige, the physician's assistant who had checked me in yesterday, sat hunched over a corner table by herself. She was writing something into a notebook.

Compared to the hustle and flow of the Channel Twelve newsroom, the clinic had a quiet, slow-mo feeling to it. There were fewer people around than there'd been the night before, when I'd checked in. It looked like the doctor's murder had scared off a lot of people.

The manager, Marjory, waved to me apologetically

when she spotted me standing in the doorway. "Oh Kate, the kitchen just closed," she said. "But don't worry—I'll grab you a plate."

Marjory disappeared, then returned with a plate of grilled turkey, some tomato wedges, and even a tiny wheat roll. No sign of Piss Paste.

"Ooh, real food," I said, taking the plate. "Thanks, Marjory."

My stomach growled appreciatively. I realized I'd been too busy this afternoon working to notice that I hadn't eaten since this morning's orange. That was a first. Except for my near-miss with the vending machines, I hadn't thought of food for hours.

"Dr. Thornburg is already changing a lot of things, including adding more calories and protein to the diet," Marjory said.

"Well, my stomach heartily approves," I said.

"Yeah, I know. It's a good thing," Marjory said, then hesitated. "It's just—it's weird to see everything change all at once."

"I'm so very sorry about Dr. Hoffman. Did—?" I stopped speaking as tears rose in Marjory's eyes.

"Thanks," Marjory said, dashing them away. "Whoa, I've gotta stop crying. I'd better go." With an embarrassed look on her face, she turned away and hurried out of the gym.

Paige had remained seated during Marjory's meltdown, quietly observing her.

Carrying my plate in front of me, I approached her. "Hi Paige, okay if I interrupt?" I said, sliding into a seat.

Paige, who'd looked startled by my sudden approach, quickly overlaid it with a welcoming nod. "Of course. I'm afraid Marjory's still a bit emotional," she replied. Whatever emotion Paige had about the murder, she did a good job controlling it.

"Well, that's understandable," I said. "I'm sure this is difficult for everyone."

"Oh, yes. It's been very difficult." Paige looked at me square on.

My initial impression of Paige as mouselike had not been accurate. She was actually quite pretty—it was her tamped-down manner that made her fade into the woodwork.

Paige rubbed her fingertips against her forehead. "I'm reworking the schedules," she said. "This is the only place to work on it right now. Our offices won't open again until tomorrow."

"Does that mean the regular dining room will re-open, too?" I asked her. "It just seems *wrong* somehow, to be eating inside a gym."

Paige pressed out a faint chuckle. "Yes, hopefully things should start getting back to normal—the *new* normal, I guess," she said. "Dr. Thornburg will address the patients after breakfast tomorrow and lay out her plans for the clinic going forward. She'll be in charge now. She's already making a lot of changes."

My stomach was thrilled with one of them, I thought as I took a bite of the turkey. Heaven. "That reminds me," I added. "I know it's terrible timing, but I need to ask Dr. Thornburg about the weight loss story I'm supposed to be taping," I said to her. "In our original plan, a camera crew was going to meet me here tomorrow morning. Do you think—"

Paige looked taken aback. "Oh, I don't know," she said. "We probably will have to reschedule because of . . . everything, you know."

"Oh dear," I said, donning a concerned expression. "Because it's a weight loss transformation story, we really need to get my near-starting weight for it to make sense. That is, if you think she'll still want me to do the story. I mean, I'm sure we can do the series at another one of the clinics in town. Is the clinic going to stay *open*?"

"Oh, of course it'll stay open," Paige said hastily. "I'm sure she'll want to reschedule. I'll remind her about it in the morning." Paige reached for a small, spiral-bound appointment book that was on top of her paper stack. "Dr. Thornburg probably forgot. She's had so much on her mind today."

"I know, this must be so rough for all of you," I said. "Have you worked here a long time?"

"Oh, yes." Paige pulled in a breath. "I've been here ten years."

Ten years? That was surprising. Paige didn't look old enough to have worked at the clinic that long.

"There don't seem to be many people around to-night. Have many checked out because of the murder?"

"A few." Paige's eyes went opaque. "I didn't hear . . . did the police say it was definitely a *murder*?"

"Well, they didn't have to," I replied. "Evelyn and I were the ones who found Dr. Hoffman's body on the porch this morning. I thought everyone knew that."

I'd said that in a blatant attempt to provoke a re-sponse. I wanted to hear from anyone who had regular contact with Hoffman. Anyone who might know something.

Paige stared at me. "No, I didn't know you found his body," she said. "That must have been terrible for you. I can't imagine."

"It was." I glanced down at the book in front of her. "So you handle the doctors' appointment books?"

Paige shook her head. "Only Dr. Thornburg's," she said. "Victor never kept a book. He thought it was something only undisciplined minds needed." She glanced away.

I noted the familiar way she'd called Hoffman by

his first name. "Wow. He must have had a great memory," I said.

"Well, he'd forget appointments sometimes, but then he'd say it was my fault because I didn't tell him about them." Paige flashed a grin, which was followed immediately by a startled look. She rolled her eyes around guiltily, as if checking to see whether anyone had overheard her being disloyal.

"Do you have any idea what time Hoffman left the clinic Sunday night? I'm just trying to maybe tie it in with some noises I heard outside my room. Maybe there's a connection to the murder, I don't know," I rambled, trying not to sound too much like I was pumping her for information.

"Um, he left for the night after dinner, I think. After his last appointment—I think it was with Billy Harris."

Billy Harris was the driver of the careening Camaro that had almost run me into the ditch. And according to Amber and Jack, Billy had said he wanted to "kill" Hoffman. *And* he'd been AWOL all day today. Had something happened between Billy and Hoffman during that last appointment—something that led to the murder?

"Did Billy ever turn up today, do you know?" I asked.

But Paige's expression had shut down. "I really don't know." She shrugged and gathered up her papers. "I have to go. I'll speak with Anita about your weight loss story first thing in the morning." Hugging her papers to her chest, she glided gracefully out of the dining room.

I watched Paige go. I'd obviously been as smooth as lumpy pancake batter with my questions. "Way to drive 'em off, Kate," I muttered under my breath.

I glanced around the room. Other than me, the only person left was the bulldog-faced waitress, who shot me a look that let me know she didn't appreciate my still being here. I dumped the rest of my food into a napkin, folded it up into a little hobo's square, and headed back to my room.

Bethany's door was closed as I passed by it on my way to my room. I paused in the hallway, straining to hear any sounds of life from within. But all was silent.

When I got back to my room, I had an IM message from Mimi:

Katie my love—how goes the program?

Your tips r great—really helping, I wrote back. And so they were. I don't know what I would have done without Mimi's words of wisdom over the past two stressful days.

But right then I couldn't bear to go into the whole story about the murder, or even mention Detective Reed and his charming accent (Mimi and I are both suckers for British guys). That was definitely a conversation one had to share over a pitcher of margaritas, or something stronger. So I added:

I'll catch u up on everything later. What are u up 2?

Mimi wrote back:

Just finished practicing my tip on sex as exercise. Glowing with pheromones right now.

I hadn't gotten to the tip on sexual aerobics yet, which is just as well because my immediate prospects for adding it to my daily workout seemed bleak as hell. I wrote back:

That's totally O.O.C., Mimi!

Great. Mimi was happily burning orgasmic calories, while all I had to think about was a skewered diet doctor and hunger pangs. Life certainly couldn't get much worse, I thought.

But I thought wrong.

The next morning I awoke with a start, groggy and disoriented. It was six a.m. I took a ten-minute shower, and then pulled on a khaki skort and a yellow polo shirt. I was gratified to feel that the waist of the skort was a little looser than the last time I'd worn it.

I popped open my laptop and opened a new document. I started writing down everything that had happened yesterday, starting with the discovery of Hoffman's body on the front porch of the main house. I wanted to get down the chronology of events before anything faded from memory.

I was still absorbed in my notes some time later when I heard the electric whine of a vacuum cleaner outside my room. I glanced at the clock. Shit, it was almost eight, which meant I was about to miss breakfast. Plus, I was supposed to talk with Anita Thornburg about my weight loss story this morning.

I checked my messages. There were two new ones— one of them from my dad, the other from Detective Reed.

My dad's message directed me to call him ASAP. He had his commander-in-chief tone on, always a bad sign. I wondered if he'd already gotten wind of the murder somehow. That would not be good.

I thought of the last time I'd seen my dad. He'd met me outside my Boylston Street condo in the wee hours of morning to see me off on my trip to Durham. Even when he was out of uniform, my father's silver-white hair and ramrod bearing gave the impression of a born commander. Born to command everyone, apparently, except his daughter. Over our weekly family dinner of boiled beef and cabbage days earlier, my father had argued against my trip to the North Carolina diet clinic. And lost.

Ever since Mom died when I was thirteen, Dad has been an incredible worrywart about me. Even now he has trouble letting go. I constantly have to remind him that I'm a big girl now and can take care of myself.

Reed had left a request for me to call him at the

office. I'd have to do that later. Right then, I had to hightail it to the dining room and weigh in.

Just down the hallway, the door to Bethany's room stood wide open. A thirtyish woman wearing a pink uniform was inside, vacuuming. The room was clean and empty looking, with only a trace of patchouli lingering in the air. It appeared that Bethany had moved out.

"Pardon me, but did the girl who was here leave?" I asked the housekeeper, raising my voice over the vacuum cleaner.

The woman shook her head and raised her eyebrows, as if she hadn't heard clearly.

I put a toe across the threshold into the room. "I'm really sorry to bother you, but do you know if the girl who was here checked out?" I repeated.

The woman switched off the machine and said some words that sounded like Spanish.

"Oh, I'm sorry. I don't speak—"

Dammit, why had I decided to be exotic in high school by taking Mandarin instead of Spanish? I only knew a couple of words.

"Um, the *chica* who was here? Did she *vamoose*?" I said, unsure whether "vamoose" was even remotely like Spanish or not.

Evidently not, because I received a baffled look. Glancing around the room, I had the weird sensation that someone was watching us. But that was impossible. Bethany was clearly gone. With an apologetic shrug and a wave to the housekeeper, I retreated to the hallway.

I'd barely taken a step when the overhead lighting dimmed and flickered green, as if it were about to zap out. I glanced around with a vague sense of uneasiness. I couldn't put my finger on it, but a weird vibe was building in the air.

Just as I was reassuring myself that there was nothing to worry about, I heard something slide open inside Bethany's room. Next there was a muffled thud, like a small body hitting the carpet. Then a crash, followed by a screeching wail.

It was the housekeeper. She was screaming.

Chapter 8

Bring Along a Meal Map

Planning is everything when it comes to staying on your eating course. Unexpected events can always arise, but it helps to know exactly what your next meal will be, plus when and where it will take place.

Think of your meal plan as a map that will guide you through the world of food. You wouldn't drive into a strange city without a map, would you? (Well, maybe you <u>would</u>, but then you'd wind up at the gas station asking for directions, and oh, while I'm here, gimme that king-sized bag of Whoppers. . . .)

To simplify meal planning, research shows that it's helpful to eat the exact same thing for breakfast and lunch every day. That way, the only thing you have to plan is dinner. And a snack. And maybe a low-fat dessert . . .

—From *The Little Book of Fat-busters* by Mimi Morgan

Two things happened next: First, there was a wild, scrabbling sound of claws ripping across the hallway carpet; then something low and soft streaked past my feet, grazing my ankles.

I let out a startled shriek. My eyes tracked the moving object until it reached the closed door at the end of the hallway, where a cloud of fur pulled up short. It was a cat.

I turned toward the sound of another commotion. Marjory came running down the hallway toward me. Her path was intersected by the housekeeper, who'd emerged from Bethany's room. Both women moved in on the cat.

"*Mi corazón,*" the housekeeper kept repeating, pressing her hand over her heart.

"I think Elfie scared Ana," Marjory said, stepping past me. "Elfie, you little escape artist," she said to the cat. Turning her head, she murmured a few words in Spanish to soothe Ana, who still looked rattled enough that I thought she might require a defibrillator.

Confronted with a dead end, Elfie the cat took a cue from the canine world. She flopped onto her back in a posture of utter surrender.

"People can have pets here?" I asked, feeling embarrassed that I'd shrieked like an idiot.

"Elfie was Dr. Hoffman's kitty," Marjory said, scooping up the cat. "I guess she was hiding out in the room Ana was cleaning. I've been looking for her all morning."

"That's Bethany William's room Elfie was hiding in, isn't it?"

"*Was* Bethany's room, yes."

"Has Bethany checked out?"

"This morning, yes." Marjory lifted her eyes from the squirming cat to me. She gave me a careful look.

"Do you know where she went?"

"No, I really don't," Marjory said, tucking the cat's front paws under her arm. "*Ouch.* Bad cat."

"What will happen to Elfie now?"

"Someone will adopt her. Maybe Lou will."

"Lou?"

"Lou Bettinger. He's a lawyer who used to be on the program," Marjory said. "He's—well, never mind. Not important." Nuzzling her face into the cat's fur, Marjory turned and hurried away down the hallway.

Clearly she'd been about to add something else, but had changed her mind.

It was interesting that Hoffman's cat had chosen to hide out in Bethany's room. It made me wonder whether she'd hung out in there before. With Hoffman, perhaps?

I headed outside and circled around the clinic, retracing the path I'd taken yesterday morning.

The crime scene tape around the porch was gone. Everything looked deserted, which meant the police must have finished the physical part of their investigation. Even so, I felt nervous as I climbed up the steps to the porch. Looking around, I saw that everything had been sanitized and rearranged. Someone had removed the couch glider where I'd found Hoffman's body.

Closing my eyes, I tried to visualize Hoffman's crumpled, impaled body on the glider. My stomach lurched. Oops—it probably wasn't such a great idea to try this exercise right before breakfast.

I entered the reception area and got weighed in by Paige. The scales revealed the happy news that I'd already lost three pounds.

"This is a great start, Katie," Paige said, congratulating me. Below her white physician's assistant's jacket she was wearing a pair of brocade Chinese slippers. "I haven't had a chance to remind Dr. Thornburg about your weight loss story yet. But I just don't know about bringing in a TV crew at this point. Everything's so—"

"So crazy, I know. Don't worry about it," I replied. "I'll grab Dr. Thornburg after she talks to the group."

Paige gave me a doubtful look. "Well, I guess that would be okay," she said. She marked my weight on a chart that she had fastened to a clipboard.

On my way to the dining room, a flow of dieters

was moving in the opposite direction, down the short hallway that connected the dining area to the rest of the building. The dress code was all about fat liberation: One three-hundred-pound woman's body completely overwhelmed her skimpy short shorts and red halter top. She was sporting almost a foot of cleavage between her massive breasts, but no one batted an eye.

I had a rare and glorious sensation of feeling like the skinny Minnie in the group. With just enough time to grab an unfilling-looking orange, I followed the herd into a large rectangular room that had been set up with rows of metal folding chairs.

Anita Thornburg stood next to a lectern at the front of the room. She was flanked by a nervous-looking man who wore a business suit.

Jack waved to me from the second row. "Hey, Red!" he called out. "I saved you a seat."

I dropped onto a metal folding chair next to the huge man, trying to make myself smaller to avoid cramming against his overflowing flesh.

"Where were you yesterday? You were missing in action all afternoon," Jack said to me.

"I just had some things to take care of," I said, not wanting to go into my trip to Channel Twelve. I wanted to downplay my television news role as much as possible with the other dieters. "Hey, did that Billy Hoffman kid ever turn up yesterday?" I asked him.

Jack shook his head. "I heard he switched to the Renaissance House across town. Lots of people checked out yesterday after what happened."

Anita stepped forward and rapped on the lectern, which caused the noisy chatter to ebb away. Her eyes swept the crowd.

"First of all, I want to thank every one of you for bearing with us during this difficult time," Anita spoke clearly and confidently. The doctor's blond updo and frosted lipstick appeared perfectly arranged. There wasn't a stray hair in sight.

Anita started off with a brief homage to Hoffman, praising him as her predecessor and the founder of the clinic. There would be a memorial service the next day, she announced. Then she quickly shifted gears to the clinic's future.

"Now, I know you have a lot of questions about how the clinic will cope with all this." Anita's gaze shifted to include every part of the audience as she spoke. Obviously this was a woman who was used to being in charge of a group.

"I want to reassure you that the clinic will remain open," she pronounced. "In fact, I can even announce today that we'll soon be introducing some new programs, with the university's backing." She flashed a smile at the man in the blue suit, who responded with a wan grin.

I broke the skin of my orange with my fingernail, releasing a whiff of citrus. I peeled the rest of the fruit, listening intently as Anita described her plans for the clinic. Something about her performance seemed *off,* somehow, for someone acting as a crisis manager. By announcing new initiatives in the immediate wake of the murder, Anita came across as more than a little insensitive.

Dr. Thornburg will be in charge now, Paige had said to me last night. I reflected on that statement for a minute. Maybe because it catapulted her to the top job at the clinic, Hoffman's death was *good* news for Anita.

As soon as the meeting broke up, I made a beeline for the doctor. I knew that she had seen me the day before, while I'd been sitting on the clinic's front porch after finding Hoffman's body, waiting for the police interview. At the time, she'd seemed to be glaring at me for some reason.

Anita gave me a blank stare as I introduced myself now, however.

"We exchanged e-mails about the weight loss piece I'll be working on," I said.

Deafening silence.

"I'll be working with a crew from the local TV station here, Channel Twelve," I prompted again. God, I hoped she'd be a decent interview. Her personality stank like three-day-old fish.

"Ah, right, the news producer from Boston." Anita's eyes stayed flat. "But right now we have so much going on. And with everything that's happened, I'm afraid—"

Paige came up to Anita and spoke softly into her ear. I heard her whisper something about "positive news." It sounded as if Paige were encouraging her to let me do the weight loss story.

Anita's eyes flicked back to me. "Well, we can talk about it, but not right this second," she said impatiently. "My plate is completely full for the rest of the day. You can schedule something for us tomorrow, Paige. Now I'm afraid you'll have to excuse me."

Dismissing both of us, she turned and started talking with the blue suit from the university.

"Let me look at Anita's schedule and get back to you," Paige said to me. She lowered her voice to a whisper. "I'm sorry if she seemed brusque. She's been under such a strain."

"Don't worry, I can handle it," I reassured her. "Thanks for putting in a good word for me, though." I glanced sideways at Anita, who was smiling and chatting up the bean counter like someone trying to impress a first date. It didn't seem to *me* that she was under a strain. She seemed like a woman who was enjoying her newfound role as head of the clinic.

I decided to skip the water aerobics class, which was scheduled for ten a.m. I was eager to check out the Vixen's Den, the adult store that the engineer at Channel Twelve had told me about. I wanted to learn more about the S and M scene that Hoffman had reportedly been involved with. I also needed to touch base with Beatty, to let him know we'd have to reschedule the weight loss taping. Thornburg had made it perfectly clear that today was out. I felt a little uncomfortable that I was heading out without a "meal map"—it was unlikely that I'd make it back to the clinic in time for lunch—but I had a lot to do.

Heading outside, I wandered around the grounds a while, looking for a place to sit down and make some calls. An annoying little cloud of gnats rose from the humid grass as I tramped about, making my calves feel sticky and itchy. Finally I came across a cement bench that was tucked behind a stand of giant saw palmettos.

There was a new message from Detective Reed. The fact that he'd called again sent an excited little tingle up my spine.

Down, girl. It's just his job, I reminded myself as I punched in his number.

The police secretary who picked up the line told me that Reed was investigating out in the field. I'd have to catch up with him later.

I left a message that I had returned the detective's call. Then I clicked off the phone and tilted my face back, soaking up the morning sunshine. I heard a tiny, high-pitched whine just beyond my ear, and flicked my hair. Mosquito. The one thing I'd never get used to in the South was all the bugs. That, plus the energy-sucking wet heat. The heat suffocated you like a sticky boa constrictor, which probably explained why Southerners were known for hanging out on the shade porch, sipping iced tea.

I forced myself to focus, making a mental list of all the things I needed to discuss with Reed.

Gradually, from the other side of the saw palmettos, my ears picked up a sound. There was a barely audible click, followed by a sliding noise. It sounded like something being unsheathed.

"Hello?" I called out tentatively, in the general direction of the sound. The sawtoothed leaves of the palmetto trees, shaped like gigantic fans, created a natural screen. Anything could be hiding back there.

My stomach tightened as I realized that my wanderings had carried me a good distance from the main house. A moment later I heard a rattle, followed by deathly quiet. My heart rate ratcheted up several notches.

"Hel-*lo*," I called again. No response. Rising to my feet, I took a step toward the trees. Slowly, I pulled back one of the leaves.

On the shaded ground below me, a man was sitting with his legs splayed out next to a leaf blower. He was wearing green workman's overalls, with a half-open lunchbox by his elbow. It was one of the clinic's gardeners.

The man's face drained when he looked up and saw my face staring down at him through the leaves. He was wearing earplugs and obviously hadn't heard me call out.

"Señora?" he said, wide-eyed. The guy was staring at me like I was some crazed dieter come to jack his breakfast quesadilla, or maybe take his plastic fork and drive it through his eyeball.

"Sorry, sorry. No problem." I made a mumbling apology, my second of the day to the nonnative English–speaking members of the staff. At the rate I was going, they'd have to ship me off for some cultural sensitivity training. Spinning on my heel, I hurried in the opposite direction, toward the parking lot and my car.

*   *   *

My first port of call was going to be the Vixen's Den, the alternative lifestyle store. "Alternative" in this case, I assumed, meant things like whips, corsets, and kooky sex toys. By going there, I hoped to learn something about the S and M dungeon that was rumored to be in Hoffman's basement. On the way I planned to find Hoffman's house, to get a look at it for myself. I wouldn't be able to go inside, of course, but just seeing the house might help me get a better sense of the doctor.

I didn't expect Hoffman's number to be listed, but just in case, I punched in 411 on my cell phone. Luckily, the information operator was able to give me Hoffman's number and address. Pulling the car over into a cul-de-sac, I consulted my maps. Hoffman's home was less than a mile away.

Next I put in a quick call to Beatty, to tell the news director we'd have to reschedule the first installment of my weight loss feature. Beatty promised to have a camera crew ready whenever we could get Thornburg's permission to get started. It was important that I get the weight loss story going. That feature had been my original assignment, before Hoffman's murder, and now it gave me the prospect of getting more access to the staff to ask questions. Questions that might lead to the identity of his killer.

I cruised the streets around Hoffman's neighborhood, looking for his address on Converse Drive. The area was one of Durham's older suburbs, populated with well-maintained homes on large lots. It was hard to see numbers on the setback homes, but I was able to spot Hoffman's place by the police cruiser that was parked outside by the curb.

From the street, I couldn't get a clear view of Hoffman's house. Most of the neighboring homes had lush expanses of velvet lawns and manicured landscaping, but Hoffman's place was completely obscured by elm trees and a privet hedge that was tall as a man. Between breaks in the foliage, I caught glimpses of a peaked roof that was covered in slate tile.

A boat-length, mint green Eldorado convertible sat within view in the driveway, with the top up. I remembered Jack mentioning that Hoffman always drove a green Eldorado that he called the "monster-mobile." This had to be the car he was talking about.

It seemed odd that Hoffman's car was still parked at his home, even though his body had been discovered at the clinic. If the police had found his car somewhere else, they would have undoubtedly taken it to the impound yard for processing, not brought it back here. So it seemed likely that the car had been parked at the house since the murder.

That got me wondering. Had someone else driven him to the clinic Sunday night, and then killed him? Or was he already dead when he was brought there? It was even possible that Hoffman had never left the clinic that day, I reminded myself. In that case, how had he gotten to the clinic that day, and how had he planned to get home that night? Had Bethany given Hoffman the final ride of his life, so to speak?

Everything was quiet as a church around the property. The lack of activity might mean that the police had already finished collecting their evidence. The only sign of an official presence was at the curb, where a patrolman was leaning with his butt attached to the side of his cruiser. He looked like he was counting the minutes until his code-7 snack break.

I tapped the brakes and peered through the trees at the house, trying to get a better angle. No dice—that Berlin wall of a hedge blocked any decent view. To see anything worthwhile, I'd have to get out and actually peer down the driveway. Such a move would risk drawing too much attention to my inspection, I decided.

Even my slow-mo gawk had caught the interest of the patrol officer, I was dismayed to see. He had roused to life as I approached, and now was giving me the staredown from behind his mirrored sunglasses. It wouldn't surprise me if he had been told to be on the lookout for anyone displaying special interest in the house. No matter how stupid you'd think it is, killers often return to the scene of a crime to do a status check, even while the cops are still on the scene. According to my friend Brian, who'd started his police career walking a beat, the officer on duty is always supposed to keep one eye out for a perpetrator doing an après-kill flyby.

I tried a half smile on the patrolman to reassure him, but that only piqued his interest some more. He took a step in my direction and reached into his pocket—he was grabbing for a pen. I was afraid he was going to take down my license number or motion me over. I sped up slightly, but without gunning the accelerator, so it wouldn't look like I was trying to escape. Holding my breath, I slid past the patrol car and the rest of the property without stopping.

As I made my exit, I checked my rearview mirror. The officer appeared to be writing something down in a notepad. I swore under my breath, fervently hoping that he hadn't gotten my license number.

It seemed odd that the officer had displayed such intense interest in my looky-loo drive-by. I wondered what that meant, in terms of whom the police might be looking for.

I thought over the jumble of information I was collecting, starting with Hoffman's girlfriend, Bethany, and the fight I'd heard coming from Bethany's room in the middle of the night. Then there were the rumors of S and M activity. And now, a policeman who'd practically jumped at the sight of a woman checking out the house.

Put it all together, and what did you have? I wondered. Was it possible the police were on the lookout for a female killer?

Chapter 9

Of Vice and Men

Many women use weight as a shield against the sexual attentions of men, which is completely unnecessary. Asking a man to take out the garbage, mow the lawn, or paint the bathroom will send him running for the hills faster than you can eat a Whoopie Pie. Relax. Men can be fun, and remember—sex burns calories, too.

—From *The Little Book of Fat-busters* by Mimi Morgan

I edged the low-slung TR6 into a bumpy dirt lot in front of the Vixen's Den. The address wasn't on any of my maps, but after making a series of wrong turns, I'd finally found the two-story brick shop tucked beside a ramshackle warehouse in the town of Kerashaw. A half hour's drive from Durham, Kerashaw must have once been a mill town, but the textile mill I'd passed on the way in looked like it had been shuttered and abandoned long ago. Most of the rest of the town had closed up shop and vacated soon after, judging by the abundance of deserted storefronts along the tiny main street.

A line of scruffy-looking vehicles parked in the lot indicated that the Vixen's Den, at least, was open for business. The purple neon fox that the engineer had mentioned glowed over the shop's door, which had a sign displayed prominently at eye-level: YOU MUST BE OVER 21 TO ENTER.

Inside, I fully expected to see men in trench coats lurking furtively in the aisles. Instead I found only a lone clerk sitting behind a glass counter to my left. The back wall of the shop was divided into a row of narrow doorways that might have been private viewing rooms. That's where the customers must be, I realized.

The clerk glanced up from his book and nodded as I entered. He was reading James Joyce's *Ulysses*, I was surprised to see as I drew closer.

"Good reading?" My eyes slid sideways to take in the contents of the glass case. The section nearest me displayed two neatly arranged rows of handcuffs.

"Absolutely," the man responded. "I think Molly's soliloquy is the most sensual speech in modern Western fiction, don't you?" He had a long face and heavy-lidded eyes that stared out at me from behind rimless glasses.

"I never could make it all the way through that book in college," I admitted. "Although I do recall that I dog-eared Molly's speech."

"Well, then, we can be friends." He closed the book and smiled. "I'm Gardner." I wasn't sure if Gardner was his first name or his last. "What can I get for you?"

"Kate Gallagher," I said, shaking his hand. "And actually, I'm looking for information." I was trying hard not to get distracted by a TV monitor that was hanging from the corner behind the counter. It showed a naked woman getting worked over by a guy dressed like Conan the Barbarian. A warm sensation rose in my cheeks—I once read that studies proved that everyone gets physically turned on by pornography—even women who claim to find it disgusting. I hoped my getting all flushed wasn't proof of that. "I'm work-

ing with Channel Twelve TV news. We're doing a
story about Dr. Victor Hoffman's murder. Did you
hear anything about it?"

"Just that he was killed," Gardner responded. He
paused for a long second. "Channel Twelve, huh?"
He looked me up and down. "How come I haven't
seen you on the news?"

"I work behind the camera," I told him, fishing out
my temporary ID. "Producer. Did you know Hoffman
at all?"

Gardner eyed the ID. "Yeah, Hoffman bought stuff
here," he said. "He's one of my best customers. *Was*
one, I guess." He took the remote and clicked the TV
to Channel Twelve, replacing the barbarian booty call
with a soap opera. "Say, do you know the anchorwoman over there at Channel Twelve, Linda Lander?
I'd love to get her picture. She's *feline*."

"Not personally. I'm kind of new. So you knew
Hoffman, then?" I said, trying to nudge the conversation back from Cat Woman to Hoffman.

Gardner shrugged. "Well, I never actually met the
man," he said. "He bought everything online and had
it delivered to his house. See, I got this Web site." He
handed me a card. The card had a picture of a little
purple fox wearing stiletto heels, plus a Web address.
"Most of my business is online these days. But we still
get a lot of walk-in traffic," he said, indicating his
stock with an expansive sweep of his hand.

I looked around. To my left was a rack of black
leather vests that had zippers and chains dangling everywhere. The rack stood in front of an arrangement
of hairy, flesh-colored gizmos. I hadn't the faintest
clue what *those* were all about.

"What kinds of things did Hoffman buy?" I asked.
"I heard the police found some kind of a sex dungeon
in his basement."

Gardner shrugged. "Wouldn't surprise me a bit. It's not unusual for our customers to have a playroom."

Pausing for a long second, he gave me a hard, probing look, as if he were coming to a decision. Then he lifted his hands and tapped on the keyboard in front of him. He peered at the screen, apparently looking for something. "Since you came all this way and I'm a sucker for gorgeous redheads, I'll look up his records," he said.

I couldn't believe my luck. Gardner appeared to be scrolling through screens of information. "Here it is . . . Hoffman." He looked up at me with a knowing smile. "Come over here and sit by me, sweetie. You can look for yourself." He patted the empty stool next to him.

I didn't like the "sweetie" thing.

"Can you just swing it around?" I asked him. No way was I going to step to the other side of the case. Gardner seemed okay, but this whole situation was starting to give me the creeps.

"Oh, she's shy," Gardner said in a mocking tone, but he angled the monitor so I could see.

I leaned my elbows on the case and stared at the screen. A series of invoices flashed by. There were lots of them under Hoffman's name. The records revealed that he'd purchased silk ties, Japanese love knots, and an inflatable sheepdog (*What exactly does one do with an inflatable sheepdog?* I wondered).

It seemed that Hoffman had been a most active customer, indeed. He'd made his last purchase seven days ago. That would have been five days before his murder, I calculated. These records confirmed that Hoffman had been hot and heavy into the S and M scene, and a possible zoophiliac, as well.

"Could I ask you to print those out for me?" I asked Gardner.

"What do I get in return?" He gave me a leering look.

To get those printouts, I knew I'd have to dangle a carrot.

I gave him what I hoped was an ingratiating smile. "Well, of course, I can never *guarantee* how a story will develop," I said. "But we might want to use your storefront as a visual. Maybe even do an interview with you."

That was a true statement—this proof of Hoffman's S and M activity added a racy angle to the murder story. When we ran the story on the air, the Vixen's Den would get a prominent mention.

"Oh, yeah, it'd be great to show the outside of the store," Gardner responded enthusiastically. "Not the inside, I guess," he said, nodding toward an aisle of neon-colored dildos. "We don't want to get the Bible-thumpers riled up."

After a couple more keystrokes, the printer behind Gardner kicked to life.

In addition to getting this piece of the Hoffman story on the air, I reminded myself, I still needed to keep digging into who his killer was. *That* was the real story here.

"You said Hoffman never came into the store," I said to Gardner. "Did anyone else have dealings with him, do you know? Any relationships you know about?"

Gardner laughed dismissively. "The good doctor didn't make the local scene, because he didn't need to," he stated flatly. "Word around town is he had his own supply at the clinic—there was always a willing woman around."

"You mean among the dieters?" I asked him. "Or do you mean staff?"

"Either, I guess." Gardner shrugged again. "Heavy women can be very sensual, you know?" Giving me a suggestive look through his hooded eyes, he handed me the printouts.

I glanced through them. These invoices gave me something we could use on the air immediately. This would be a tabloid-style piece—not the kind of classy story that would win me another award, that's for sure. It would play more like "KGO News," as it's known in the broadcast industry—"Kickers, Guts, and Orgasms." I don't blanche at the idea of running a blatant scandal sheet story. I'm not proud of the trait, but there's a calculating lobe in my producer's brain that actually *enjoys* the prospect of airing something that will make people's jaws drop over their TV dinners.

Now that I had the records, I was free to escape. First, however, I felt compelled to ask a couple more questions. Gardner was turning out to be a good source.

"You say Hoffman didn't make the local S and M scene," I said to him. "Where is that scene, exactly?"

Gardner gave another laugh. "Oh, it's everywhere, more places than you'd imagine," he said. "But you'll find the biggest crowd at a club in Chapel Hill, a place called the Razor's Edge. In fact"—Gardner blinked as if a lightbulb had just gone off in front of his eyes—"I heard that one of Hoffman's old girlfriends still works there as a bartender. Cheryl something, I think. Yeah, that's her name. She's a former dieter, or maybe she worked at the clinic. . . . I can't remember."

The name Razor's Edge rang a bell. Amber had told me that Hoffman and Bethany had been seen entering that club. That added an interesting wrinkle.

A customer emerged from one of the back rooms carrying a DVD under his arm. He laid the box on the countertop.

"Thanks, man," Gardner said to the man, who was wearing a pair of ancient gray overalls. "I have some

great amateur stuff coming in from China next week."
The man grunted and left.

Gardner glanced down at the box with a look of
distaste. "I really hate it when they come back all
sticky." He reached down and pulled out a bottle of
Lysol and a roll of paper towels that he evidently kept
at the ready.

My stomach made a nauseated cartwheel. However,
I was determined to gather all the information I could
before leaving.

"By the way," I said as Gardner misted the box
with the disinfectant, "have you ever met anyone from
the clinic staff?" I wanted to make sure I'd covered
all the bases.

To my surprise, Gardner nodded. "Well, I don't
know if she was *staff*," he said. "One night I guess
Hoffman needed something in a hurry. Someone came
over in a big green car, but it definitely went on his
account. She had bushy brown hair, I recall. Tons of
freckles."

Bushy brown hair, freckles . . .

"That sounds like Marjory, the clinic's manager," I
said to Gardner, who shrugged.

I found the idea a little shocking. Marjory seemed
so wholesome and down-to-earth. I couldn't imagine
anyone less likely to be running as a bag woman to a
porn shop.

"Do you recall what she purchased?" I asked
Gardner.

"I can't really remember," he said with a shake of
his head. "I don't think it was anything unusual." He
tilted his head left as if trying to jog loose a memory.
"Might have been a spreader, come to think of it."
He snapped his fingers. "That's right. They needed
a spreader."

"A spreader?"

"Think of your last Pap smear. That'll give you the basic idea," Gardner explained, tagging on a smirk.

Ick.

Behind that giant hedge that shielded his house from prying eyes, Hoffman had been conducting a very randy practice, indeed. From what I'd learned so far, at least one dieter, Bethany, and a staff member, Marjory, were involved. And there were probably others.

I remembered that Jack had called the Hoffman Clinic "a real Peyton Place." From everything I was learning, the scene was more like something straight out of Sodom and Gomorrah. Hoffman had played the starring role, but now his role had been extinguished.

As I drove away from the Vixen's Den, my stomach was sending up smoke signals that spelled HUNGER. On the Richter scale of hunger, I was at six-point-five.

I got so focused on thoughts of food that it was a while before I noticed the beige-colored sedan that had fallen in behind my car. It stayed about thirty yards back—no closer, no farther—as I drove the sparsely traveled stretch of road between Kerashaw and Durham. It might have been the very blandness and nondescriptiveness of the car that first caught my eye. When I made a ninety-degree turn onto the rural highway toward Durham, the sedan turned, too. Nothing too unusual about that—probably Durham was the major destination for travelers from Kerashaw. Nevertheless, something about the vehicle piqued my curiosity.

Just to see what would happen, I slowed to a crawl. The sedan slowed down, too, remaining behind me at the same distance. That did seem strange—usually, the guy behind you moves up when you slow down. And then honks.

Peering into my side mirror, I tried to get a look at the driver. It was too far back to see clearly, but the driver appeared to be male. I jammed the accelerator, speeding up until I was doing almost seventy. Again, no change—the car remained exactly the same distance behind.

Getting concerned now, I kept my eye out for a side road. A few minutes later I spotted a gravel road just ahead to the right, marked by a black-and-white wooden signpost. I came up on the intersection. As I reached the road I jerked the steering wheel right, barely slowing down as I made a sharp right-hand turn.

The hind end of the TR6 swung out wildly as it hit the rough gravel, spewing out rocks and sending up a plume of powdery white dust. If the TR6 didn't have such a low center of gravity, it would have certainly flipped over.

Cursing myself for taking the corner so fast, I wrenched the steering wheel into the spin—no easy feat in a car that lacked power steering. With great effort, I managed to regain traction on the slippery surface. Pressing the accelerator, I checked my mirror again.

At first I couldn't see anything except the suspended cloud of gravel dust I'd left in my wake. Then I felt my heart take a free fall.

The beige sedan emerged from the dust cloud behind me. No longer hanging back, now it was gaining speed, closing in.

There was no more doubt—I was being followed.

Make that, pursued.

Chapter 10

Visualize the New You

*Visualization is a powerful tool. Seeing yourself as a
toned, sexy creature can help you attain your fitness
goals. Find a picture of someone you'd like to look
like (pick a healthy role model, not a heroin chick),
and hang it up on your wall. Focus your thoughts on
transforming yourself into that image. It helps if you
hang the picture next to a photo of a hot-looking guy.
Your imagination can take it from there!*

—From *The Little Book of Fat-busters* by Mimi Morgan

My pursuer's car was closing so fast I could hear its
engine screaming. Mashing down on the accelerator,
I simultaneously popped the clutch—the TR6 leaped
forward, its front end practically lifting off the gravel.

I shot ahead down the gravel road, praying that I
hadn't managed to turn down a dead end. I flicked
my eyes to the side mirror to get another look at what
was bearing down on me. It was then that I caught
sight of a flashing light—the light was strobing from
the car behind me.

It was a flashing blue police light.

Police . . . it's an unmarked police car, I realized all
at once. Instantly releasing the pressure on the accelerator, I felt a jittery surge of relief wash over me.

I pulled my car all the way over to the right, almost into the gulley. Then I waited, sucking down gravel dust while the sedan swooped in behind me. The fear slowly drained out of my muscles, and was quickly replaced by a new anxiety. *What's this about?* I wondered.

Checking the mirror again, I recognized a familiar face at the wheel of the sedan. It was Detective Jonathan Reed. He was holding a police radio in front of his mouth, which prevented me from seeing the expression on his face. Something told me it wasn't pleasant.

Reed emerged from the driver's side. As he walked toward my car, his footsteps made little crunches in the gravel. Watching him approach, I had an odd sense that everything was moving in slow motion.

Reed leaned forward and placed his hands along the top edge of my door, looming over me with his arms spread out in a V.

"Miss Gallagher," he said. The detective had his shirtsleeves rolled up in the humid heat, and wore his weapons holster and detective's badge fastened to his belt, right at my eye-level. "Quite the queen of dramatic driving, aren't we?" Reed's tone made me feel like an errant schoolgirl who had just been chased down by the headmaster.

"Hello, Detective Reed," I said, struggling to keep my voice even. "I didn't know it was you following me. The police, I mean." A rush of prickly sensations swarmed into my hands and feet.

Reed fixed on me with a depth-charged look. "When I got a report that a redhead with Massachusetts plates was poking around this part of town, I figured it was you," he said. Reed's voice had a crackling intensity that I hadn't heard yesterday. "You were sighted at Hoffman's house, then the Vixen's Den. Why?"

His question meant that the police must be watching the Vixen's Den, in addition to Hoffman's house. It also meant that the cop in front of Hoffman's house had gotten my plates.

I shrugged, trying hard not to show how rattled I felt. "I'm just doing my job—gathering information," I said. "You have a watch on the Vixen's Den, then?"

"I'll ask the questions right now if you don't mind," Reed responded in a reproving tone. "So what *were* you doing at the Vixen's Den?" His eyes swept me up and down. "Shopping for a corset?" he asked curtly.

Hold on—was he implying that I *needed* a corset? I felt my scalp turn hot pink, which always happens when my Irish temper starts to rise. Reed's nice-guy persona of yesterday had vanished somewhere into the ether layer, and now he seemed intent on shaking me up. Well, bollocks to that, as the British would say. It was time to turn the tables and do a little cage rattling of my own.

"What was I doing at the Vixen's Den?" I echoed the question. "I was learning that Hoffman was one of their best customers." I met Reed's gaze without flinching. Let's get everything out in the open, I thought. I might even be able to provoke a comment on the story I was working on.

"I've confirmed that Hoffman was a big player on the S and M scene, and according to my sources, you found a sex dungeon in his basement," I said. "Care to comment? And that's *on* the record, by the way." I knew my tone was going to raise the detective's hackles. But right now, that's just what I wanted to do. Reed's hot pursuit and new, tough-cop tactics had taken a big toll on my nerves.

Reed's face darkened perceptibly. "What the hell?" he said. "Are you running a bloody *news* story about this?" He tapped out a tense, two-finger rhythm on the door. "Look, I won't have you and your cohorts spreading half-baked rubbish all over the telly before we nail this dollymop."

When he got riled, I noticed, Reed slung his British slang thick and fast.

"I don't report 'rubbish,'" I said. "This is my job, and I'm very responsible when working with the police."

"I've yet to see evidence of that," Reed snapped. "All I see is you getting in the way." Bending his elbows, he lowered himself forward until his face was in mine. "I could take you into protective custody as a material witness, you know. You discovered Hoffman's body, after all."

"You mean, slap me in jail?" Was he *serious*?

Before Reed responded, I heard a scrunch of tires on the gravel behind us. Glancing back, I saw a black-and-white police cruiser turn onto the road. Behind the wheel was the cop with the mirrored sunglasses I'd seen standing watch outside Hoffman's home.

The cruiser pulled up alongside us. "Everything okay here, Detective?" The patrolman leaned across the front seat and spoke through the passenger-side window, which was partly rolled down.

"Yeah." Reed half turned toward the other officer, but without breaking eye contact with me. "On second thought, Benny. Check to see if there's a matron on duty right now, would you?"

"You got it, sir." Officer Benny edged the cruiser a few yards ahead of us. Through the cruiser's rear window, I saw him pick up the radio.

A police matron, he must be talking about. Reed really was taking me in. Oh my God. I tried not to think about what my father's reaction would be to his daughter getting hauled off to the hoosegow, even if it were for her own "protection." And, what exactly did I need protection *from*? It seemed like a blatant intimidation tactic—the whole thing was enraging.

Abruptly, Reed reached down and opened my door

with an imitation of a gentlemanly flourish. "Why don't you step into my mobile office?" He nodded toward the beige sedan.

"Do I have a choice?" I asked him.

"Negative."

It took some effort to climb out of my low-slung convertible, which was listing toward the edge of the road's drop-off. As I stepped out, my ankle wobbled on the loose under footing.

Reed reached out, placing a steadying hand on the small of my back.

I flinched away from his touch and tried not to notice again how attractive he was. I didn't want to be distracted from my righteous sense of outrage over the way he was handling me.

I held tightly to my composure as we got into the sedan. As soon as the sedan's doors shut, Reed inserted the ignition key and clicked on the air conditioner. Then he turned to face me. A moment passed.

"You know, if you were in lockup, at least I could call your father back and let him know you're safe," he said, at last.

"You could what—*what*? My father called you? No, my father did not call you . . . did he?"

Reed nodded. He was grinning, the bastard.

I grabbed both sides of my hair with my fists. Releasing a deep groan, I scrunched my eyes shut. "Dammit, that's what this is really all about. The long arm of the chief. *Arrgh!*" Slowly and rhythmically, I pounded my forehead against the dashboard, like one of those water-dipping bird toys. "Wherever I go, he thinks I need a guardian. Did he call you about Hoffman's murder? How'd he find out about it?"

"Word spreads fast in the cop community." A glint had risen into Reed's eyes. "And he might be right about your needing a guardian," he said. "After all, I had to force you to ground."

"Force me to ground? You mean like fox hunting?" How dare he *enjoy* this?

"Let's start over, shall we?" Reed said, downshifting his tone. "You see, the beastly thing is, I have this problem."

"So, what's *your* problem? I've got my own. A Father Knows Best on steroids." I sat crabbed-over in a self-protective position. Claws out.

"Well, right now, you're my problem," Reed said, his expression turning sober. "If you run a story right now about Hoffman's S and M activities, you could scare off the person who killed him."

"Do you have a suspect?" I asked him.

Reed eyed me warily. "*Off* the record now, are we?" he asked.

Well, thank God, at least he wasn't arresting me, and seemed to be treating me seriously again. Maybe Dad's call wasn't a total disaster. Now that Reed knew I came from a cop family, it might make him trust me a little bit.

"Off the record, of course," I responded. I would never expose anything I'd agreed to hear off the record. That's an ironclad rule of journalism ethics.

"I can't comment on specific suspects. All I can tell you is that the next few days could be critical to the investigation." Reed focused his gaze into my eyes. "And if you've turned up anything, anything at all, I need to know about it, Kate."

When he said my name, my breath caught in my chest.

"Word is you're good at that," he added.

Now it sounded like Reed was asking me for *help*. I felt unsettled inside, off center. And my heart rate was still recovering from the double whammy of the chase and the arrest threat.

"And sorry for making you think I was about to jug you," Reed continued, although he didn't look sorry at all. "It was just a little rough play, police style. I thought you could handle it, since you're such a fan of the Vixen's Den."

"Rough play has to be consensual," I retorted.

"Well then, I'll have to improve my game." With an abrupt motion, Reed reached across me toward the glove compartment. The back of his arm grazed my breasts.

Was that grazing an accident? It didn't feel that way. I felt a rippling in my nipples where he'd brushed against me. Embarrassed by my reaction, I stiffened, willing my body not to react. I would not give this faux-arrester the satisfaction of knowing I was attracted to him.

Opening the glove compartment's door, Reed withdrew a small object and stuck it into his shirt pocket.

"I'll make a bargain with you," he stated. "You hold off on your story for just a wee bit, and I'll call you when we're close to making an arrest. You'll have plenty of time to get your camera crew ready. Sound like a deal?"

A deal? Normally, I don't favor deals with the police. It's usually their way of putting you off long enough for them to bury a story. But maybe it was worth discussing in exchange for an early heads-up.

"How long do you need me to hold the story?" I asked him.

"Just seventy-two hours."

"I can promise twenty-four. After that they might run it on their own," I said, thinking fast. I'd need at least twenty-four hours, anyway, to collect interviews and footage for the Hoffman piece. Reed's deal gave me the promise of getting the story and an exclusive on the arrest, to boot.

I could tell by Reed's expression that he was surprised I was negotiating with him. "All right, then, twenty-four," he finally said.

"Deal," I said firmly. This was fantastic. The promise of an exclusive on the arrest was more than I could have hoped for.

The only real danger at this point was that another media outlet might run the Hoffman story first. I wasn't too worried about that possibility, though. From what I'd observed, the rest of the local media mostly ran no-brainer stories, the kinds that were based on press releases churned out by PR types. Durham didn't exactly seem to be a top destination for Columbia J School grads.

"Now I need something from you. You left me a message last night." Reed reached for a pen and pad that were fastened to a clipboard on the dash. "What's come up since yesterday?" He'd turned all business again.

I paused to collect my thoughts about everything that had happened since the murder. "Okay, then," I said. "That boy I told you about who got upset with Dr. Hoffman the night before the murder? His name is Billy Harris. Evidently there was some kind of quarrel between him and Hoffman. And Hoffman's last appointment at the clinic Sunday night was with Harris. After the murder, Billy transferred to another clinic, the Renaissance House."

Reed scrawled some more notes.

Outside the car's window on Reed's side, Officer Benny pulled up in the black and white.

Reed cracked the window. "Hold on a second," he said to me.

"Do you want that police matron to call you on the radio?" Benny called through the window to Reed.

"No, you can cancel that request—I won't need her after all," Reed said. "Thanks Benny."

Benny looked past Reed at me with a curious glance. "No problem, Detective," he said, then shrugged. "I'm going for a ten-two." Police code for a snack break. He shifted the cruiser into gear and slid past us, headed back toward the highway, no doubt in the direction of the nearest doughnut shop.

Reed turned back to me. "Okay, what else have you got?" He was sounding impatient, as if he thought I was burying the lead.

"I found out that the woman staying next door to me at the clinic is—was—Hoffman's girlfriend, Bethany Williams," I told him. "The night before I discovered Hoffman's body, I heard shouting come from her room. I think I told you yesterday that I'd heard a quarrel next door in the middle of the night, but I didn't know that it came from Hoffman's girlfriend's room."

"Right." Reed's tone made it sound like he already knew about Bethany and Hoffman. He must have already put two and two together about the fight I'd heard.

I wondered what else he knew about Bethany—was she his prime suspect?

"Bethany has checked out of the clinic. Do you know where she went, by the way?" I asked him.

"Someplace safe," Reed replied, giving me a look that said "don't ask."

"Oh. Well, when I spoke to Bethany about Hoffman . . . ," I began.

Reed's spine stiffened as though someone had shoved a curtain rod down it. "You *spoke* to Williams?" He stared at me incredulously.

I must have struck a nerve. There was an unmistakable note of disapproval in Reed's voice. Oh, oh, here comes the cop's eye again, I thought.

"Yes, I did," I responded.

There was a long pause. "What did Williams say when you talked to her?"

"Not much—she really freaked, though, when I asked her about the shouting I heard the night before," I told him. "Our conversation got cut off by this friend of hers, Reno. He's kind of a gorilla. Really creepy."

"You saw Reno O'Malley in Bethany's room the morning of the murder?" Reed raised his eyebrows. I hadn't mentioned Reno's last name, so it appeared the detective was already familiar with him.

I shook my head. "Actually, it was the afternoon. She told me you'd already interviewed her. So, was Hoffman drugged before he was stabbed?" I asked him, determined to get something I could use in my story. "I mean, I can't figure out why he didn't put up more of a fight. Those fondue forks were stuck through his eyeballs like perfect bull's-eyes. The stabbing was done postmortem, wasn't it?"

"We'll have to wait for the results of the autopsy." Reed slapped shut his notebook. "And besides, you know I wouldn't tell you anyway," he added. "But there *is* something I want you to keep in mind."

I leaned slightly forward, waiting for what would come next.

Reed reached his hand into his shirt pocket. "Remember what I said to you yesterday? That I didn't want to be combing you out of my hair?" He plucked something from his pocket and laid it on the bench seat between us.

It was a man's tortoise shell comb.

Using his index finger, Reed slowly pushed the comb across the front seat toward me. "Don't make me whip this out again," he said, his expression deadpan.

I had to squelch a big silly grin. Reed's reprimand had sounded playful, maybe even flirtatious. Then I got buffeted by a counter-rush, this one fueled by self-doubt. If Reed knew that I was attracted to him, it occurred to me suddenly, he might be indulging in some fun at my expense, like "Let's make fun of the chubby Anglophile." *Delete that thought,* I told my brain sternly.

"Is there anything else you want to tell me?" Reed scanned my face.

"I just want to ask one more thing," I said, taking a deep breath. "You called the killer a 'dollymop' before—that's slang for 'woman,' isn't it?"

Reed shifted in his seat. "Kind of vulgar slang, I'm afraid. Sorry for that." He sounded almost embarrassed.

"Are you thinking it was a woman who killed Hoffman?" I pressed. It made perfect sense that Hoffman's killer had been a woman—his mutilated corpse had passion murder written all over it.

"We're looking at all angles very carefully, including that one," Reed said. It sounded like a careful reply. He reached to the arm panel and flicked a button that noisily unlocked the sedan's doors. No doubt about it—I was being released.

Reed escorted me back to my car. He opened the door for me again—only this time, there was no mockery in the gesture.

Reed stood over me, looking down. "Remember we were off the record, and the twenty-four hour hold. Don't forget," he said.

"I won't," I assured him. "What's given to me off the record, stays off the record. You can trust me on that."

"I suspect I'll find out whether I can trust you, soon enough." Reed reached out and gave me a light pat on my forearm.

I felt another tingle where his fingers touched my bare skin.

As I drove away from that encounter, images from the porn video I'd seen at the Vixen's Den invaded my thoughts. In the frames that flickered through my head, the starring roles—Conan and the ravished maiden—were played by Reed and me.

I flushed with embarrassment at the fantasy, and spent the next few seconds trying to chase it away. But then I remembered Mimi's tip: Visualization is a *good* thing.

Chapter 11

Don't "Supersize Me"

American restaurants typically serve about four times the recommended portion size. Using our tools of the broadcast trade for comparison, here's a rule of thumb for normal portion sizes:

- *Average bagel: Size of the camera lens*
- *3 oz. meat: Size of an audio cassette tape (not a videotape, which is the equivalent of a gut-busting sirloin)*
- *Small potato: Size of a computer mouse*
- *2 tbs. peanut butter: Size of the head of a microphone*
- *1 cup pasta: Fills that Styrofoam to-go coffee cup you pick up on the way to cover a smoky fire at three a.m.*

—From *The Little Book of Fat-busters* by Mimi Morgan

My midsection beat out a bongo rhythm as I drove away from my run-in with Reed. There was a giant bat cave where my stomach should be. I was also beginning to feel light-headed, which meant it was way past time to get some food.

I glanced at my watch. It was almost two-thirty. Way too late to grab lunch at the clinic. Reluctantly,

I decided to look for somewhere to stop. I'd have to order carefully to avoid blowing the diet, though.

I pulled into a Shoney's, a Southern casual dining restaurant that had a menu filled with slick, colorful pictures of its entrées. Most of them deep-fried.

After being seated I gazed soulfully for a while at the picture of the cheeseburger platter (I could practically *taste* the seasoned fries, with lots of ketchup). Then, stiffening my resolve, I set aside the menu with a sigh.

"Can I get grilled chicken without the skin?" I asked the chunky-armed waitress. The woman's hair was cut supershort on the sides and teased into a smooth, puffy crown on top, a style that seemed popular with Southern women of a certain age.

"We got a real nice chicken sandwich," she said, nodding. "You want the sandwich?"

"No plain chicken?"

"Uh-uh, ma'am, sorry."

It felt funny to be called "ma'am" by someone older than me. "Okay then, I'll take the sandwich," I said reluctantly. "But hold the mayonnaise. And hold the fries. And hold the . . . bun."

The waitress looked appalled. "Hold the *bun*?" she said. "Child, that's not enough food to feed a hamster. You want a milkshake with that?"

"No thanks, just lettuce and tomato. But do you have some fresh fruit?"

Her expression brightened. "We've got homemade peach cobbler," she said. "Local peaches. Fresh, not canned."

"That's okay." I shook my head sadly.

While waiting for the order, I reached into my purse and fished out the brochure that Amber had given me yesterday for the Renaissance House, the rival diet program across town from the Hoffman Clinic. Billy, the boy who'd threatened Hoffman, had reportedly

switched over to that program. My next move would
be to head over to the Renaissance House to look for
him there. I still needed to rule out Billy as a suspect,
even though by now I had reason to suspect that Hoffman's killer was a woman. Evelyn Brooks was supposed to be there, too. I was looking forward to
exchanging our impressions of the murder scene.

I had a personal motive for checking out the Renaissance House, whether or not I found Billy there.
I might soon have to switch over to that program myself, if I could scrape up the extra dough for it. My
Hoffman story was going to run in the very near future. There was a good chance that the clinic might
not survive the publicity and scandal that would inevi-
tably follow. Even if it did survive, I would likely become persona non grata there once the story ran.
Since I was the producer, my name would appear in
the credits at the end of the story. The staff would
have to know that I had produced the piece. I'd probably be booted from the clinic.

That would be a shame, and I wasn't thinking only
of my personal dieting prospects. Hoffman was eccen-
tric and had used unorthodox methods at his clinic,
but he'd clearly helped people like Norm and Jack
and Amber. In fact, he'd developed almost a benign
cult following among his dieters and staff. Benign, except for the person who'd driven those forks through
his eyes.

The waitress set my meal down in front of me. It
included a giant oatmeal honey bun resting on a
side plate.

"I brought this in case you change your mind," she
said, winking at me as she set down the plate.
"Lemme know if you want butter."

I stared at the bun as if it were an IED that might
explode, raining down fat. Then, with a surgeon's pre-
cision, I used a knife to divide the top of it into four

pieces. One section should equal the nano-sized portions they served at the clinic, I reassured myself.

The first bite of the bun almost knocked me sideways; it was bursting with so much flavor of oatmeal honey. Starvation must be having a steroidlike effect on my taste buds. I forced myself to eat it slowly, even though what I really wanted to do was inhale it in one gigantic bite.

From deep inside my purse came the tinny sound of "Ms. New Booty." I pawed through the bag to retrieve my cell phone.

"Hey, Katie-o." It was my friend Brian.

I was never so happy to hear a familiar voice in my life. "*Hey,* Brian." My greeting sounded squeaky and harsh to my ears.

Quickly, I filled Brian in on the major events that had happened since I arrived in Durham, including Hoffman's murder, the doctor's S and M activities I'd learned about, and my chase-down by Reed.

"I'm sure Dad put him up to it," I said. "He must have heard something about what's going on down here. Has he said anything to you about it?"

"Not yet, but I was off yesterday. Wowzer." Brian let out a low, long whistle. "And here all I expected you to talk about were hunger pangs and charley horses. Sounds like you've got a real mess down there." He sounded worried. "Are you all right?"

"Yes, I'm fine," I said. "But I've got enough going on without my father siccing local law enforcement on me. Dammit, why doesn't he realize I can take care of myself? I'm thinking it would be just as well if I didn't move back to Boston after all of this. But don't tell him I said that." I had to keep in mind that Brian worked under my father's command in the South Boston police district.

There was silence on the other end.

"What?" I asked him after a few more seconds went

by. "Do *you* think it would be better if I didn't come back to Boston?"

Brian let out a deep sigh. "I don't want to lose my best friend as a neighbor," he said, "but *as* your best friend, I have to say that it wouldn't be a bad idea to get a break from Boston. Sometimes it's better to get away from the home front for a while. Like when I went to New York after college."

"Humph," I replied. It was something to think about.

"So, it sounds like their homicide guy really gave you the treatment," he continued. "You okay?"

I let out a whooping laugh that felt uncomfortably close to turning into tears. "Yes, but oh my God, I have such a crush. I'm an *idiot*," I said, glancing around furtively to make sure I hadn't disturbed anyone with my yelp. My right hand went all trembly, which caused me to almost drop the phone. The stress and pent-up tension from the past two days came streaming out through my extremities all at once.

"You're not an idiot—you're under a lot of pressure, and from the way you described him, I'd have a crush, too, so don't worry about it," Brian said soothingly. "Want me to come down? I've got vacation days stored up the *yin yang*."

"No . . . I'm okay, thanks."

I definitely did not want Brian to come galloping to my rescue. He'd done that once before, when I was working on a news story that landed me in a tight jam with a ring of illegal alien smugglers. This time, I needed to be a big girl and handle my own problems. Starting with my father's interference.

"Don't you have a birthday coming up in a few days?"

"Yeah, twenty-six, can you believe that? It's all downhill from here to thirty," I joked.

"It *is* a thrill," he insisted. "Do you have any special plans yet?"

"With whom?" I said, surprised to hear a bitter-sounding laugh jump out of my mouth, like a toad. "I don't really know anyone down here that well to plan something. Besides, you can't celebrate without cake, can you?"

I was embarrassed to feel a painful lump rise in my throat as I said that last bit. I didn't want to come off like I was feeling sorry for myself.

Brian made a little clucking sound over the phone. "Well, I'll give you a call on the day," he said. "I expect to find you doing something wild and crazy to celebrate."

"Thanks, Brian," I said, and then said good-bye and clicked off.

The combination of food and conversation with my good friend had had a cathartic effect on me. I felt lighter and more energetic. After paying the check I headed out, leaving precisely three-quarters of my honey bun behind.

Everything about the Renaissance House was shiny and perfect looking, including the receptionist who greeted me in the lobby. The girl, who introduced herself as Naomi, was put together like a young Donatella Versace, with a deep tan and whitish-blond hair that hung down to her waist.

"You're from the Hoffman Clinic? Ooh, you'll love it here—you should definitely switch programs," Naomi said as we started on a quick tour. "Better sign up fast, though. We're nearly full," she whispered in a confidential tone.

We paused in front of a window that overlooked an enormous workout room that had state-of-the-art treadmills with individual television monitors. Every treadmill had someone on it, huffing away.

"Are people transferring here from the Hoffman

Clinic because of the murder earlier this week?" I asked her.

Naomi widened her eyes with an expression of exaggerated horror. "Wasn't that a terrible thing?" she said. "And yes, it *did* have an impact. People are flocking over here in droves now. But even before that, we were getting lots of transfers," she continued. "Ever since we opened last year, the Renaissance House has been the number one destination for people who can't handle the Fruit diet. And who can blame them? People want to be treated well, you know? And from what I've heard, that place is kind of a boot camp, you know?"

Naomi couldn't be much younger than me, but her habit of ending every other sentence with "you know?" made her sound annoyingly young and Californian.

"Have you ever heard any serious complaints about the Hoffman Clinic from the dieters who have come here?" I asked her. "Other than that they couldn't hack the diet?"

Naomi shrugged. "It's mainly a style preference," she said. "Some people were really devoted to that doctor—Hoffman, that was his name, right?—and the program over there. For the rest . . ." She made a sweeping motion to indicate the gym and the huffers.

We made our way outside. Just as Amber and Jack had described, the Renaissance House was the polar opposite of the Hoffman Clinic. Located in a pristine medical park, the campus resembled a posh private hospital. The main buildings were shaped like random cubes and rectangles. They whirled out from a sunken garden that served as a kind of floral centerpiece for the clinic.

As Naomi and I strolled through the garden, my nose picked up a lulling whiff of lavender. It was no wonder that patients from the Hoffman Clinic were stampeding over to this program. Even before his murder, the Hoffman Clinic must have been losing ground to the new competition.

Naomi led me through a pair of metal doors. "So, here we have our dining room," she said.

The dining room looked as if it belonged in a four-star hotel. It featured lots of pale maple and floor-to-ceiling windows that overlooked the sunken garden. A few patients lingered at the tables, which had centerpieces of fresh snapdragons. I'd bet anything that the diet meals here would be fresh and gorgeous, too. Quite a contrast to the Hoffman Clinic's groady cafeteria.

I spotted a familiar face at one of the tables. It was Evelyn Brooks. The last time I'd seen Evelyn was on Monday morning, right after she and I had discovered Hoffman's body on the clinic's porch.

I glanced at Naomi. "I see someone I know. Do you suppose I could break off?" I asked her.

Naomi hesitated, but then nodded. "I guess that would be all right. Come back to the front when you're ready," she said, before heading back in the direction of the lobby.

As I approached the table where she was sitting, Evelyn's eyes met mine. Her jaw dropped.

"Kate?" She squealed. Her chair rolled back as she stood up and threw her arms around me with an enthusiastic hug. "I've been planning to call you," she said. "I knew you'd wind up here sooner or later."

Even though it had been just a couple of days since we'd last seen each other, Evelyn looked different. She had a new, shorter haircut that framed her face, and she appeared visibly thinner.

"Hey, you look fantastic. I can already see a big difference in your face." Evelyn held me by the elbows and looked me up and down. "How much have you lost? Are you starting the program here?" she asked.

"Three pounds. And, possibly," I said, smiling. It was hard not to respond to Evelyn's buoyancy. "Actually, right now I'm following up on Dr. Hoffman's murder for a local news station, Channel Twelve," I added in a quieter voice. For some reason, I felt inclined to be honest with Evelyn. Maybe it was because we'd shared the traumatic experience of discovering Hoffman's body.

"That's right, I forgot that you're a . . . what? A news producer? Let's go over here," Evelyn said, leading the way to an empty table tucked away in the corner.

"So, what all did that homicide detective say to you?" she asked, once we settled into a couple of chairs. "Reed—that's his name, right? And by the way, wasn't he the absolute most adorable guy on earth? Didn't you love that British accent?"

"I have to agree. He's very cute," I said. However, I was here to discuss the murder, not Reed. "He warned me to move away from the clinic—he told you the same thing, I suppose?"

"Yes," Evelyn said, taking a sip of her coffee. "I'm still having nightmares about that whole thing." She grabbed my hand and clasped it in both of hers. "It was so sickening. Do you remember those horrible eyes?"

"Unfortunately, yes." I said, batting away the mental image. "Actually, I came here hoping to find someone else who used to be in the Hoffman program. A boy named Billy Harris."

Evelyn nodded. "Oh yes, I know Billy. He checked in the day before me, in fact."

"I'd like to ask him some questions, if you think he would talk to me," I said to her, trying not to sound too eager.

"About the murder?" Evelyn gave me a startled look. "You don't think that Billy had anything to do with it, do you?"

I shrugged. "Not that I know of. I'm just asking lots of people questions right now."

"Let's go find him. I know where his room is," Evelyn said, rising from her chair. "Ooh, this is like one of those crime dramas, and I'm the friend with information," she added, grinning. "When it's made into a film, make sure I'm played by someone gorgeous and sexy, like Angelina."

I laughed at that—Evelyn had a wonderful sense of fun. I followed her out of the dining room and down a covered walkway. After a series of turns, we arrived at the entrance to a rectangular building. Pushing a metal bar on the door, we stepped inside and headed down a hallway. Finally, we stopped in front of a door, which Evelyn announced was Billy's room.

Within seconds of my knocking, Billy opened the door.

"Billy, this is Kate Gallagher," Evelyn said, introducing us. "She's a Fruiter, but thinking about becoming a Renaissance woman. Thought you could give her an idea of what it's like to switch programs."

"Oh sure," Billy said, giving me a polite but perfunctory smile. He was about twenty years old, tallish, with the oversized belly that was typical of the male dieters. His arms and legs were muscular and solid. Beneath the sleeves of his light yellow polo shirt, you could see bulging triceps. A tennis racket hung over his shoulder on a strap.

Beyond Billy I could see a young girl sitting on the made bed. She was making notes in a small journal.

Billy squinted slightly at me as if trying to recall my face. "I don't remember seeing you at the clinic," he said.

"I just started on Sunday," I explained. "And then,

well, you know what happened. . . ." I trailed off, letting the implication sink in.

"Oh, yeah, I know." Billy's eyes widened as he waved us in. "Can you believe, Dr. Hoffman was killed the night I left? Was *that* ever creepy." He gave an uneasy sounding laugh.

"So, you were already checked in here by the time the murder happened?" I tried to make my question sound casual as I followed Billy into the room. Evelyn trailed behind me.

"No, that night I was stuck in a motel room with my parents, trying to talk them out of sending me home. This is Mandy, by the way." Billy dropped onto the bed next to the girl.

"Hi," Mandy said without looking up from her notes. "How am I supposed to know this stupid stuff for the diet journal? Like how many calories in a half cup of applesauce?"

"Fifty," Evelyn and I chimed in together.

"I didn't know that you had been planning to go home, Billy," Evelyn added.

"Well, I didn't *want* to go home, of course," Billy said, shifting the racket so that it rested on top of his knees. "My dad's this GI Joe type. He kept saying I'd washed out of the Hoffman program, so I should just come on home. Like I'd failed or something." He started bouncing his right knee under the racket.

"What do you mean, 'washed out'?" I asked him. "Hoffman was kicking you off the program?"

Billy nodded. "Old Doc Hoffman told me he was booting me because I wasn't losing weight fast enough. And I'd already lost twenty pounds. Can you believe that?" He slapped his hands against his abdomen for effect. It made a hollow sound. "Plus I'm working out a lot and building muscle, which everyone knows weighs more than fat. It totally wasn't fair."

Two high, red spots had risen in Billy's cheeks as

he spoke. "And to make it worse, my parents were in town to visit," he said. "I had to go right over to their motel and tell them I was being fired from the program. My father went nuts."

"What did you say to Hoffman when he told you that you were out?" I asked him.

Billy dropped his eyes. "Nothing, really," he said.

Mandy giggled and looked up. "You *know* you yelled that you were gonna kill him, Billy," she said. "And then it was so weird the way he died right after."

Then it seemed to dawn on her. "But it's not really funny, I guess," she said, her cheeks reddening. She lowered her face again over the journal.

Billy glared at the top of Mandy's head. "Well, maybe I did yell at him, but I didn't *kill* him, okay?" he snapped.

There was a beat of silence.

"You must have been pretty upset, though," I said.

"I was, *kinda,* until Dr. Anita helped me out," Billy said, shrugging. "She talked to my parents. She told them Doc Hoffman was being too strict, but that he wasn't going to be with the clinic much longer, and I could come back after he was gone. I guess he was retiring or something."

Retiring? That was completely new information.

"Thornburg told you that Hoffman was retiring soon?" I said.

Billy nodded. "Well, he was pretty old—at least fifty, right? But I'd never go back to the Hoffman Clinic now. I mean, they won't even give you diet Jell-O over there for dessert. That's how whacked they are. The Renaissance House has got, like, low-cal pudding and diet Cool Whip. Way better stuff."

No way could I disguise my next question as casual. I was just hoping he would answer it. "Did Detective

Reed interview you about the murder, the way he did with Evelyn and me?" I asked him.

Billy's eyes flew open. "No," he said. "A detective? Why—was he looking for me?" He sounded alarmed.

"Not that I know of," I responded evenly. "But the police have been talking to a lot of people."

Mandy tossed aside her journal. "Hey, aren't we going to go hit some balls, Billy?" she interjected peevishly.

"Yeah, okay." Billy rose to his feet. "I'm so *totally* glad to be away from all that psycho stuff at the Hoffman Clinic." He turned to face Mandy, who had remained sitting on the bed. "You know that old flick, *Psycho*?"

Raising his fist, Billy held up an imaginary knife. He fixed his gaze on Mandy. "You're the bad girl, Mandy! *Bad!*" Emitting a series of staccato, piercing screeches, Billy fell upon her. Using repetitive, slashing motions, he pretended to stab her.

What in blazes?

Billy and Mandy rolled back and forth on the bed, laughter mixing with screams. Billy seemed to be acting out the shower scene from the film, *Psycho*.

Evelyn rolled her eyes at me and shrugged. Neither of us seemed to know what to make of Billy's performance. It seemed supremely strange that he would pick this moment to playact a vicious knife attack, right after discussing Hoffman's murder.

Billy grinned up at us from the bed, one arm still flung around Mandy. "*God!* I loved that film," he said, looking from me to Evelyn. "Hey, you guys bring rackets? We could play doubles." His tone was back to being completely casual, as if a manic interlude had not just taken place.

"Actually, it's time for me to be getting back," I said, shaking my head slowly.

After stopping by the front desk to tell the receptionist Naomi that she would take over my tour, Evelyn showed me around the rest of the Renaissance House. No doubt it would be a great place to be, if I could possibly swing it financially.

When we reached yet another garden, we removed our shoes and dipped our lower legs into a bubbling Jacuzzi. I could feel my calf muscles relaxing in the steamy water—God, I really *would* love this place.

"So, what did you think of Billy's *Psycho* routine?" I asked Evelyn.

"Well, it was weird, but I think Billy's really a nice young boy," Evelyn responded. "You don't think he had anything to do with Dr. Hoffman's murder, do you?"

"I certainly hope not," I said.

If Billy had truly thought that he was being sent home, perhaps that would have caused him to kill Hoffman. It just didn't seem like enough of a motivation for murder, though. Plus it wouldn't explain the *way* Hoffman had been killed. I would expect an enraged young man to kill quickly, using blunt force trauma. I wouldn't expect him to go ghoulish by filleting the corpse with fondue forks.

However, as I said good-bye to Evelyn and returned to my car, my mind kept returning to Billy's admission that he'd threatened Hoffman, and the way he'd unexpectedly reprised the shower scene.

To Billy and Mandy, his miming of the role of a psychotic killer seemed to have been done in a spirit of good fun.

I had a different take on his crazy-eyed slasher routine, however.

To me, his performance had been chilling.

Chapter 12

Separate Hunger from Appetite

Many of us who have gained and lost weight have forgotten what real hunger is. We may even have forgotten that it's <u>okay</u> to eat when you're hungry! Here are some basic guidelines:

1. *My stomach is stuffed; I feel sick. (Definitely not hunger. Avoid eating for at least six hours. Maybe seven.)*
2. *I'm comfortably full. (Not hunger. Don't eat anything for about four hours.)*
3. *I have a slight sense of appetite; I could use a bite. (Probably not hunger. Try not to eat anything for fifteen minutes. If the feeling goes away, it wasn't hunger.)*
4. *My stomach is growling a little, feels empty. (This is hunger. It's OK to eat!)*
5. *My stomach is making noises like an oompah band, feels like it's going to cave in. (Oops, now you're <u>too</u> hungry. It's OK to eat, but avoid snarfing.)*

—From *The Little Book of Fat-busters* by Mimi Morgan

When I pushed through the heavy oak front door of the Hoffman Clinic an hour later, the manager greeted me with the news I'd been waiting to hear.

Marjory touched my arm as I stepped into the lobby. "Oh, Katie," she said, flashing me a wide smile. "Dr. Thornburg left a message for you. She's cleared her schedule so that she can meet you here first thing tomorrow morning for an interview. Eight thirty a.m."

"Fantastic," I said, returning an equally broad display of teeth. Tomorrow's meeting with Anita would give me the opportunity to kill two birds with one stone, so to speak. I'd be able to snag some footage for my weight loss story, plus sneak in a few questions that might shed light on Hoffman's murder.

I was starting to go a little nuts from the pressure of developing two stories at the same time: my weight loss piece, plus the Hoffman murder. I was feeling anxious about the murder story on several levels. My journalist's intuition told me that the story was going to break wide-open soon, whether I was ready or not. It was time for me to kick-start things into forward motion.

"So . . . I got lost today and wound up in this little town called Kerashaw," I said to Marjory. "There's nothing much there but a place called the Vixen's Den. Ever hear of it?"

I kept my eyes pinned on hers as I rambled through my question, trying unsuccessfully to sound casual and conversational. What I really wanted to do was provoke her reaction to the information I'd learned from the clerk at the Vixen's Den, that someone matching Marjory's description had bought sex toys at the shop on Hoffman's account.

"It's a funny place—kind of a funky sex shop. Although I guess they would prefer to call it an 'alternative lifestyle' shop," I said.

Mentioning the Vixen's Den risked raising alarm bells or alienating Marjory as a source. However, at this point I didn't think I had a choice. I had to confirm that part of the story. If she had purchased items on behalf of Hoffman, that information would tie the clinic into the story and widen its scope, making it more than simply a lurid gossip piece about the murdered doctor. In the same way that a detective or a prosecutor builds a case, I was building my story.

Marjory's friendly, open expression evaporated. She dropped her eyes. "Um . . . no, what did you call it? The Vixen's Den?" She lowered her voice so much that it was barely audible. "No, I never heard of it."

I arched my eyebrows deliberately to communicate disbelief. "No?" I said. "Actually, the clerk there seemed to know quite a bit about Hoffman. He said someone from the clinic bought stuff for him there. Someone who drove up in a big green car. Someone with curly brown hair and lots of freckles."

In the gaps between her freckles, Marjory's skin drained to a pasty white. She remained silent for a long moment. When she finally lifted her eyes to meet mine, the expression in them had soured.

"Why—? Okay, I know what you're getting at. . . . Let's go over here," Marjory said, leading me to her desk. "All I can say is that this is a *good* job. They pay me really well. I could never earn 45K anywhere else in town for what I'm doing." She took in a deep breath. "I didn't ask questions about every little errand, okay?" Riding out on the exhale, the *okay* came out with a bit of a snap, like she was starting to get mad.

"Of course, you need your job." I said. I understood jobs where you didn't look too closely at your assignments if you wanted to see your next paycheck. The same could often be said of journalism, come to think of it.

"How many times did Dr. Hoffman send you to the Vixen's Den to purchase things?" I asked her.

"Just the once," Marjory responded. Her tone was prickly. "All I had to do was pick something up. I really didn't know what it was all about, to tell you the truth," she concluded with an elaborate shrug of her shoulders.

It didn't take a psych degree to tell she was lying. "Then let me ask you this . . . ," I began.

Scraping back her chair, Marjory stood up. "No. I don't want to say anything else. It's not anyone's business, anyway. Not *your* business," she said, practically hissing the word. "Please don't tell Dr. Thornburg," she continued, shifting from anger to a pleading tone without missing a beat. "And, *God,* you won't put anything about this in your TV story, will you?" She stared at me with an appalled expression. "I've gotta go." Turning on the heel of her blue canvas sneakers, she practically sprinted for the hallway that led out from the rear of the lobby.

I remained standing there in the lobby for a moment, thinking over Marjory's reaction to my question. I hoped she wouldn't go running to Anita Thornburg about me. As soon as Anita found out I had an agenda on the murder story, I'd probably get booted off the program. I'd have to tread very carefully in my interview with her tomorrow. That is, assuming Marjory hadn't busted me by then.

Marjory's reaction had implied that she didn't think Anita knew anything about Hoffman's recreational activities. If it was true that Anita was in the dark, there was an upside for me, I figured. If Marjory were trying to hide her own role, she probably wouldn't squeal on me about the kinds of questions I was asking.

Who among the clinic's staff would have known about Hoffman's sexual proclivities? His actions must have been common knowledge among the staff, unless he'd been extremely careful. And, witness the fact that Hoffman had been making booty calls with a skank like Bethany, I suspected that he had not been very careful at all.

Hoffman might have had one or more "closed loops" among the staff, some loops that included people who were in the know and others who were not. If Anita had been in the dark, it implied to me that she might be at a certain remove from the clinic's dark side, and possibly therefore less of a suspect. At least I had been able to confirm that Marjory had purchased sex toys at the Vixen's Den for Hoffman.

I stopped in the dining room for dinner, which consisted of overdone chicken and some steamed spinach. Dessert was a cup with nine grapes in it. I counted them—nine grapes, exactly. Not exactly low-cal pudding and Cool Whip, but hey, at least there *was* a dessert.

I pressed my hand to my stomach to gauge my hunger level—it was only a level three, not critical. So I packed up the chicken in a to-go plate and concentrated just on the fruit. Peeling each grape lovingly to prolong my encounter with it, I lingered over coffee, chatting with Lila and a few other stragglers. From the conversation, it seemed that everyone who was planning to leave in the wake of Hoffman's murder had already gone, and the dieter population had stabilized at a smaller but loyal core.

An hour later, my looming work deadlines drove me back to my room. I needed to devote the rest of tonight to preparing for tomorrow's taping and interviews. I now had two stories to produce simultaneously. The murder story would air in the local market as soon as the twenty-four-hour hold I'd agreed to with Reed was up. Once it was aired, the story would probably get snapped up by other news markets, possibly even the network. It would be just the kind of salacious story that news managers were clamoring for.

I should be ashamed to admit that I was even starting to groove on the kinkier aspects of Hoffman's story. As I made my way back outside to the wing where the guest rooms were, a random series of ridiculous story promos floated across the surface of my brain . . . *The death of Dr. Dildo—news at eleven.*

I perched on the edge of my bed and made a quick call to Channel Twelve. I needed to arrange for a camera crew to meet me the next morning for my appointment with Anita Thornburg.

The news director, Beatty, was out for the evening, but an assignment editor assured me that she would write me into the white board schedule, which is how TV newsrooms keep track of their reporters and camera crews. A news van and crew would meet me in front of the clinic at eight a.m. the following morning, which would give us half an hour to prep for the Anita interview.

I was hunched over, concentrating so much that my back was starting to hurt. I looked around for my favorite down pillow, the one I'd brought with me from Boston. The pillow appeared to have been removed. I glanced around for it, wondering whether housekeeping had taken it. How annoying.

Giving up on the pillow, I grabbed my laptop and opened a file. I needed to gather my thoughts and sketch out some notes for my interview with Anita. From what I'd gleaned so far, she was the person who had benefited the most from Hoffman's murder. She might have had her own motive to get rid of Hoffman, one that was completely separate from the sex games that had been going on at the clinic.

Meanwhile, I had my weight loss story to consider. Even though people didn't know me here, I cringed at the idea of having my "before" self splashed all over the tube. I'd have to endure the sight of me being weighed-in wearing shorts, thunder thighs fully on display. Well, there was one consolation: I'd already lost some weight since arriving in Durham. Before you knew it, I'd be svelte and wearing chic, killer suits. *I'll look back on my fat former self and laugh with the rest of them,* I reassured myself. Still, a sense of dread clutched my soul at the very thought of exposing my body to public ridicule.

A grinding-gears noise emanated from my stomach, announcing the arrival of level-four hunger. Time for the chicken. After getting up to wash my hands, I clicked on the bathroom light.

The first thing I noticed were white feathers floating in the air. Then I gasped.

Something was hanging from the curtain rod. It looked like a person, but not a person. It was a hanging figure, made of clothes. Clothes that were stuffed and held together with duct tape. *My* clothes.

Someone had carefully stuffed and arranged one of my outfits—my Celtics jacket, sweatpants, even my fanny pack—taped it together with duct tape and hung it from the shower rod with a rope.

It was a horrible scarecrow, dressed like me. Only where the head should have been, someone had stuffed my down pillow into the collar.

And slashed it to shreds.

Chapter 13

Sleep Your Way Skinny

Research shows that people who get eight to nine hours of sleep are less likely to be overweight than those who skimp on their z's. This benefit appears to be related to the impact of sleep hormones on appetite.

So it's a good idea to hit the hay earlier. When you're skinny you'll have more room to roll in it, too. . . .

—From *The Little Book of Fat-busters* by Mimi Morgan

"Jesus fucking Christ."

Gingerly, I reached forward and touched the crude figure with my fingertips. It swayed under my touch. My Celtics windbreaker and sweatpants had been stuffed with newspapers and stapled together to look human. A twisted manila rope cinched the slashed-up pillow to the jacket's collar. The figure dangled from the neck, looking like a life-sized voodoo doll that had been assaulted and then lynched.

Spinning on my heels, I bolted to the bedroom. I checked the door to make sure I'd locked it behind me on the way in. It was secure. A prickly crawling sensation spread over my skin. I tore about the room, checking to see if anyone was lurking. No one hidden behind my clothes in the tiny closet. No one under the bed.

The floor-length curtains over the bedroom window were drawn. Dammit, why hadn't I noticed that earlier? I always leave curtains open during the day. I must have been too distracted by my work to see it before. Had it been the maid who closed them, or my intruder?

A Gordian knot of apprehension grew in my stomach. I studied the curtain for a long moment, looking for any telltale lumps that would reveal someone standing behind it. After flailing at the fabric to make sure, I pulled back the curtain and looked out the window at the pool area. The serene surface of the lap pool glowed like an aquamarine, reflecting underwater lights. No one around.

Returning to the bathroom, I checked the narrow sliding window over the shower. It was locked. Even if it had been open, it would have taken an anorexic contortionist to get in that way.

By now I was panting. I forced myself to slow down and take a deep breath. Someone had carefully stapled together the nasty thing in the shower to throw a scare into me, successfully. The fact that the room had been locked meant my intruder must have a key.

The first person who leaped to mind was Marjory. Maybe she was warning me about poking around into her trips to the Vixen's Den. She could have assembled and hung the scarecrow while I was lingering over my nine grapes and coffee.

I opened my cell phone to call Reed. When he picked up, I could hear a police radio squawking in the background—it sounded like he was in the middle of an investigation.

"Don't touch anything. I'll be right over," he promised after I described my shower creature to him. Just hearing the soothing cadence of .his British accent was reassuring.

When Reed rang from the side entrance twenty minutes later, I buzzed him in from the room's phone.

I opened my door and saw an older man standing next to Reed in the hallway, clutching an equipment bag in his right hand. The man was completely bald except for a stubborn fringe of white hair.

"This is Senior Criminalist Corley," Reed said. "We were wrapping up another call when you phoned. He volunteered to take some prints."

Corley extracted a pair of latex gloves from his bag and snapped them on. "Couldn't resist tagging along when buddy here said he had to go check out a scarecrow," he said. "Bathroom?" He was already moving past me.

"Yes," I said, pointing.

Reed dogged Corley, who'd paused at the doorway of the small bathroom. They stood for a moment, eyeing the figure hanging from the shower rod.

Corley set down his investigator's bag. "This is an inspired one," he said. "At least it's not another Red Roofer."

Reed chuckled.

"Red Roofer?" I echoed.

Corley pulled out a camera. "We just came from a call where the guy slit his wrists in the tub and left the water running," he said. "Imagine that coming through your ceiling."

Ugh.

"Any thoughts?" Reed asked me as Corley started taking pictures.

I shook my head. "The only person I can imagine doing this would be Marjory Cash, the manager. She got angry at me earlier when I tried to ask her some questions. But this . . . this is so off-the-charts weird."

"What about these particular clothes? Do they have any significance?"

I tried to clear my head. "This is the outfit I was wearing the morning I found Hoffman's body on the porch," I said slowly, realizing that fact for the first time. My knees went squishy at the thought. "Oh my God—that's it, isn't it? This is a warning from Hoffman's killer. He's letting me know he saw me?"

"Possibly."

Corley pulled more supplies from the bag—some squares of white paper, a brush, plus a jar of black powder and a roll of acrylic tape.

"Let's dust the doorknob and get whatever else you think looks promising," Reed directed.

"Okay, Boss."

Taking the brush, Corley dipped it into the jar of powder and dusted the bathroom doorknob. With a strip of tape, he lifted an impression and transferred it onto a sheet of white paper. Next, he scrutinized the tile at the back of the shower.

"If the maid did a decent job cleaning before our perp strung up Scary Crow here, I might get something off the tile," Corley said to Reed. "Then should I cut her down to bring her in?"

Reed nodded, then led me around the bedroom on a quick tour. "Anything missing?" he asked me.

"It doesn't look like they touched anything," I said. "Everything's locked, too. So that means they had a key, right?"

"Right. And probably still have it. Kate, this is a serious threat." Reed fastened his eyes on me. "A sane person would find someplace else to sleep tonight."

"True, but we broadcast types aren't all that sane; didn't you get the memo?" I joked, trying not to sound the way I was feeling, which was scared stiff. "Remember, we're the ones who stand outside during hurricanes, shouting into a microphone." I mimed a reporter battling a headwind. "Well, Anderson, the wind is really starting to blow now!"

A grin cracked through Reed's on-the-job face. "You're right, you people *are* insane," he said.

Corley emerged from the bathroom. He had my stuffed clothes draped over one arm the way someone would carry a dry-cleaned garment. The crime scene bag was in his other hand, packed up and ready to go.

"Scary Crow and me are off to get hitched. I'll see you back at the barn after the honeymoon," he said to Reed. "Bye, Dorothy." He winked at me on his way out.

"Dorothy?" I looked at Reed, rocking back on my heels.

"Scarecrow. Wizard of Oz."

"Of course."

Reed shrugged. "Corley's a tad rummy, but there's no one better at lifting prints," he said. His expression turned serious again. "Is there someone you can call to stay with you tonight?" A slight pause. "You have a boyfriend, no doubt?"

"No. I mean, I *had* one, up in Boston. He broke up with me just before I came down here."

"Then he must be insane, too."

Before I had time to digest the insane boyfriend remark, Reed reached past me. With his fingers, he flicked the security chain on the door. "Don't count on this to keep anyone out. You should—"

"Batten down the hatches?"

"Precisely. I'll send around a patrol car every hour to keep an eye on the place," he said. Then he left.

After securing the door as much as possible, a process that included shoving the spindly guest chair under the doorknob, I fell back onto the bed. My mind was racing.

Reed was right. Staying at the clinic tonight was

risky, and yet leaving now would mean giving up my access to the story and my investigation into Hoffman's murder. Neither was an option I would consider. Someone was trying to drive me out, but I'd already moved beyond feeling scared. I was starting to get pissed.

I reviewed the clinic's staff people I'd had meaningful encounters with so far, trying to think of anyone who might have hung that horrible scarecrow. Beyond the obvious, which was Marjory, who else had a key to my room, plus a motive to murder Hoffman?

Topping the list was Anita Thornburg, the new queen bee of the Hoffman Clinic. So far, I didn't know much about Thornburg, except that she had assumed control of the clinic in the wake of Hoffman's death. Somehow I couldn't imagine Thornburg lowering herself from her haughty high horse to perpetrate a stunt like this one. If she was involved, she'd probably directed someone else to do the dirty work.

Then there was Paige, Thornburg's smooth and mouse-meek assistant. I've never felt comfortable with people who are as reserved as Paige. I still didn't know what her agenda was, if any.

Of course, I mustn't forget Billy, the boy who loved *Psycho*. The more I thought about the way the mannequin's pillow "head" had been shredded, the more it reminded me of the slasher routine Billy had acted out earlier today. Perhaps he'd found a way to get into my room, and hung the scarecrow as some kind of sick adolescent prank. Or a warning.

And finally, Bethany or her evil sidekick Reno could have returned and gotten into the room somehow. I knew that Bethany had checked out of the clinic, but not where she'd gone.

I stayed there on the bed with all the lights on for a couple of hours, fully dressed, staring open-eyed at the ceiling. Then I grabbed my sleep shirt from the hook on the back of the bathroom door and took my laptop with me to bed, but felt too fragmented to do any work. Around two a.m., I must have finally crashed.

I fell into a collage of dreams. In one of them, I was climbing back up the steps to the clinic's front porch with Evelyn. There was Hoffman's body again. I saw the bloodied forks protruding from the black mush of his eyes, and once again that horrible mass of ants, seething across his mouth. Streaks of something shiny and viscous looking were smeared all around the edges of his lips, like honey.

All at once Hoffman sat straight up, à la *Dawn of the Dead*. Raising his arm straight out, he pointed at me with a bony, accusing finger.

"Are you new?" Hoffman croaked. A black waterfall of ants poured from his mouth, like vomit. The ants swarmed onto my arm, stinging and biting.

I snapped out of my sleep, waking up in a sitting position. I was drenched in sweat. My right arm, which I'd evidently tucked under me, had fallen asleep. It prickled and tingled as it came back to life slowly. That explained my dream ants.

So much for the idea of getting any more sleep. I looked over at the clock. It was four a.m. On top of everything else, I was going to be sleep-deprived the next day.

My eye fell on a hardbound book that was lying next to the clock. It was the complimentary copy of Hoffman's book, *Follow! Follow! Doctor Hoffman's Diet Rules,* which had been in my room since I'd arrived. I'd skimmed the book when I checked in, but to prepare for today's taping I really needed to do a more thorough read-through.

As is my habit when starting a book, I opened it to the cover page.

I read Hoffman's inscription: *To the lovely Anita T.*

My partner in love and war. Handwritten across the bottom of the page was another message: *From your Victor.*

The message struck me as oddly ambiguous. Hoffman had dedicated his book to Anita Thornburg, I felt sure. How many other "Anita T's" could be connected to the clinic? But what kind of relationship was defined by both love and war?

I studied the rest of the book. Hoffman's message to fat people was simple: To be thin, they must follow his program without question and without deviation. Well, no surprise *there*. According to Hoffman, the only way to permanently change one's metabolism was to adopt a rigorous regimen of extremely low-calorie, low-protein intake.

Yeah, followed by regular lashings with a cat o' nine tails, I added silently.

Tossing the book aside, I went into the bathroom. I grabbed a washcloth and started to step into the shower, only to get brought to a full stop by the thought that the last person in there had been my creature-hanging nemesis. An image of Billy Hoffman flashed into my mind. Earlier that day he'd acted out the shower scene from *Psycho,* and hours later I'd found a scarecrow in my own shower. Was that a coincidence?

Rejecting the shower, I took a washcloth bath—my mother used to call this type of ablution a "French bath," for reasons I never understood. An unsettled feeling had been nagging at me for a while now. It felt as if I'd forgotten or overlooked something that had a bearing on Hoffman's murder. I reflected on the previous day.

It had started with Anita's presentation to the dieters about Hoffman's death. Then I'd driven past Hoffman's home. Spooked like a deer by the sight of Benny the cop whipping out his notebook, I hadn't been able to study the outside of the house very long. As I'd passed the driveway, I'd seen the back of Hoffman's green Eldorado convertible, parked at an angle—a rear angle, from my point of view.

Parked at a rear angle . . .

The vehicle's back fenders had a pair of old-fashioned, half-sphere taillights in the middle of them. Round taillights. Just like the taillights on the car I saw driving away from the clinic's parking lot, the morning of the murder.

As I wrung out the washcloth, the answer dawned on me. On the morning I'd discovered Hoffman's body, I'd seen the murderer leaving the scene of the crime.

The killer had driven away in the murdered doctor's own car.

Chapter 14

Weigh Every Day

Contrary to some generally held diet wisdom, it helps you keep on track to weigh every day. Just don't let minor fluctuations on the scale throw you into a "this isn't working" panic attack. By plotting your weight on graph paper, you can see the downward trend over time. If you're doing things right, your weight loss graph should resemble the bear market of the mid-1970s. (But if your graph looks more like the crash of '29, you're not eating enough.)

—From *The Little Book of Fat-busters* by Mimi Morgan

Early the next morning found me standing on the doctor's scales in the lobby, confronting my ultimate nightmare—getting weighed on television.

I was wearing my skort and a tank top, the lightest outfit I could find. To prepare for the taping, I'd gone to the bathroom and taken off my shoes. During a fit of pre-weigh-in panic, I'd also removed my watch and necklace. If I could've tied helium balloons to my wrists to lighten my load some more, I'd have done that, too.

Reggie, the Channel Twelve cameraman who was assigned to work with me, stood a few inches off my shoulder with his camera rolling.

Paige was doing the weigh-in honors. She moved the metal slider along the top bar of the scales to get my weight. She tapped the slider to the right. Tapped . . . and then tapped some more.

"One eighty-nine," Paige announced when the scale finally balanced. "Fifty pounds above your ideal weight," she added, a bit unnecessarily, I thought.

One eighty-nine. Oh, happy day! Oh, joy! Down five pounds from one ninety-four in just two days . . . a whole new decade. (Only fat people calculate their weight in decades, in case you didn't know.) I had to tamp down my glee for the camera though, because for the series we were pretending this was my first day on the program. I couldn't look like I was already celebrating.

Following the weigh-in, Reggie and I got some great footage in the dining room, where Jack and his cohorts hammed it up for the camera. Then we left for our appointment with Anita Thornburg, whose office was located along a short hallway that separated the clinic's main house from the guest wing.

From the moment Anita greeted the two of us at her office door, you'd have thought we were on a mission to extract one of her molars.

Anita began by reading me the riot act about "ground rules."

"Just so we're clear, I'm only going to discuss the weight loss program today," Anita announced as Reggie clipped a lavaliere microphone onto the lapel of her white doctor's coat. She regarded me coolly across her desk. "I won't talk about anything to do with the clinic's recent . . . difficulties. Nothing about Victor Hoffman."

"Oh, absolutely . . . ," I began to reassure her, but Anita waved me off impatiently.

"I've been pestered to death by reporters since poor

Victor's death," she said. "Especially from that station you're working with, Channel Twelve. What's that reporter's name over there? Greg Silver? I'm not even sure I should still do this interview, since you have a connection with him." She flicked her hand toward the camera with its Channel Twelve logo on the side. "You have to give me assurances that nothing we discuss will be misused in any way."

I groaned inwardly. I'd warned Silver to back off and let me collect information about the murder quietly from the inside, but it sounded like he'd bulled ahead on the story anyway.

"Well, I appreciate your meeting with me," I told her. "I'm sorry if my colleague has been a pain. But as you know, this interview is for a completely separate assignment, my weight loss feature. Of course, I'll keep my questions to that one topic."

"You see to that," she snapped, crossing her arms.

Anita's guarded attitude and body language were frustrating. She seemed unwilling to discuss anything at all on camera.

And from that crabby start, the interview slid rapidly downhill. Anita acted as if every syllable she dropped might run back and stab her. The whole experience was a TV journalist's nightmare. The reporter is asking questions, lights and camera all set up, while the subject barely ekes out one-word responses.

Even though Thornburg was a difficult subject, I knew I was at fault, too. I'm used to working behind the scenes as a producer, not face-to-face as an interviewer. Experienced reporters and anchors make the on-camera stuff seem easy. Trust me, it's not.

After she delivered a couple more terse rounds of "yes" and "no" in response to my questions, I heard Reggie sigh behind the camera. It was clear he thought the interview was a flop.

A burning sensation rose in my cheeks. Cameramen hate it when reporters can't control their interviews. And here I was, losing control.

I'd been clutching my complimentary copy of Hoffman's *Follow! Follow! The Hoffman Diet* in my lap. Desperate to get something going for the story, I reached forward and slid the book across the desk.

"So, I wanted to talk about the program as it's outlined in your diet book . . . ," I began. I planned to slip in a question about the strange dedication Hoffman had written to Anita on the cover page.

Anita eyed the book as if it were a bowel movement I'd deposited onto her pristine white desktop. "Where'd you get that?" she said.

"It was in my room when I checked in," I said, confused. "Aren't they in all the dieters' rooms?"

With an abrupt motion, Anita scooped up the Hoffman book, then opened a desk drawer and dropped it in. "That book's out of date," she said. "We've been revamping the program to include newer methods." She swiveled around in her chair and plucked another book from the shelf behind her. "*This* is the book you should reference in your story," she said, handing it to me.

I turned the book over in my hands. It had a cover with the bold red title *Svelte!* A picture of Anita was displayed prominently on the back of the dust jacket. She was wearing a white doctor's coat and leaning against a bookcase.

Cracking the book open, I scanned the copyright page. The first printing of her book had taken place earlier this summer, in May. Two months before Hoffman's murder. Anita wasn't the type to let moss grow under her feet, that was for sure. Already she was replacing Hoffman's book with her own.

"So, when did the clinic replace Dr. Hoffman's book with this new one? Was that Dr. Hoffman's

idea?" I watched that question sail across the desk
and land in Anita's lap.

"Well, no, in fact, Victor didn't—" Anita paused.
She darted a glance toward the camera. "Look, this is
getting into an area I said I wasn't going to discuss."

"I know you said you didn't want to discuss Dr.
Hoffman's death, but we're just talking about the program, and how it's changed," I said evenly. Or *were*
we? If Anita and Hoffman had quarreled over whose
book to use, or how to run the program, that was a
possible motive for murder.

Anita's alabaster skin had flushed a rosy pink just
under the surface. "Well, I'm just not comfortable
with your question," she snapped. "In fact—" She
fumbled with the microphone that was pinned to her
jacket.

Just as I thought she was going to cut off the interview, a vibrating noise came from somewhere
overhead.

The three of us—Anita, Reggie, and I—lifted our
eyes toward the sound, which seemed to be coming
from the sky. It was a vibrating *thwump* . . .
thwump . . . *thwump* sound.

It was a helicopter, I realized—and a damned close
one, at that. It sounded as if it was going to land right
on top of us.

Anita's face lit up. "That must be Lou!" She pushed
back her chair and took a step toward the window. "I
didn't know he was coming today! Oh, Kate, you'll
have to talk to Lou for your story. Lou Bettinger.
He's one of our greatest success stories," she explained, looking back at me over her shoulder. In her
enthusiasm about this "Lou," Anita momentarily appeared to forget her antipathy toward me.

Anita practically toe-shoed her way ballerina-style
outside to the parking lot, with me trailing behind.

Reggie was already way out in front of us. While

Anita had been extolling the virtues of "Lou," he'd grabbed his ENG camera from the tripod, hoisted it onto his burly shoulder, and was now taping the helicopter as it settled down into a clearing in the wooded lot behind the residential wing.

Watching Reggie in action, I was impressed as always by the way a good cameraman can shift into hyperspeed while wrangling tons of heavy equipment.

The chopper noise had attracted curious dieters and staff from every cranny of the clinic. They clustered in small knots at the edge of the clearing, just beyond the wind wash of the rotors as they circled and slowed to a stop.

A murmur ran through the onlookers.

"Isn't that Lou?"

"Did you know he was coming today?"

The way everyone was carrying on, you'd have thought the president of the United States was about to pop out of that whirlybird.

When the cabin door finally opened, a dark-haired man emerged. As he turned his head and directed a few words to the pilot inside the aircraft, I could see he had the face of a man in his early forties, with just enough gray at his temples to give him a distinguished look.

"Hey, stranger!" He grabbed hold of Anita Thornburg, who had stepped forward to greet him, wrapping her in a giant bear hug. And to my utter astonishment, Thornburg was hugging him back.

With one arm around Anita's waist, Lou turned his head and took in the sight of Reggie's camera.

"Press conference in my honor?" Then, I swear, he winked at me. "You shouldn't have, Nita."

"Not a press conference, Lou, silly." Anita slapped Lou's lapel lightly with her palm. "Kate's just started on the program, and she's doing a feature about it for Channel Twelve here in Durham. Kate . . . *Gallagher,* right?" She sounded as if she were slightly unsure what my last name was, much to my annoyance.

"Lou Bettinger." He smiled into my eyes as he shook my hand. Then he looked at Reggie, who was standing by with the camera poised on his shoulder. "How're you doing today?" he said to him. "Reggie, right? Haven't bumped into you in a while."

"Yeah, last time was that Pinkston Power case," Reggie said. He shot a glance sideways at me. "I covered that story with Mike Owens. Lou headed the team that defended that nuclear power company."

I remembered that case. It had gotten a modest amount of national publicity. The defense had proved that a disgruntled ex-employee had swiped some radiation seeds from a cancer lab and planted them in the swamp to make the company look guilty of polluting the environment. Looking at Lou's face more closely, I realized that he looked vaguely familiar. I must have seen him on some of the national news reports.

"Are you coming to the memorial service tonight?" Anita asked Lou.

"You know I wouldn't miss it," he said. "I'm going to check in to the hotel and then I'll come by for a visit. Talk with you about some things. I know it's been a tough week," he added in a low voice.

"I'd like that." Anita's voice cracked, and moisture rose in her eyes.

Were miracles possible? Anita was morphing into a human being before my very eyes.

"Hey, I have an idea." Lou looked from Reggie to me. "Why don't the two of you come up with me for a quick tour? You can get an aerial shot of the clinic from the bird. Is that something you could use for your story?"

"Hey, cool." Reggie's voice rose with enthusiasm. "An aerial would be a great establishing shot for the series. And we'd never get the budget for a chopper out of Beatty." He was already making his way forward, lifting the camera over the cabin door's threshold. "Hey, isn't this a Blackhawk?" I heard him say to the pilot as he disappeared inside the cabin.

I held back, not sure what to make of this stranger who had suddenly dropped from the skies, with his helicopter and invitation. What's this guy's angle? I wondered. But there was a more important reason for my hesitation. I don't like to admit it to people, but I have a deathly fear of flying. Especially in small craft. Lou's helicopter resembled nothing more than a metal dragonfly. It seemed impossible that such a bizarre-looking contraption could actually hoist me into the air.

"You're coming, right?" Lou looked at me.

I balked, trying to think of an excuse. "I don't need to go," I said.

"Of course you need to go," Lou replied. He had this maddening air of confidence about him.

"What do you mean?" I countered.

He held out his hand to me. "You need to conquer your fear."

I felt warmth rise in my cheeks. Who was he to accuse me of being afraid? And how did he know?

I looked down at the ground for a moment, considering. What the Devil was I getting into? It felt like something more than just a helicopter tour.

Beware of strangers bearing helicopter gifts, I heard a voice say in the back of my head.

Then, ignoring both the voice and Lou's outstretched hand, I brushed past him and stepped through the helicopter's cabin door.

I'd met a lot of movers and shakers during my years working as a journalist, but I'd never met anyone like Louis Alders Bettinger. A top-tier corporate lawyer who had argued many successful cases before the Supreme Court, he projected a sense of confidence and . . . and *safety,* is the only way I can describe it. After our helicopter ride, I could see why corporate bigwigs were willing to fork over top dollar to hire Lou as their attorney—it felt as if no harm could befall you when you were in his presence.

Of course, I didn't feel very safe at the beginning. In fact, I'd almost had a heart attack as the helicopter lifted off. Without saying a word, Reggie had propped open the cabin door and flung his legs over the side so that they dangled above the chopper's landing rail. He'd leaned precariously far out, rolling with his camera as we hovered hundreds of feet in the air. I'd grabbed awkwardly on to his jeans waistband and hung on to him for dear life.

"Got what you need?" Lou said when Reggie finally leaned back inside. Lou was sitting in the seat next to the pilot, a man who spoke few words and had a military bearing about him.

"Yeah, great stuff," Reggie said. "Thanks, man." Reggie's legs still hung over the side as we settled gently back to earth. Giving my heart another shock, he dropped to the ground while we were still hovering a foot or so above it.

"Yes, thanks," I said somewhat stiffly to Lou, preparing to follow Reggie. "You going to be around later today? Because I wanted to get—"

"An interview, right? I knew Nita'd sic you on me," Lou said, looking pleased.

"Well, yes, I'm doing . . ." I launched into my spiel about the weight loss feature.

Lou cut me off. "Tell you what. Why don't you let Reggie go do his thing for now," he said. "I'll go over some background with you one-on-one. We can do the on-camera part later."

"Well . . . ," I started to object. I didn't feel comfortable with the way Lou seemed to be assuming control of things.

"Works for me, Kate. I've gotta hustle back to the barn, anyway," Reggie said without looking up. He was bent over the camera, unhooking its cable from the sound deck. "Beatty's got me scheduled to do a live shot in an hour. And then remember, you'll be producing the live shot with me and Silver tonight at the memorial service," he said in a quieter voice.

"You'll be back in plenty of time for that. We'll be back before lunch, in fact," Lou interjected. "I wouldn't dream of depriving someone on the program of one of their meals," he added with a grin.

"All right, then, fine," I said, still reluctantly. I already had my reporter's notebook with me from my interview with Thornburg, so I could use that. *Fine.*

"Let's head to my home office. My pilot Kurt'll have us there in a jiffy. You take the passenger seat this time." Lou put his hand on the small of my back as he steered me toward the front of the chopper. "It's got the best view."

"Where's your office?" I asked as I eased into the passenger seat.

"Atlanta."

"Atlanta?" I gasped. Atlanta was a long, long way away. An eight-hour car ride away.

"Just a puddle jump for us in this thing," Lou said.

Too late for second thoughts, I realized. The ground was already pulling away below us.

Chapter 15

Make Every Calorie Count

Don't waste a single calorie eating anything you don't like, just because it's "diet" food. Wouldn't you rather have a quarter cup of M&M's than two dried-dung fat-free cookies? I know I would! For average women, the new USDA food pyramid allows 132 to 195 "discretionary" calories every day. Make 'em special ones!

—From *The Little Book of Fat-busters* by Mimi Morgan

Lou told me his story on the way down to Atlanta.

"The first time I came to the Hoffman Clinic was five years ago. I was over four hundred pounds. Heavy smoker, high blood pressure, the works. *And* I'd already had a heart scare," he said. "Other doctors always pussyfooted around with me, but Old Doc Hoffman gave it to me straight. Said I had to finish the program, or I'd be dead within six months. And he was right," he added soberly. "I dropped everything to make it work. Delegated my cases, gave up cigarettes. Victor Hoffman literally saved my life."

"Five years, wow," I said. It hardly seemed possible that Lou, trim, suntanned, and athletic-looking, had once been like Jack or Norm—morbidly obese.

My initial impression of Hoffman was that the doc-

tor had been totally overbearing. Lou's story cast new
light on the man. Some patients had obviously benefited from Hoffman's hard-line methods.

"Nowadays, the second I gain more than ten
pounds, I drop everything and come back to Durham.
It's the only way I've been able to keep it off long
term," he said. "Because I still love to eat," he added
with an amused glint in his eyes.

I'd thought his eyes were brown when we first met,
but now I saw that the centers of his eyes were green,
ringed with rods of gold. Calico eyes.

"There it is." Lou pointed down through the window. We were closing in on a sprawling edifice that
seemed to cover an entire hillside.

"It looks more like a house than an office," I
observed.

"It is a house," Lou said. "I work out of my home
most of the time. I did say 'home office,' right?" He
tagged on that confident grin again.

An irritated flush rose in my cheeks. "But I thought
you meant . . ." Lou seemed to be presuming an awful
lot, bringing me down here to his house. *If he thinks
this tour will extend to his bedroom, he has another
think coming,* flashed snippily through my brain.

I needn't have worried. As soon as we landed (on
the heliport that was right next to the grass tennis
court, *natch*), Lou led me to what must have been the
business wing of his house. After making our way
down a short hallway that had glass walls on both
sides, we entered his book-lined office. The furnishings
were mostly expensive antiques, from the look of
them.

Through a long rectangular window on the right
side I caught a stunning view of the Atlanta skyline.
Scattered about were pictures that showed Lou in
court, shaking hands with senators, and golfing with

Bill Clinton. No family pictures. Maybe those were in a different wing.

Lou pointed me to the guest chair. "Have a seat right there," he said, sitting behind an imposing teak desk the size of a Ping-Pong table. All it had on it was a sleek computer array and leather portfolio.

As soon as we sat down, Lou stiffened. With a deliberate motion, he reached for the leather portfolio and opened it in front of him. He slid a couple of manila file folders from the portfolio and held them between his hands. The friendliness in his tricolored eyes drained away, and was replaced by something flat and expressionless. "So tell me," he said, his eyes boring into mine, "why are you poking around into Hoffman's death?"

I drew back as sharply, as if Lou had reached across the desk and flicked my cheek with his finger.

"What makes you think—"

Lou held up his palm to cut me off. "Look, I play golf with Beau Keller, okay? Beau and I go back a long, long way. So let's you and me just cut through the goose crap here."

Beau Keller was the General Manager of Channel Twelve. Had he actually told Lou that I was looking into Hoffman's murder for the news station? That seemed grossly out of line.

"I know that you're looking into Hoffman's murder in addition to that other story about the weight loss," Lou said. "Beau suggested I talk to you."

"Why?" I folded my arms. I planned to call Beatty as soon as this meeting ended to verify Lou's story about having spoken with the general manager. If Beatty even knew about it, that is.

"I know that you found Hoffman's body, and that you're collecting information about the murder for the news division. I have some information you can use for your story. In exchange, perhaps you can help me."

"Help you? Hold on a second." Was that Lou's real motive for practically hijacking me down to his Atlanta office? I was starting to feel surly. "Why is Hoffman's murder your business, and why talk to *me* about it, anyway? Why not talk to the police?"

"I did," Lou said. "You know how that goes. And I want to know who killed Hoffman." Lou rose and circled around the desk, holding a file folder under his right arm. He stopped in front of the window with the fabulous view of Atlanta and stood there for a moment, staring out over the distant skyline. "I *need* to know who killed him," he said in a grim voice.

"Why do you need to know?" I demanded. "What's this all really about, anyway?"

I resented the fact that Lou had hauled me down here to his house under false pretenses. He'd obviously been playing games with me up until now, and I didn't appreciate that, not one little bit.

Lou spun about to face me. "Good question. Here's your answer," he said, thrusting the folder at me.

I opened the folder and quickly scanned through its contents. It contained a thick sheaf of documents. At first glance, they appeared to be some kind of real estate contract. As I flipped through the pages and read further, the meaning of the contract became clear. It was an agreement between Bettinger and Hoffman for the purchase of a piece of property. I recognized the property's address—59 Palmetto Street. That was the address for the Hoffman Diet clinic.

"You're purchasing the Hoffman clinic?" I blinked rapidly, confused. These documents appeared to indicate that Lou was buying the clinic. But Lou was an attorney, not a doctor. How could that be?

"I *was* purchasing the property," Lou said. "Hoffman died before he signed the final papers." He pointed to the pair of signature lines at the bottom of one of the pages. Lou's name was signed at the bottom, but the line above Hoffman's printed name was blank. "Hoffman was supposed to sign them this week, but before he did, he was killed."

"I still don't understand." I shook my head, trying to make sense of what he was saying. "If Hoffman had been planning to sell his clinic to you, does that mean you were going to run it?"

Lou shook his head. "I wasn't going to run the clinic itself. I was just buying the property. Hoffman was planning to move the clinic's operations across town. He'd found a spot where he was going to build a more modern facility. The purchase was part of a plan to raise capital for the move," he continued. "I was going to renovate the house and flip it back on the market. Now, of course . . ." He trailed off. "Everything's in limbo."

So, when Hoffman was murdered, he'd been in the process of selling his clinic's current property to Lou, and relocating to another facility. I wondered whether Anita, as the new head of the clinic, would move ahead with the sale despite Hoffman's death.

As if sensing my unspoken question, Lou shook his head. "I have to discuss all of this with Anita later today. If I know Anita, she'll probably go through with the sale, though. She seemed onboard with it before. In fact, she's—" He cut himself off, but it was clear he'd been about to add something else.

"So, what exactly do you know about Hoffman's death so far?" I asked him, feeling my way cautiously. "Tell me more about that."

"Well, it's only preliminary, but I have a good indication of how Hoffman was killed," Lou said.

"You know how he was killed?" My pulse quickened.

"He was poisoned," he said.

I'd worked on enough murder stories to know how long police lab analysis took. "Toxicology reports take at least a week," I said. In a smaller city like Durham, I suspected, they'd have to send the lab work out of town, which would mean it would take even longer.

"The *official* toxicology report takes at least a week."

The Cheshire cat grin had staged a comeback on Lou's face. And frankly, it was beginning to get on my nerves. "But I have a buddy who's a Diener at the morgue," he said, dropping back into his chair. A Diener was an assistant to the pathologist who conducted the autopsy, such as the one that was being conducted right now on Hoffman's body.

I knew that Lou had just taken a risk by telling me about the Diener, his inside source. That could get him into big trouble if it got out. I wondered whether he'd done that deliberately, to establish the beginning of a bond of trust between us. "Do they know what kind of poison?" I asked him.

"Again, it's only preliminary, but the spectrograph results showed organic residue in the liver—some kind of extremely toxic floral extract. They're thinking it might be *Onvallaria Majallis*," he said. "Known commonly as 'lily of the valley.' "

"Lily of the valley? The *flower*?" I stifled a surprised guffaw. "I always see lily of the valley in bridal bouquets. It seems like such an innocent little flower. It's poisonous?"

"Evidently, quite. Six out of six on the toxicity scale. Something for grooms to consider, I guess," Lou added dryly. "It also looks as if Hoffman ingested a good deal of honey before he died, but they're not sure yet whether that's connected with the poisoning. They haven't finished that part of the analysis, yet.

Then, after he was dead or maybe while he was dying, the bastard stabbed him through the eyes."

An image of Hoffman's face swam before my eyes. The gooey-looking streaks I'd seen on his lips, which had been crawling with those disgusting black ants—that must have been the honey Lou spoke of just now. Honey that the doctor ate just before he was killed. The memory made my stomach lurch all over again.

I glanced down at the Oriental carpet that was directly under my feet, which spread out in some kind of Tree of Paradise design. Hand-knotted silk, from the look of it. Curling my fingers together, I dug my index fingernail into the pad of my right thumb, a habit I have when concentrating. I tried to fit together this new information from Lou with what I already knew about the murdered doctor, attempting to come up with a mental picture of the killer's actions.

Unbidden, another image bobbed to the surface. It was the cover of an old Earth, Wind and Fire album that had belonged to Brian's older brother. As kids, Brian and I had hooted over the cover, which showed the breasts and upper torso of a reclining, naked woman. The entire surface of her skin had been slathered with honey. The woman's nipples, stomach, her whole body, presumably, was dripping with the golden honey.

Honey . . . Sex games . . . Poison . . .

"What are you thinking?" Lou prompted me from across his desk.

"About the type of poison that was used, lily of the valley. It seems so delicate. So unlikely. Like something a jilted lover might have dreamed up." I recalled how Reed referred to the killer as a "dollymop"—slang for a woman. "Plus, there's something else. When I found Hoffman's body on the porch, there was something smeared all over his face," I told Lou.

"There were all these gooey streaks. . . . It very well could have been honey that was on his lips. There were hundreds of ants all over his mouth." I touched my fingers to my lips.

"If it was honey, that would have attracted the ants," Lou looked thoughtful. "A woman, huh? If it was a woman, any ideas who could have done it?"

I shrugged. "The rumor around the clinic is that Hoffman had a young girlfriend among the dieters, and word on the street is that he was heavily into S and M. So, who knows? I'm looking into several people right now who might have been involved." No way was I going to share my list of suspects with Lou. His story sounded plausible enough, but I had no reason to trust him yet.

I silently reflected on all the other women I knew about so far who were connected to Hoffman: Bethany, Marjory, Anita, Paige—who knew, maybe even the cleaning woman.

Lou expelled a puff of compressed air, as if he'd been holding his breath. "I guess I always knew Doc Hoffman was a randy old goat," he said slowly. "That was pretty common knowledge. Among the men, anyway." He rubbed the side of his thumb back and forth across the surface of the leather portfolio. "But I always thought he kept his affairs private, that he found his partners outside the clinic. But then, it's been a few years since I was on the program. Things might have changed since then." He tilted way back in his leather chair and gave me a considering look, as if he were thinking something over.

"Let me put you in touch with this guy I have on my staff, Lionel," he said, leaning forward. "He does background checks for us. He's really good—around the office we call him the Grand Inquisitor."

"A useful employee, especially when you need to

discredit a prosecution witness, I assume?" I said, my tone arch.

"Touché," he said, grinning at me. "You'd be a good attorney, you know. Did you ever consider a career in the law?"

"Actually, I was prelaw at Wellesley, for a while," I said. "But I was also editor of our newspaper. Journalism seemed a lot more exciting, I guess."

"Wellesley College—no shit? I went there on exchange during my junior year from Amherst. It was supposed to be a surefire way to meet intellectual hotties, but all that happened was that I got my heart slammed." He winced at the memory. "But I loved the classes there. I was a few years ahead of you, though. More than a few."

"Yeah, I guess we missed each other there," I said, feeling myself warming to Lou. For the moment, though, I pushed aside the friendly thoughts. I needed to pump him for any information he had that might help me solve Hoffman's murder.

"So, tell me about Anita Thornburg," I said, meeting his gaze. I was curious to know what the Snow Queen was all about in real life. Lou must know her pretty well, judging from the way she'd flung her arms around him earlier today.

"What about her?" Lou gave me a guarded look.

"Well, for one thing, as the new head of the clinic, Anita directly benefits from Hoffman's death," I said in a level voice. "For another, she's been acting prickly and paranoid as all get out." I described my abortive interview with Anita earlier today, including how she'd welcomed me with about as much enthusiasm as she would have greeted the arrival of termite season.

"There's something you don't know," Lou said, after pausing a moment. "And it's another reason for

my coming up today in addition to the memorial service. Anita told me that there have been some . . .
incidents, since Hoffman was killed."

"Incidents?" I straightened in my chair. "What kind
of incidents?"

"She hasn't told me much, yet." Lou shook his
head. "That's why I came up to the clinic so early this
morning. I'm going to meet with her when we get
back to find out more. I've never heard her sound like
this. I should probably tell you that . . ." He hesitated.
Whatever it was he was going to add right then, he
appeared to change his mind. "Well, anyway, she's
definitely scared. If she seemed off-putting during your
interview this morning, I'm sure that's why. Right now
she doesn't know which way is up."

"Why are you telling me this?" I asked him. Lou's
information had sent my thoughts running like a computer that was maxing out its CPU. I couldn't tell
where he was coming from.

"Because I need your help," he said simply. "That
is, Anita needs your help." Again with that word,
"help."

"I did some checking up on you after hearing about
you from my friend Beau." Lou opened the leather
portfolio he had on the desk in front of him again,
revealing a yellow legal pad inside. "In Boston, you're
known as someone who gets the story, but you do
it quietly."

"Thanks, I guess—I just wish my ex-employer could
hear that. But what does that have to do with helping
Anita?" If he was leading up to a request that I not
report the information he'd just given me, as Reed
had done, I wasn't going to bite.

"I just want to ask you to keep an eye on her. Do
some digging around the clinic. Find out if anyone
around her might be a threat to her safety at this
point."

"What about the police?" I asked him. "Aren't they doing that job?"

"They've got a good investigator on the case, that detective Reed, but I want someone inside the clinic." Lou cupped his hands together for emphasis. "Closer at hand."

So this is what Lou was really after. He was trying to protect Anita. And he wanted my help to do it. The idea was intriguing, but first I needed to set some journalistic boundaries.

"I can help you investigate by looking into the murder, but I won't let it compromise anything I report on the air," I said to him.

"Done." He nodded tersely. "You won't have any interference on your reporting."

"And I'll need to be able to interview everyone at the clinic, plus have access to all the confidential files." I might as well shoot for the moon and get as much access as possible.

Lou hesitated, but only for a moment. "I'll fix it with Anita," he said. "But anything you use from patient records can't be attributed to the clinic," he said. "Otherwise we get into a problem with patient confidentiality."

"Done," I said, equally tersely. "And one more thing," I added, eyeing the notes Lou had spread out in front of him. "Since you researched all that information about me, you already knew I went to Wellesley College when we talked about it a couple of minutes ago, didn't you? You weren't surprised at all."

"First rule they teach you in law school." Lou tossed me another enigmatic smile. "Always know the answer before you ask the question."

On our way back to the helicopter, Lou insisted on showing me the rest of his house. As I'd expected, the house had another entire wing, one that reflected the private Lou. The tour didn't include his bedroom, thank God, but along the way we turned down a long hallway that was lined with personal pictures. We stopped in front of one of the pictures, which showed Lou with an attractive brunette, and a young boy and girl who might have been twins.

"Your family?" I ventured.

"My sister Jo and her little monsters, Jennifer and Brett," Lou said affectionately. In one of the pictures, Lou and his nephew Brett stood on a platform in the middle of a jungle somewhere, feeding bananas to a giraffe. "I took them on a photo safari to Africa last year. Jo lost her husband a few years ago, so . . . you know, I try to do stuff with them here and there." He scuffed the floorboard with the tip of his leather shoe.

One section of the hallway didn't contain any pictures. Lou caught me examining the empty space. "Haven't gotten around to doing that part of the wall yet. Who knows, if I'm lucky, maybe someday that's where the wife and my kids will hang."

So Lou wasn't married.

"Guess I've always been too busy to find the right girl so far," he added with a sheepish grin, as if he'd read my thoughts.

On our way out the back entrance, heading toward the helicopter, we passed a picture of a group of people standing, holding skis in front of some kind of winter resort. One of the women in the group was blond and wearing dark round sunglasses. We passed too quickly for me to get a good look, but the woman in the picture looked very much like Anita. I turned my head to shoot a questioning glance at Lou, but he had already hustled ahead and was going over the flight plan with Kurt the pilot. That was just as well— it would be better for me to find out for myself what type of connection Lou and Anita had going.

Lou was certainly an interesting man. I found him attractive, but he was a bit older than the men I usually dated. When I got back to Durham, I'd have to spend some time reflecting over exactly what to make of Louis Alders Bettinger.

Settling back into the helicopter's passenger seat next to Kurt the pilot, I gripped the edge of the cushions and braced to get hit with the familiar white-knuckle fear. My dread of flying centers mostly on takeoff. That particular phobia started back when I was a junior in college and took an island puddle jumper during spring vacation. The pilot had gone down the line of waiting passengers, asking them their weights before boarding in order to calculate the takeoff load. When he got to me, God help me, I lied. I lied by at least thirty-five pounds. As we'd rolled down the runway that day, I'd been positive that those unreported pounds were going to ditch us into the aqua waters of the Caribbean. I've been terrified of crashing on takeoff ever since—and having it all be my stealth fat's fault.

I felt Lou's hand on my shoulder. "You'll be okay," he said calmly. "Kurt here flew choppers in Afghanistan. He can hang this thing on top of a church steeple like a Christmas star, if I need him to. Right, Kurt?"

The stiff-jawed Kurt gave an almost imperceptible nod in return.

As we lifted off, for the first time ever, I was pleased to note that the panicky sense of an elevator dropping in my stomach didn't come. In fact, as we rose into the air, I found myself actually enjoying the sensation of lifting away from the earth.

Something had changed. Perhaps this unexpected detour to Atlanta in the company of a relative stranger had enabled me to conquer my fear, as Lou had suggested I needed to do, earlier today.

It was much too soon to tell, of course, about these things. But for the first time since setting foot in Durham, I had the sneaking suspicion—the hope, even—that I might actually be making a friend.

Chapter 16

Eating on the Run

Don't even get me <u>started</u> on the TV reporter's bête noire, which is trying to make good eating choices during a hectic workday. Two keys to survival: One, eat five smaller meals a day, not three big ones; and two, keep a mental list of the fast food places that serve healthy stuff, like McDonald's fruit and yogurt. That way, when the cameraman grabs his fries, you can grab something that won't torpedo your waistline.

—From *The Little Book of Fat-busters* by Mimi Morgan

On the return ride to Durham, I called Beatty to let him know I was developing a fresh angle on the Hoffman story. Amazingly, there was a signal even though we were flying a thousand feet in the air. Shouting over the copter noise and without revealing Lou as my source, I told him that the cause of Hoffman's death had most likely been poisoning.

Beatty leaped at my information the way a spawning trout snatches a fly hook. He ordered me to include the poison information in our coverage of Hoffman's memorial service, which was scheduled to begin later this afternoon. I would need to have the entire story ready by then.

Beatty's sudden deadline threw me into maximum

scramble mode. As soon as Lou's helicopter touched down back at the clinic, I jumped into my car and double-timed it to the station, ignoring my growing hunger. There wasn't time to even think about lunch. Lou, meanwhile, went off to meet with Anita, to find out more about the incidents that had been troubling her since Hoffman's murder. He said he'd set up a meeting for all three of us tomorrow morning, so that I could get caught up to speed on everything.

Upon reaching the studio, I hastily swerved my car into an empty spot under a row of elms that lined the street in front of the studio's main entrance. I didn't even take the time to go around back to park inside the gated lot. Moments later I turbo-charged through the door to the newsroom, almost colliding with a young woman who had a stack of tapes balanced precariously in her arms.

"Hey, it's about time you got here, Gallagher," Beatty called out as I dodged my way between workstations in the bullpen.

Beatty and a jumpy-looking producer were hunched over a long metal desk next to the assignment board. They were arranging sheets of script into three neat columns, each sheet a placeholder for a news story or feature that would run in tonight's six o'clock broadcast.

"Your story goes on the air in"—Beatty paused to check the digital wall clock, which displayed 2:02 p.m. in large red numbers—"in four hours. No problem, right?" He gave me a questioning look over the top of his aviator frame glasses. "Are you under control?" he added.

"Right, no problem, Beatty. Under control," I lied.

"Under control" is how every news director I've ever known lovingly refers to his la-la land expectations of reporters. Expectations that don't always get met in real life, I should add. Reporters are "under control" when they have all their information perfectly gathered, written up, produced, and ready to burst forth onto the air as a blockbuster story, all without a hitch. Needless to say, "under control" was a phrase that did not remotely apply to my current state of readiness.

The twitchy-eyed producer who was standing next to Beatty shot me a glance as he shuffled pages in and out of three columns on the table in front of them. The columns represented the major "blocks" of the broadcast—news, sports, and weather.

"Oh, so you're Kate? Ducky. I'm Rob," he said.

Rob's pasty skin and edgy eyes made him look as if he had a habit of spending way too much time in the control room under conditions of extreme stress. You could practically see the vein tapping out stress signals on his forehead.

"We've bumped Hoffman's memorial service story with Silver up to the lead, since you have breaking info," Rob told me. "And we're running long, so keep the intro tight. Don't let it go more than twenty seconds. At the out cue, we'll have the anchor throw to Silver for a live shot outside the church," he continued. "And you'll need to give him a question to ask."

Rob meant that I needed to provide the anchorman with a question to ask Silver at the end of the live shot. Those "spontaneous" exchanges between anchors and reporters that you see during broadcasts are usually scripted, as this one would be.

"Okay. And do you already know there's a follow-up story for the eleven o'clock?" I asked Rob.

During my earlier conversation with Beatty from the helicopter, we'd made the decision to hold back the information about the Vixen's Den and Hoffman's S and M activities for the later broadcast, the one that would run at eleven o'clock tonight. The late-night audience would be more receptive to the randier aspects of the story, was our thinking. Besides, it wouldn't be seemly to run that part of the story during the murdered doctor's memorial service. Even journalists have to observe certain rules of propriety.

"Let's make it through the six o'clock first." Rob waved an impatient hand. "*Dammit,* not there! That's sports," he muttered to no one in particular as he snatched a page from the first column and slapped it on top of another one.

"But, FYI, you'll have the lead at eleven, too," Beatty said to me. He gave Rob a wary sidelong glance, as if the producer was a cherry bomb that might explode at any moment.

"Okay, got it," I said. "Will do." Having both my stories run in the lead spot meant that they would get more notice—but it also meant there was more pressure to make them strong. And as always in broadcast news, there was never enough time for perfection.

I did a mental rundown of everything I'd need to accomplish over the next few hours. At the very least, I shouldn't have to worry about the wrath of Detective Reed when my story ran. As of two o'clock this afternoon, just two minutes ago exactly, the twenty-four-hour agreement I'd made with Reed to hold off on the Hoffman story had expired. Just to make sure, I pulled out my cell phone and checked my messages. Nothing from the detective. Good. I was free to go with what I had on the air now.

I glanced up at the list of crew assignments on the whiteboard. At the top of the list was the notation, *Gallag-Silver/ENG #3.* Roughly translated, it meant that Greg Silver and I would be working with camera crew number 3, aka Reggie.

"Silver's on the horn with the Durham PD in my office right now, getting a reaction to your poison tip," Beatty said to me, nodding his head in that direction.

Through the glass window of the news director's

private office, I could see Silver hunched over the phone. He had a scowl on his face, as if he were arguing with the person on the other end.

When I entered the office where he was sitting a moment later, Silver clicked off the phone with a sigh.

"Okay," he said to me, skipping over a conventional greeting. "The desk sergeant checked and came back with a 'no comment' on your poison information. That was all I could get." Silver ran a hand through his moussed blond wavelets. He gave me a hesitant look, as if waiting for my reaction. "What do you think that means?"

"It means just that, 'no comment,'" I responded. "But if we were wrong on the story, believe me; they'd be screaming all over our butts with calls to Beatty and upper management."

"Okay cool, that's what I thought," Silver said. His cheeks had an excited flush.

More than excited, I realized. The skin on his face looked blotchy, as though he was getting sick. Sweat was dripping down the side of his neck.

"Hey, you okay?" I asked him.

"Yeah, yeah," he said, scratching at a gland. "So, we've got the lead—did Beatty tell you?" Silver made that announcement with a breathless air, as if he'd just learned we'd won an Emmy. Well, he'd certainly be ready to walk the red carpet, if the day ever came. Today Silver was wearing another one of his overly thought-out outfits, this one involving ostrich skin cowboy boots and a gray linen shirt that precisely matched his eyes. Patches of sweat showed through the shirt in places.

"Yeah, I heard." I shrugged. Producing the lead story was not unusual for me. "Here are a few notes I put together about Hoffman you can use in your live shot," I said, handing over the notes I'd written up on the way back from Lou's house. "I'll get the scripts back to you as soon as I look at what we've got on tape."

"Thanks," Silver said as he flipped through the notes. "I got a brief on-camera yesterday with that police spokes-hole, too. Might be something on it we can use. Hey, it's great having you producing this story, you know?" He glanced up at me. "Normally I have to do my own research and writing and stuff."

Maybe that's why you're not used to getting the lead, my brain replied snarkily.

Next, I located the production editor, Julia, in her editing booth, a tiny cigarette box of a room that opened onto the hallway just outside the newsroom. Julia showed me a video reel she'd already put together.

"This tape has everything you've shot so far with Reggie, plus there's an interview with the police that Silver got yesterday," she explained to me as she popped a cassette into the editing machine.

I grabbed a wooden stool and sat down on it next to Julia. Together, we scrolled through the video.

The first segment showed some establishing shots of the clinic, including the aerial views that Reggie had taken earlier today from Lou's helicopter. Just behind those pictures was the footage that was taken the morning of the murder, earlier this week. They showed a couple of rangy EMTs holding Hoffman's sheet-covered body on a stretcher, carrying it down the clinic's front steps.

"That's great stuff—we can use all of that part," I said to Julia, referring to the body's removal. I opened my reporter's notebook and reviewed the rest of the notes I'd made.

"Okay, so I know I'll need"—I whispered aloud one of the sentences that I planned to use in the story, watching the wall clock simultaneously to time how long it took—"I'll need about seven seconds of the receipts from the Vixen's Den to cover this part," I said slowly. *"Shit,"* I exclaimed. It had suddenly occurred to me that I was missing something. "I need Reggie to grab a quick exterior of the Vixen's Den," I said to Julia. That part of the story wouldn't run until eleven o'clock tonight, but we'd need the shot right after six for promos we'd be running throughout the evening.

"You can use that phone to call the desk." Julia pointed to a red phone attached to the wall. Someone had stuck a handwritten label with the words *Ass Desk* onto the phone's receiver, to indicate the assignment desk. The Ass Desk label was stuck to the front of the receiver with a little sticker of a kicking jackass.

Almost before it had a chance to ring, Jumpy Rob picked up the phone.

"Desk," he barked.

Without mincing words, I gave the producer instructions to relay to Reggie so that he could get the shot we needed. I included directions to the Vixen's Den.

"And, this will be obvious to Reggie when he gets there," I told the producer, "but tell him to make sure he gets a close-up of the purple neon fox in the window, the one wearing stilettos."

"Purple neon fox. Stilettos. Got it," Rob said without missing a beat. I'd expected to get some flack from him over my last-minute request for more camera work, but none came. Handling such last-minute emergencies was probably what had made him so jumpy in the first place.

Last on Julia's video reel was Silver's interview with the community liaison officer at the Durham police department, which he and Reggie had taped yesterday. As I watched, I realized that the liaison officer had said a whole lot of not very much about the ongoing investigation. However, there was one decent sound bite we could use. In that part, the officer had described some of the standard police procedures that were employed following a homicide, including toxicology tests. Once I wove that sound bite into the story, it would sound as if the officer had been commenting directly on my information from Lou Bettinger about the poisoning.

I noted down the in cue and out cue, so that Julia would know which part of the interview to insert into the story later on. There was just enough material here to cobble together a decent story, I realized with a surge of relief.

Making my way back to the newsroom, I found an open desk with a computer and wrote up two brief, concise scripts that covered what we knew so far about Hoffman's murder, one for the six o'clock broadcast, and the other for the eleven. In the six o'clock story, I described the stabbing with the fondue forks, plus the preliminary indication of poisoning, which I attributed to a confidential source. In the script that would run during the later broadcast, I piled on innuendo about Hoffman's S and M activities, as evidenced by the Vixen's Den receipts that proved some of his purchases. The latter story would include a prominent close-up of the receipt for the inflatable sheepdog. We'd leave 'em scratching their heads over *that* one, I thought, grinning to myself.

I pulled the pages of my scripts from a nearby printer and reviewed them quickly. They were imperfect, but sufficient, I decided. Next, Silver would go into the sound booth and voice the stories I'd just written. Then Julia would combine the narration with the images from the video, and insert the sound on tape from the interview with the liaison officer. And then, voilà! Breaking news.

I turned at the sound of loud voices behind me. Beatty and Silver were arguing.

"I'm telling you I'm fine!" Silver's words rose over the din of the newsroom.

Silver's face looked like it had been hit with a red-hot waffle iron. His face was completely covered in spots.

"Chicken pox," I heard whispered in my ear. Julia had come in from production, and was standing just behind me.

"Dammit man, you look like a spotted turtle," Beatty said to Silver. "I'm sending you home *now*."

"But what about the live shot?"

Chuck glanced around the newsroom. Then he caught my eye. "Gallagher will do it," he said, crossing his arms as if to ward off a blow.

"*Gallagher* will do it?" Silver directed his glare at me, then back to Beatty.

"*Gallagher* will do it?" I echoed. My pulse took a little skip. I'd produced many pieces involving live shots, but I'd never done one myself in front of the camera before. My whole reason for coming down to Durham was to make the switch from producer to reporter, so Beatty's live shot seemed like an opportunity that had just dropped from the heavens. So why were my RPMs redlining all of a sudden?

"Yeah. She's the one with the real goods on this story, anyway," Beatty said.

Silver looked at me. "Have you ever done a live shot in your *life*? See, she's not a reporter," he argued to Beatty, without waiting for my reply.

"Neither are you, Silver, if you don't get your ass home and see a doctor," Beatty snapped.

Muttering something under his breath, Silver made plenty of noise as he grabbed a few things from his workstation. Then he stopped and stood perfcctly still for a long moment, staring down at the surface of his desk as if the chicken pox vaccine might be hidden there somewhere. Finally, releasing a deep sigh, he approached me.

"Here are my reporter's notes," he said, handing me his notebook as solemnly as a knight passing Excalibur. "You can use them."

"Thanks, Silver. I appreciate it. Hope you feel better."

"I'm sure you'll be fine doing the live shot," Silver said, but his tone implied otherwise. "Stand at a three-quarters angle to the camera. It's more flattering."

More *flattering*? The spotted ass. "Don't worry about me. I'll be fine," I said, a tad snappishly.

As soon as Silver left, Beatty looked at me.

"This means you're going to have to voice the story, too," he said.

"No problem," I said, trying to ignore the sudden fluttering in my stomach. *Scram,* I told the butterfly, giving it a mental swat.

I glanced down. Silver's "flattering" jibe made me consider the camera appeal of what I was wearing. Fortunately I had actually put some thought into getting dressed earlier this morning while I was getting ready for my interview with Anita. I was wearing my sapphire blue V-necked top and a relatively flattering black skirt that I called my "magic" skirt, because it fit me whether I was up or down my seasonal fifteen-pound weight fluctuation. All things considered, the sartorial situation could be worse. All I'd need would be to slap on some makeup.

As it turned out I wouldn't have much time to think about how nervous I was getting. There was just enough time to put the whole thing together.

After getting Beatty's approval on the copy, I entered the sound booth and read my first script aloud a couple of times, practicing it. After a couple of false starts, I had something that sounded acceptable, I thought.

When I finished voicing both scripts, Julia popped her head into the sound booth. "Hey, you've got great pipes, Kate. You sound like network," she said, giving me a smile.

I suspected Julia was trying to reassure me. I'd mentioned my lack of on-camera experience to her while we were getting set up for the recording. A good production editor's booth is like a priest's confessional. You can reveal all your sins and shortcomings, and it won't come back to haunt you.

"Reggie's already back with that footage of the Vixen's Den," Julia said. "He must've broken some land speed records getting it. He's waiting for you out in the lot."

"Thanks," I said. "Just make sure you put in a good cut shot of the neon fox."

"I will."

Reggie and I would have to head over to the memorial service while Julia was still putting together the story. I wouldn't be able to see the finished product until it aired. Gathering up my courage along with my scattered notes, I headed out the door to meet Reggie in the parking lot.

In contrast to the tawdry violence that had ended his life, Victor Hoffman's memorial service was a hushed and dignified affair. While Reggie was busy outside getting his equipment set up for the live shot, I stood in the back of Our Little Chapel of Blossoms, watching as a procession of dieters and clinic staff filed their way down the center aisle. The giant chandeliers that hung overhead were dimmed low, so that the most striking lights were colored streams that came through the stained glass windows along the sides of the chapel. Everyone was dressed in variations of black except for the heaviest dieters, who wore their usual muumuus splashed with flowery prints. Every armpit was sweating from the late afternoon heat, which washed down the aisle each time the chapel door opened.

In the front pew where the family would normally sit, Anita took her seat next to Lou, flanked by Marjory, Paige, and various other members of the staff. Judging from the seating arrangements, one would have to conclude that his coworkers at the clinic were the closest thing Hoffman had had to an actual family.

I scanned the backs of the mourners, wondering whether one of them was faking it, and was secretly Hoffman's murderer. Then I glanced down at the rose-colored program that had been thrust in my hand on the way into the church. Slated were a prayer service and a couple of solemn-sounding funeral songs, followed somewhat incongruously by one called "I Love to Tell the Story." Reading that song title, I had to squash an inappropriate and almost irresistible urge to start giggling, right there in the back of Our Little Chapel of Blossoms.

"Kate!" Reggie signaled me just beyond the propped-open doorway at the back of the sanctuary. His appearance meant that it was time to do the live shot.

As I turned to follow Reggie outside, out of the corner of my eye I caught sight of someone sitting in the upper gallery. The gallery was a narrow balcony that overlooked the main sanctuary, housing the giant organ pipes and a couple of rows of seats. In the dim light, I could just make out the profile of a man wearing a dark suit, his features obscured by the shadows. He sat there alone, quietly studying the mourners below. As I stepped forward to look closer, the man leaned back into the shadows.

Something about the man seemed somehow familiar. I wanted to get a closer look, but Reggie stood in the doorway making increasingly frantic gestures.

Mouthing the words, "Two minutes!" Reggie held up two fingers and rounded his eyes dramatically. That meant it was two minutes to six.

With a last, lingering look up at the shadow in the balcony, I spun on my heel and followed Reggie outside.

Chapter 17

Plan Ahead When Eating Out

To avoid descending into a feeding frenzy when eating out, you'll need to develop a strategy ahead of time. Here are some tips:

- *Banish the bread basket. Or at least put it next to a BSP (Born Skinny Person) across the table.*
- *Order a broth-based soup or a salad (with low-fat dressing on the side) as an appetizer.*
- *Stick to simple entrées that are grilled, baked, or steamed. If none are listed, don't be shy about asking the waiter for what you want.*
- *If you order dessert, try berries. They're always ripe and sweet at restaurants.*
- *Limit your alcohol intake. Alcohol has tons of calories, plus it releases your inner food demons, who'll whisper into your ear, "Aw, c'mon, just enjoy yourself tonight, honey, heh heh. . . ."*

—From *The Little Book of Fat-busters* by Mimi Morgan

I trailed Reggie outside to the Channel Twelve live truck, then stood stiffly while he hooked me up with a molded earpiece. Even though pale lemon twists still lingered in the evening sky, the van's roof-mounted spotlights were turned on, throwing a patch of gauzy brightness onto the grass lawn. From the camera's per-

spective, the outside of the chapel would be the back-
drop as I delivered my live shot.

"Okay, Kate. Ready to go?" Reggie asked as soon
as he finished taking a white balance. He handed me
a microphone, which sported the red-and-blue flag of
the Channel Twelve logo.

"Yep. Ready." I clutched the microphone with my
fist in front of my chest, counting on it to cover up
any visible signs of a hammering heartbeat. Stepping
gingerly over a coiled nest of cables, I assumed my
position under the lights. After taking a look at myself
on the closed-circuit monitor, I shifted my shoulders
around from the waist slightly. I hated to admit it, but
Silver was right—a three-quarters angle *was* better.

Through the pushed-back sliding van doors, I
watched as another monitor broadcast the opening of
the Channel Twelve Action! Newscast. Pressing in on
the earpiece so that I could hear the audio clearly, I
listened to the lead story as it came across—it was
the story I'd written earlier today about the murder's
aftermath, including updates on the police investigation. It looked pretty damned good, especially considering how little time I'd had to throw it together.

Then the story ended, and the anchorman's face
reappeared on the monitor.

"At this hour, mourners are attending a memorial
service for Victor Hoffman at Our Little Chapel of
Blossoms in East Durham," the newscaster announced. "We have special reporter Kate Gallagher
live outside the memorial with the very latest. Kate?"

"And two . . . *one.*" Reggie pointed at me with his
finger, indicating that we were now live.

The moment Reggie pointed at me, as if by magic,
all the stage fright I'd been feeling about the live shot
fell away. Swallowing deeply, I focused in on the black
lens in front of me. Without glancing down at my
notes, I spoke directly to the camera, speaking to it

as if I were talking to a good friend, telling her about the memorial service that was going on behind me. I can't even remember the exact words—I just remember the way they flowed out naturally, the way you tell a story to someone you're comfortable with.

When I finished, the baritone-voiced anchorman, whose name was Hal, posed the question that I'd written for him earlier.

"So Kate, have the police said whether they have a suspect in the doctor's murder?"

"No, Hal, right now the police aren't saying much on the record," I said. "But I'm told that detectives are aggressively pursuing every available lead. Unconfirmed reports indicate that Hoffman was poisoned to death with a concentrated extract of a toxic flower, possibly lily of the valley, before his eyes were stabbed. For now the police won't comment on that information, but the official toxicology report is due back within two weeks. Back to you at the studio, Hal."

"And . . . *out*." Reggie gave me a thumbs-up. "Great job, Kate," he added. "You really nailed that sucker all the way."

"Thanks, Reggie," I said, removing my earpiece. I was riding a huge surge of relief, a kind of high, really, that my maiden live shot had gone so smoothly. I've seen first-time live shots go horribly wrong—the reporters get spacey, or they forget what they're supposed to say entirely and freeze up in front of the camera the way a hairy-footed gerbil gets hypnotized by a cobra. It felt like a weight had rolled off my shoulders—if I ever got another chance to work on-camera, I would be okay. Better than okay.

After the live shot, Reggie and I hung around to catch some interviews when the memorial service concluded. It was getting dark by the time people began to spill through the lighted, open double-doors of the church. A few made their way across the lawn toward the news van, drawn as if by a magnet to the lights and electronics.

"Hey Kate, interview me!" I heard Jack's voice boom across the grass. "I wanna be a star!"

I was quickly surrounded by Jack and Amber and a couple of other women dieters. In response to their excited questions about what I was doing with the Channel Twelve camera crew, I explained that I was filling in for a reporter who had gotten sick, Greg Silver.

"Ooh, I've seen him. That Greg Silver is *hot*." Amber grabbed my wrist. "But isn't he gay?" she added in a worried tone.

"I don't think so," I said, trying not to laugh. Behind me, I could hear Reggie chuckling. Amber's question about Silver would be all over the newsroom by tomorrow morning. Newsies love nothing more than to make fun of their prima donna colleagues behind their backs.

I kept glancing toward the entrance to the church, trying to spot anyone resembling the shadowy figure I'd seen lurking in the balcony area before the service. Something about his dark profile had seemed familiar, but I couldn't put my finger on it.

Looking toward the door again, I spotted Lou and Anita leaving the memorial service together. Lou waved to me, his other arm circled protectively around Anita's waist as he escorted her toward a black town car that slid silently to the curb. Watching Lou and Anita exit as a couple, I wondered again whether they were a romantic item. The idea caused an unexpected twinge in my gut. It felt suspiciously like jealousy.

What the freak? I demanded of the twinge. It wasn't as if I were starting to *like* Lou, right? He was too old for me. And anyway, I had a crush on Reed. Right?

Picking up the microphone again, I interviewed a

couple of dieters to get their reactions to Hoffman's death. I was struck by how heartfelt their stories were. One of the people I interviewed was Lila, she of the abundant skin. Lila had tears in her eyes as she recalled how Hoffman had "cured" her morbid obesity. I could see that in death, Hoffman was quickly assuming a mythic stature among his former patients.

Reggie and I were breaking down the equipment when Jack approached me again.

"Hey, you gonna come with us, Kate? We're all heading out to celebrate Dr. Hoffman's life."

"How are you going to celebrate?" I asked him.

"How else? With the all-you-can-eat buffet at the Hungry Shores restaurant," Jack said with a wicked grin. "It's over in Gorgetown—that's what we call Restaurant Row. Wait until you see the staff get all frightened when all us super jumbos come piling through the door. Historically, we've cleaned them out when we descend in packs."

"Well . . ." I suddenly realized that the twinge I'd felt at the sight of Lou and Anita together had morphed into a tornado-sized twister of hunger. In my rush to get the story done today, I had skipped all thoughts of lunch. By now I was so famished I was beginning to feel light-headed. "Can I get a ride?" I said to Jack. "My car's back at the station."

"No problema, señorita." Jack made a sweeping gesture, accompanied by a gallant bow. "Your chariot awaits."

I felt a hand on my shoulder.

"Pardon me, Kate?"

I turned to see Paige standing off to one side.

"Anita asked me to let you know she can meet with you tomorrow morning at nine," Paige said. She looked apologetic that she'd interrupted me.

Typical Anita—rather than walk twenty feet across

the lawn to tell me about the appointment herself, she'd sent her assistant.

"Thank you, Paige. I'll be there at nine."

Paige remained standing, a hesitant look on her face.

"Is there something else?" I lowered my voice and gathered myself in, mirroring her self-contained body language.

"Umm . . . actually, I was wondering if I should mention something," she said.

"Let's go over here," I said, steering us a few paces away from the rest of the group.

"Remember you asked me about Bethany, about whether she'd checked out?"

"Right."

Paige blinked, hunching her shoulders forward. I waited patiently for Paige to summon up the nerve to tell me whatever she had on her mind. She reminded me of a little hunkered-down bunny. Thin as she was, she probably ate like a bunny, too.

"I didn't see your story because I was still inside the service." A tiny crease appeared between Paige's eyebrows. "Have the police found a suspect yet?"

"Not that we know of," I said. "The police haven't confirmed anything about specific suspects or cause of death."

"Cause of death? So then, they don't even know how he *died,* yet?" Paige pressed a hand to her chest with her fingers fanned out.

"Not officially, yet, but early indications are that he was poisoned before he was stabbed."

Paige's eyes went blank. "Oh," she said. "That's terrible. Well, at the staff meeting this afternoon, Anita said you were working on something for her, and that everyone should cooperate with you."

That meant Lou must have already worked his persuasive magic on the Snow Queen.

"So there's something I should probably let you know," Paige continued. "Remember when you asked about Bethany Williams, and whether she'd checked out of the clinic?"

"Yes, I remember," I said, feeling my pulse quicken.

"Well, after you asked me about her, I found out that she left the clinic without telling anyone on the staff why, or where she was going. Everyone thinks the way she took off was kind of strange."

"Do you know if anyone has seen her since she left?" I asked.

"Someone mentioned they saw her in a club downtown. It's this kind of sketchy place. Called the Razor's Edge, I think."

That was interesting. Amber had mentioned that Hoffman and Bethany had once been spotted at the Razor's Edge together, and now Bethany was evidently frequenting the place again. The clerk at the Vixen's Den had mentioned that a former employee of the clinic worked there, too.

"Why were you asking about Bethany?" Paige asked. "Does she have something to do with all of this? With Dr. Hoffman's death, I mean?"

"Possibly. My understanding is that Bethany was sleeping with Dr. Hoffman," I said. "That she was his girlfriend. Is that true?"

An appalled look washed across Paige's delicate features. "No, not at all," she said. "Why would . . ." To my surprise, she looked as if she were getting upset. "Believe me, what you heard must have just been a rumor," she continued, collecting herself. "People at the clinic are such gossips. Most of it's completely bogus."

"Did he have a girlfriend or a relationship at all, do you know?" I persisted.

Paige fixed on me with a cool stare. I felt sure that

she was about to tell me to shove off. But then she drew in a breath and held it in for a long second.

"Dr. Hoffman was . . ."—Paige sounded as if she were choosing her words carefully—"kind of an ascetic man, you know what I mean? He was always surrounded by women, but I don't think in an intimate way. Certainly not with someone like Bethany." She sniffed delicately.

From the way Paige spoke about Bethany, I could tell there was certainly no love lost between the two women.

Paige glanced swiftly over her shoulder, as if checking to see whether someone was standing there. Over by the broadcast truck, Jack and the other dieters were peering inside it, taking in the array of monitors. They weren't paying any attention to us.

"I feel like I can trust you," she said, as if reassuring herself. "The other night at dinner, you asked me about Dr. Hoffman's schedule."

"Right." I nodded. When I'd asked Paige about Hoffman's schedule, she'd told me that the doctor's last appointment on Sunday had been with Billy Hoffman, the boy who loved *Psycho*.

"Well, when I woke up yesterday morning, I suddenly remembered that I *did* see Dr. Hoffman late in the day on Sunday. Or rather, I saw his car. Marjory—you know, the clinic manager?" Paige's words tumbled out in a nervous rush. "She was driving it away from the parking lot. At the time, I guess I just assumed she was doing an errand for Dr. Hoffman."

"You saw Marjory in Hoffman's car?"

I registered Paige's information. If the freckled clinic manager had been seen driving Hoffman's car just before the doctor was murdered, that would vault her right to the head of the list of suspects. It might also explain why Hoffman's body was found on the clinic porch, while his car was parked at his home

across town. Perhaps Marjory had driven it back there
after the murder.

"Yeah, Marjory drove his car a lot," Paige said.
"Do you think that's important?"

"Yes. You should tell the police about what you
saw," I replied.

"Do you think so?" Paige sounded reluctant. "I
mean, they might wonder why I didn't say anything
about it *before*. I just didn't think it was important.
Now I'm worried about what to do. I feel like I'm
going to get in trouble with either the clinic or with
the police."

"Absolutely, you should say something." I reached
into my purse and fished out Reed's card. "That's how
the police connect the dots in a case like this." I
handed her the card. "And don't worry about not having said anything before this." I attempted to sound
reassuring. "They always expect that people will recall
more details after a traumatic event."

"All right, thanks." Paige pocketed the card.

I realized something then. The man I'd seen sitting
alone up in the balcony before the memorial service, the
one who'd been studying the mourners—that had been
Reed. That's why the man had looked vaguely familiar,
even though I hadn't been able to see him clearly. The
detective must have been observing one of the mourners
as a suspect. But the question was, which one?

Behind us, I heard the van's engine power up.
Glancing away briefly from Paige, I told Reggie I was
getting another ride and wouldn't be heading back
to the station, and then turned back to talk to her
some more.

But Paige was already gone.

To celebrate the life of Victor Hoffman, Jack and
the assembled Fruiters set about eating the town red.
And then some.

During the first part of what would become a blow-out session at the Hungry Shores buffet, I tried to restrain myself. Really I did. As I started my journey down the buffet line, I laid a modest quarter-broiled chicken on my plate, along with the kind of fruit and vegetables I might have expected to receive during a regular meal at the Hoffman Clinic. A few green beans, a cup of mandarin oranges, that was all. Unfortunately, the final buffet stop was an entire table filled with nothing but hot, yeasty bread and muffins. As I paused in front of the table, somehow a piece of cheese bread leaped onto my tray.

I stared at the offending carb long and hard. My mouth watered involuntarily. I could actually *feel* the hot cheesy bread on my taste buds. *Banish the bread-basket,* I heard Mimi's voice reminding me, followed by a mental image of myself standing at a three-quarters angle to the camera. With a reluctant sigh, I picked up the square of bread. Dangling it from two fingers, I dropped it into a nearby trash can. Better to banish those calories than throw them into *me*.

Meanwhile, the rest of the Fruiters were busy heaping leaning towers of pizza and every other food imaginable onto their plates. They kept returning to the buffet for more and more, followed by more.

As everyone devoured their feasts with abandon, I cruised the tables, asking questions about Hoffman and Marjory. I wanted to know what the clinic manager's background was, and whether there was any history between her and Hoffman.

No one had a bad word to say about the clinic manager. Norm, the manatee man, said he thought she'd started working at the Hoffman Clinic several years ago.

"She loves working outside in those gardens—when I first started, there was nothing out there in the back lot but weeds," Norm explained between huge mouthfuls of fried chicken. "She hired all these gardeners and put in exotic plants. Really spruced up the place."

As the manager of the landscaping crew, Marjory would know a lot about plants, including the poisonous kind. But why would she want to kill Hoffman? Perhaps she'd resented having to run the doctor's sex errands, or perhaps she'd been involved in something even more lurid. But so far, I was missing any real sense of a motive.

Wondering what Norm's attitude toward Hoffman had been, I asked him about an incident that Jack had told me about, in which Hoffman had made a DON'T FEED ME sign for Norm to wear around his neck.

To my surprise, Norm dismissed the whole sign-hanging episode.

"Dr. Hoffman had kind of unorthodox methods, but that was his genius," Norm said. "I mean, what else you gonna do with us? Look around you." He gestured to include the people around us, who were busy gobbling down platters of food. "We need a kick in the pants sometimes. I'll gain nine pounds tonight, you watch."

Judging from the amount of food that was rapidly disappearing from his plate, Norm was probably right.

Everyone seemed to agree that Hoffman had been like a stern shepherd, keeping them on track toward weight loss.

But somewhere inside his flock, there was a wolf.

I asked Jack to drop me off at my car on the way to the group's next destination, a hotel lounge they'd nicknamed the Crisco Disco. The Fruiters were planning to assemble there for a night of dancing. I wanted to pick up my car so I'd have the option of crashing early. My dinner had hit my system like a load of cement, making me suddenly realize how tired I was. It felt like a million years since I'd gotten up this morning to do the interview with Anita, followed by the trip to Atlanta, plus all the pressure of producing the story and doing my first live shot. It felt like I'd just completed a triathlon. I was shaky with tiredness.

"Thanks for the ride, Jack," I said to him as he pulled his enormous SUV in front of the station.

"See you at the Crisco. They're having a seventies night tonight. I do a mean Hustle," Jack said, rocking his shoulders back and forth and snapping his fingers.

"I don't know about dancing," I said. "My college roommate once accused me of doing the 'white girl bop.' Not a compliment."

"Don't worry," Jack assured me. "The only people there will be Fruiters and a few chubby chasers. We don't even bop—we jiggle."

The cool night air was moist on my skin as I climbed out of Jack's car and watched the taillights recede down the street. My car was parked right where I'd hastily pulled in along the street at one this afternoon. Ten hours ago exactly.

I'd left the top down on my convertible when I'd parked earlier, as I usually did in the summer. Drawing closer, I spotted some white streaks on the black leather edges of the dashboard. I leaned over the side of the car, then reached forward with my fingers and ran my fingertips across the streaks. Then I jolted back.

The white streaks were gashes.

It took a moment for my brain to grasp the information. Someone had vandalized my car. Using a razor, or maybe a knife, they'd slashed my dashboard all to pieces. It looked like a saber-toothed cat had gotten hold of my car and ripped out its stuffing.

I threw open the driver's-side door to get a closer look, and saw something on the seat. Something that the vandal had evidently left behind.

Several flower stems, tied together with a ribbon,

lay on the driver's seat. It looked like a nosegay that had been dropped by a drunken debutante. Peering in closer, I caught a whiff of something cloyingly sweet. Then I recognized the tiny flowers on the stems, and jolted back.

They were the delicate white bells of lily of the valley.

Delicate, white, and deadly.

Chapter 18

Seek Out Sources of Emotional Support

Research suggests that people who have a strong support group lose more weight and keep it off longer than those who go it alone. Nowadays, support can be as close as your computer. Online support groups have grown exponentially in the last decade, and the reason is—they help!

Of course the best emotional support comes from a loving, supporting partner. But hey, I'm a single gal in broadcasting, so I don't ask for the moon. I have the stars—online.

—From *The Little Book of Fat-busters* by Mimi Morgan

I didn't know which discovery was more horrible—the slice-and-dice job on my car, or the telefloral nasty-gram that had been dropped on my front seat.

I gaped down at the flowers. There were two stems bound together with a thin black ribbon. Just two stems—that seemed like an odd number. My imagination kicked into morbid overdrive. Was Hoffman's killer implying that there would be another murder? Of me?

My first reaction was to dig out my cell phone and punch in Reed's number. To my profound relief, he picked up on the first ring.

"Reed." I heard the detective's clipped greeting.

"It's Kate," I blurted. "My car's parked outside Channel Twelve. On Irwin Street. Someone hacked up the dashboard. They left flowers behind—lily of the valley. It might be some kind of stupid prank from someone who saw my story on the news."

"Are you alone?" he asked me quickly. "Is anyone there with you, Kate?"

"No one's here, but I'm right across the street from the Channel Twelve studios . . . ," I started to explain.

"Go inside," he commanded tersely. "I'm going to send a cruiser and then head over myself. But I'm across town—it may take a while."

"But . . . ," I began.

"Get inside *now*." He used an urgent tone I hadn't heard before. It was the tone weathercasters use to tell you to take cover when radar shows a tornado bearing down on your neighborhood.

"Okay." I reflexively clicked off the phone and then immediately wished I hadn't. Reed's warning had underscored how vulnerable and exposed I was, standing there. I cursed myself for not taking the time to park in the gated lot earlier today, rather than parking hurriedly here on the street in front of the studio.

I glanced left and right. Beyond the studio building, an overhead canopy created by urn-shaped elm trees blocked the feeble street lighting. Everything around me was shrouded, impenetrable. I pulled in a stitchy breath and tried to settle my nerves, acutely aware of the sound of the air passing through my nostrils.

I heard a sharp crack. Behind me, there was a cascading crash, followed by a push of air, and finally a thud as something landed hard on the pavement.

Startled, I sprinted across the street, then practically levitated my way up the whitewashed brick steps to the studio building. I reached the main door and grabbed frantically at the handles. It was locked.

"Dammit!" I kicked at the brass doorplate in a panicky fit. Moving right, I peered in through the angled slats of the window blinds. A security guard was striding across the lobby, headed for the door.

Scrabbling in my purse for my ID badge, I rolled my eyes wildly over my shoulder. The next thing I expected to hear was the sound of an attacker's footsteps pounding up the stairs.

"Miss?"

The security guard had cracked open the front door a slice, and was now peering out at me. "Are you okay?"

Up close, the guard looked well into his seventies, older than I'd thought. His nose was liberally cross-stitched with a network of broken capillaries. The guard stared at me warily; obviously he was convinced he had a crazy woman on his hands.

I brandished my ID at him. "My car was vandalized on the street out front here, attacked . . . the police are on the way," I announced breathlessly.

The guard motioned me inside.

Just before ducking inside the lobby, I took a final, lingering look over my shoulder, searching for any signs of an assailant. I half expected to see someone with his fist raised and grasping a knife, poised to slash me up so that I'd match my dashboard.

But the street was empty.

With the security guard in tow, I crossed the lobby and headed down the corridor that led to the newsroom.

The newsroom was deserted except for a young girl who was hunched over some wire service copy at the assignment desk. Everyone else must have been tied up in the control room producing the eleven o'clock broadcast.

"Is there a videographer available?" I asked the girl, who returned a blank stare. I wanted to get a shot of the flowers before the police arrived. I might need the footage in a story down the line.

"Um . . . I can ask them after the broadcast?" the girl said in that irritating way younger people have of punctuating a statement with a question mark. Probably an intern. "Who are you?" She looked back and forth from me to the security guard, as if she thought I'd stormed the studios and taken him hostage, and that she might be next.

"Kate Gallagher. I'm a contractor. And never mind about the camera." I'd already spotted an ENG camera on a shelf near the production area. "I can take the footage myself."

Grabbing the camera as well as an extra battery and a field equipment bag, I dashed back to the lobby. Meanwhile, I fielded a series of excited questions from the security guard.

"What got you so spooked out there?" he demanded, trotting along behind me.

"I thought there was someone," I said, taking a moment to peer cautiously out the lobby window again. "Possibly whoever slashed up my car."

"Well, everything looks clear now. I can ride shotgun until the police get here, if you like," the guard announced, as if he were Superman rescuing Lois Lane. He didn't appear strong enough to bring down a litterbug, much less a slasher psycho. He wasn't even *armed*, for Pete's sake. But I went with the safety in numbers theory.

Using a torch flashlight he'd retrieved from the lobby desk, the guard lit the way as we crossed the street to my parked car. He swept the beam of light back and forth across the pavement.

The beam caught the edge of a six-foot-long tree branch lying on the ground. The branch hadn't been there earlier, so it must have dropped from one of the nearby elms. A falling tree limb—that's what had scared the stuffing out of me. Not an attacker after all.

After inserting a fresh battery and fishing a white balance card out of the equipment bag, I hefted the camera onto my shoulder.

"Can you hold up this card for me a second while I get a color balance?" I asked, handing the card to the guard.

"Sure thing, Miss. Hey, am I gonna be on TV?" The guard grinned inanely while holding the card in front of his chest.

I focused in with the lens. Although I'm no equipment expert by any means, I was familiar enough with this particular type of camera to get what I'd need for a story later on. It was important to record the flowers and the damage to my car, even though I wasn't comfortable with the idea of mentioning the attack on the air. With the possible exception of Geraldo Rivera, reporters generally don't like to become the center of the story they're covering. But now the attack was part of the murder story's narrative.

I panned across the car, and then zoomed in for a close-up of the flowers on the driver's seat.

"Jesus, Miss. Your car's a total mess." The guard gave a low whistle. He seemed increasingly wound up. Tonight was probably the most excitement he'd had in his entire night watchman career. "Somebody must've been all pot-likkered up to do that," he said, looking at me. "Boyfriend?"

"No," I said through gritted teeth. I was already wigged out from the attack and the little forget-me-not bouquet, and now the guard's asinine remarks were making things even worse.

A patrol car careened around the corner onto the street in front of the studio, sirens blaring. It slammed to a halt in the middle of the street alongside my car.

An older-looking cop emerged. His face was dominated by an old-fashioned handlebar mustache that made him look like Sir Arthur Conan Doyle.

Within moments, another car pulled in from the opposite direction. I recognized the plain-looking beige sedan that Reed had been driving when he'd chased me down the day before, as I was returning from my trip to the Vixen's Den.

Reed climbed out of the driver's seat. He gave me the five-minute sign and then spent a few minutes consulting with the patrol cop. While the uniformed officer ran back to the cruiser to grab something, Reed stood silently over my car, staring down at it. Finally, he approached me, waving a hand to get me to lower the camera.

"Did you misinterpret the words 'Go inside'?" Reed wasn't wearing a jacket, but nonetheless he was dressed impeccably again, this time wearing a sage green tie knotted over a pale yellow Oxford shirt.

I was beginning to suspect that Reed must spring out of bed in the mornings, fully garbed and knotted to go. I set the camera down. "You said to go inside if I was alone." I nodded in the direction of the security guard, who was now nattering away at the uniformed cop, embellishing his words with looping air gestures. I arched my eyebrows as if to say, *See? Not alone.*

Reed rolled his eyes. "Just tell me what happened," he prodded.

"Well." I took in a deep breath. "I left the car here today at about one o'clock, and got a ride back at eleven. The dashboard was slashed up, just like you see it here."

"Did you touch anything after making the discovery?"

"No." I shook my head. "Whoever ripped up the dash left behind these lilies on the seat," I added, gesturing toward the flowers on the front seat. "What do you make of that?"

"What do *you* make of that?" he parried back.

"C'mon, Detective." I released a frustrated sigh. I was in no shape to play a Q&A tennis match right now. "You and I both know that Hoffman was poisoned by lily of the valley, or some derivative of it. These flowers must have been put here as a warning by whoever killed him."

"I heard about that little poisoning theory you put out on the air, earlier tonight. Where'd you get your information? We haven't released the cause of Hoffman's death yet," Reed snapped. In response to an elaborate shrug by me, his expression darkened further. "I can see I'm going to have to plug a leak in our laboratory staff. But you're right about one thing," he added flatly. "The person who did this might be connected to Hoffman's murder. We have to treat this as a threat against you."

"On the other hand," I countered, playing devil's advocate, "is it possible that the vandalism could have been some kind of prank, by someone not connected to the murder?" During my live shot at six o'clock, after all, I'd told the entire city that Hoffman was poisoned by lily of the valley. The attack could have been done by someone who happened to see the broadcast, and recognized my car.

"Possible, but not likely." Reed shook his head dismissively. "This has all the earmarks of a targeted attack."

I had to agree with Reed. Even as I'd posited my prankster theory, my gut told me the truth—Hoffman's killer had just sent me a message.

"Pardon me one moment." Reed walked over and consulted with the mustachioed officer, who had dropped the flowers into an evidence box he'd retrieved from the patrol car. Reed and the officer huddled over my TR6, talking something over in low voices. I saw the officer nod and then reach across his chest for a microphone that was attached to his shoulder.

"We're calling in for a police tow," Reed announced to me when he returned. "I'm afraid I'm going to have to impound your car for a couple of days."

"You're not taking my car," I protested in a squeaky-sounding voice.

"I need to get prints and some other tests," Reed replied. "And right now the conditions here aren't good for processing."

I groaned. Shit, I'd have to rent something, which was the last thing my budget needed right then.

"Don't worry." His eyes deepened with those little creases around the edges again, the ones that had rendered my knees all kanoodly the first time I'd met him. "I'll give you a ride home."

"You gonna tuck me in, too?" The instant those flirty words escaped my mouth, I wanted to snatch them back. Good God, I sounded like I was channeling Lauren Bacall in *To Have and Have Not*. Next thing you know, I'd be prancing around in a dangerously overstuffed wiggle skirt, telling Reed to pucker up his lips and blow.

Thankfully, Reed appeared to take my comeback as a joke.

"Not on this drive," he said, looking amused. With everything that was going on, this was no time for me to discover my inner vamp.

Before taking Reed up on his offer of a ride, I extracted the video and dropped off the camera inside the newsroom. The only person still there was the night side anchor, who was pulling on his jacket as if he were preparing to leave for the night. He nodded at me in a vaguely friendly way, but didn't ask me any questions as I replaced the camera on the shelf and pulled out my tape. The newsroom lacked windows, and the staff normally used a back entrance that led directly to the covered parking lot on the other side of the building, so it was entirely possible that no one even knew the cops were parked out front. Probably the only person who knew what was going on was the security guard, and he was still outside pestering Reed and the patrol cop.

After pausing to drop the video into the top drawer of my desk and retrieve a manila file folder, I left without making any comment to the anchor. I didn't feel like launching into a whole discussion about the incident involving my car with someone who didn't know the background—there'd be plenty of time to brief Beatty tomorrow, to let the news director know about everything that had happened.

Reed grilled me with questions the entire way back to the Hoffman Clinic. He wanted to know exactly whom I'd spoken to today, and where I'd gone. He listened closely as I described my day, which had started out with my interview with Anita Thornburg. I remembered to mention the quick helicopter side trip I'd made to Lou Bettinger's house in Atlanta. I *didn't* mention that Lou had asked me to help protect Anita, by figuring out whether there was a murderer close at hand at the clinic. I knew Reed would go ballistic if he heard that part. Then I described how I'd returned to the Channel Twelve news station to work on my story.

"At six o'clock tonight, I did a live shot at Hoffman's memorial service at the church," I added slowly. "But then, you already know that, don't you?" I kept my eyes glued to Reed's profile as he drove. "Wasn't that you I saw up in the balcony before the service? Watching the mourners?" I'd suspected that the detective had been up there in the shadows, studying the people who'd attended the service. This seemed like a good opportunity to confirm that.

"Yes, I was there," he said, keeping his eyes level and straight ahead on the road. "Why do you ask?"

"Do you have a suspect?" I said. "I mean . . . are you watching anyone in particular?"

Reed shot a sideways glance at me.

"Maybe I'm watching *you*." The front end of the car bumped up and down as we pulled into the gravel parking lot of the Hoffman Clinic. We stopped in front of the entrance that opened off the lot. "Did you ever think of that?" Reaching forward with an abrupt motion, he switched off the ignition key.

"Oh, right. Like I'm a suspect?" I tried to tag my retort with a dismissive laugh, but it came out sounding more like a sickly *heh-heh*.

"No, but it serves you right for asking me questions about the case, when you know I won't answer," Reed said with a tight expression. He turned in his seat to face me. "I think I should have someone posted outside your door tonight, just to be on the safe side." He reached for the radio.

"Please don't do that," I said quickly. "I really don't want that." Even though I was shaken up, the last thing I wanted was to have uniforms hanging around. I might as well move out, in that case.

"Well, at the very least I'll have extra patrols come by here again tonight—they'll swing through every couple of hours."

"What can happen in a couple of hours?" I asked with a shrug of my shoulders.

"A lot." Reed's expression remained stern. Despite the fact that the air conditioning was still running on battery, the windshield was beginning to fog up around the edges. "That story you ran tonight . . ." Reed shook his head. His voice sounded grim. "You've put yourself right under a spotlight. The killer very well might think you know something. They probably attacked your car to get you to back off the story."

"But of course, I don't know who *did* it," I protested in a small voice. "My job is to report the news. That's what I do."

"Well, you've just managed to make your job much more dangerous than it had to be." Reed's tone was getting testier by the second. "And that's a problem for me—I mean, for the police. Because we have to protect you."

"I get that lecture all the time from my father," I snapped. "Thanks for your concern, but I'll be okay." I tried to pull up on the door handle, but my hand slipped, and the handle sprang back with a *thwack*. It was evidently on autolock.

Reed opened his door, got out, and circled around the front of the car. Then he opened the door on my side.

"Pardon the correction, but I *do* recall receiving a distress call about an hour ago, from someone named Kate Gallagher. Was that not you?" Reed lifted his eyebrows and extended a hand to help me out of the car.

"Sarcasm noted. It won't happen again." I slid sideways on the seat. I used my card key to open the glass door to the residential wing, which was locked at this hour.

"At the risk of further provoking the famous Irish temper, I'll go in with you to make sure everything's okay," Reed said. "Hold a second."

Sliding past me as I opened the door to my room, Reed took two long strides into the room. As he did a quick check around, his hand hovered over the area of his jacket that would be covering his weapon.

I'd halfway expected to discover the room upended or torn apart, like my car. However, there appeared to be nothing unusual. The room appeared quite undisturbed.

Reed appeared to be satisfied. "It's clear."

I was already feeling sorry for snapping at Reed. "Thank you. For bringing me back I mean." To my dismay, I heard a hiccupy sound break underneath the word "back." It sounded suspiciously soblike. *"God."* Squeezing my eyes shut, I bit back a wild impulse to giggle hysterically. "Bad time to fall apart. Guess it was a bit too much for me tonight."

"It's all right."

I felt first one, and then the other of Reed's arms wrap around my waist, and then squeeze me gently. Relaxing into the swift embrace, I leaned my cheek against his shoulder. The cotton shirt and his shoulder had a soothing, woodsy scent. Like KL, my favorite men's cologne.

"Uh-oh." I tilted my face back after a moment, opening my eyes. "I think I got snot on your shoulder." For some reason, this struck me as insanely funny.

"That's okay. Will you be able to get some sleep now?" Reed smiled down at me, holding me lightly at the elbows.

"I think so."

"Just the same, I'm going to stand outside your door for a while." Reed reached for the guest chair that was next to my bed. "Or sit, rather. Mind if I borrow this chair?"

"Not at all." I tried to imagine the reaction my fellow dieters would have if they passed my door and saw Reed sitting there. I'd have a thousand questions to answer by morning.

I closed the door behind Reed and locked it. Peeling off my clothes, I changed into a T-shirt and my favorite oversized pajama bottoms, and then stopped off in the bathroom to scrub my face. After drying off, I returned to the bedroom and tossed back the sheet. Slipping between cold layers of covers, I lay there for a few minutes. Despite the trauma of everything that had happened to my car earlier this evening, I felt oddly, deliciously relaxed.

The idea of Reed sitting right outside my door, keeping guard, lifted a weight off my shoulders. As I drifted off to sleep, another kind of slow, syrupy feeling stole through my muscles. I knew the reason for it.

When Reed had held me in his arms, comforting me, I'd felt the curving outline of an unmistakable bulge beneath his belt buckle. It was a bulge that answered the question I'd been wondering about.

And the answer was this: Reed liked me, too.

Chapter 19

Don't Eat the Grapes of Wrath

There's an old saying: Scratch an anger, and you'll find a depression. Well, scratch an overweight woman, and you may find an angry one underneath. Many of us eat to repress angry feelings—over a rotten childhood, over a chintzy news budget that doesn't cover wardrobe expenses . . . you name it. We've got plenty to be angry about. Learn to express anger in a healthy, assertive way. Which <u>doesn't</u> include diving into a pint of Chunky Monkey.

—From *The Little Book of Fat-busters* by Mimi Morgan

The next morning, I felt a surge of anticipation as I set off for my scheduled appointment with Anita and Lou. I hadn't the faintest clue what to expect during this meeting. Yesterday, when I'd tried to interview Anita for my weight loss story, the doctor had come off like a royal Bitch Queen from hell. The interview had been a total nonstarter. But now I knew the reason for her prickly behavior—she apparently felt threatened.

My breakfast of a half grapefruit and oatmeal goop, which I'd choked down during a brief stopover in the dining room, had hardened into a sourball in my stomach by the time I arrived at Anita's office at nine. At least there'd been banner news at the morning weigh-in. I was down nine pounds in less than a week. Nine pounds! Granted, most of that loss was probably initial water weight, but, H_2O or no, nine pounds down felt utterly fantastic. I could already feel the beginnings of a new looseness around the yoke of my chevron-striped blouse and my black skirt, which I'd donned once again in order to look professional for this meeting.

Anita's office lay along a long, tiled corridor that connected the clinic's main house to the residential wing. Checking up and down the hallway, I didn't see Paige or any staff in sight. No one at all, in fact.

The second I tapped on Anita's office door, Lou threw it open.

"Kate. Welcome!" He greeted me with a warm smile. Above the smile, however, his eyes were tense. "I really appreciate your coming." He ushered me to one of two brocade-backed guest chairs inside the office, his right hand guiding me under my elbow in the manner of an old-fashioned swain. He held his leather portfolio under his opposite arm. Wearing an elegant navy suit, Lou was all spiffed-out this morning, as if he'd dropped by on his way to make a presentation to the Supreme Court.

I remembered that Lou had been planning to spend last night at a hotel, although maybe he'd wound up at Anita's place, if I was right about the two of them being a couple.

"Hey, Lou," I said to him. "Anita." I nodded hesitantly.

Anita sat erect and stiff-shouldered on the other side of her ash-colored desk. She had her hands folded precisely on top of the desk blotter in front of her. There was a taut watchfulness about the angle of her back in her chair.

"Yes, of course! Kate." Anita looked slightly startled, as if suddenly realizing she was required to say something. "Lou tells me you have some background in investigative research, and might be able to offer us some assistance." This effusive outburst was followed by an awkward pause.

"I'm happy to help in any way I can," I said, settling into the guest chair. I was concerned that Lou might have given Anita some big buildup about my investigative abilities, and that I wouldn't be able to live up to it. But it was nice to have Anita acting semi*friendly*, for a change.

"First of all, Kate, I must apologize if I came off a bit . . . *uncooperative*, perhaps, during our interview here yesterday." It seemed to take an effort for Anita to keep her eyes level with mine as she spoke. "But please understand that I've been going through a difficult ordeal." She ground to a halt again.

"Why don't you tell me what's been going on?" I said cautiously, struck by how anxious Anita seemed today. Her imperious attitude of yesterday had disappeared entirely. She seemed to be a nervous wreck, in fact.

"Anita's had a string of things happen since Hoffman's death that she's found to be a little . . . unsettling," Lou interjected. He pushed forward with his hand in the air, as if trying to prime Anita's verbal pump.

"Right." Anita kept glancing at Lou before shifting her gaze back to me, as if seeking assurance from him.

Anita's tropism toward the lawyer was disconcerting, but it would probably help move the conversation along. I was glad Lou was sitting in.

"Since Victor was killed, I've had this weird feeling I'm being followed," she said. Her face looked embarrassed, as if it were hard for her to sound vulnerable, especially to a stranger.

"Can you tell me any specifics?" I prompted her.

"Okay, this may sound silly, but when I came home day before yesterday, my cat was sitting outside in the middle of the driveway." Anita shook her head. "I *never* let Pyewacket—that's my cat—out, because I had her declawed when she was a kitten. And I live alone. No one else has the key except my sister, who lives across town." All of this information came out in a series of agitated bursts. "And I already checked. It wasn't her."

"Was anything disturbed when you went inside?" I asked her.

Anita nodded. "This is the creepy thing," she said. "Someone came into my kitchen and made tea for themselves, evidently. The teapot was on a different burner than usual, and there was a cup in the sink— my Hoffman Clinic mug. It smelled like tea."

"Perhaps it was a burglar?" I suggested, with a sideways glance at Lou. "Was anything missing from your house?"

"No, nothing," Anita said. "What kind of burglar makes tea and doesn't steal anything? Am I dealing with a *stalker,* do you think?"

"Possibly, but I wouldn't jump to conclusions," I said.

"How can I help it?" Anita shook her head, looking frustrated.

"You feel scared when you think your house has been violated," I said to her gently, switching deliberately into active listening mode. I use active listening mode when it's critical to understand fully what a person is saying, as well as their *feelings* about what they're saying. Boiled down to basics, active listening is a two part sentence: You feel (*insert a feeling*) when (*insert a situation*). The technique is a cheat I learned from a therapist I interviewed once. It works wonders with people who don't feel comfortable expressing emotion.

"Yes, that's just the right word—violated." Anita's frosted-over eyes met and held mine for the first time since I'd entered her office. Her eyes were ringed with thick, dark eyelashes, which made them appear to pop out of her face. In contrast to her light coloring, the effect was attractive, if somewhat startling. "And that was just the first thing that happened. Night before last, I had a bunch of hang-up calls in the middle of the night. Then yesterday morning, someone tacked a bunch of flowers to my door."

I felt a cold front move through my stomach. "What kind of flowers?" I asked, my words almost getting stuck in my throat. I could predict the answer.

"They were lily of the valley," she said, burying her face in her hands. "That's how Victor was poisoned, right?"

"*Possibly* it's how he was poisoned," Lou interjected again. His voice sounded distressed. "As we discussed before, Nita, that was a preliminary result from the toxicology lab. We won't know with absolute certainty until the police report comes back."

"You say you found those lilies on your door yesterday morning?" I asked Anita thoughtfully. "How many stems were there, may I ask?"

"Two."

Anita had gotten two flowers, just like my "gift." That was no coincidence. She'd gotten her flowers before my report about Hoffman's cause of death went on the air at six o'clock last night. That settled the question about whether my flowers had been left by someone who'd seen my story and put them there as a sick prank. They'd been put there by Hoffman's killer—just like Anita's.

"Have you told the police about any of this?" I asked her.

"Not yet." Anita pressed her lips together tensely. "Until now I've been afraid the police would think I was imagining things. I mean, a tea tippler lets my cat out, then I get some phone calls and a stupid bunch of flowers? It's *ridiculous*," she insisted.

I could tell Anita was a woman who didn't like to appear ridiculous. "You should definitely tell Detective Reed exactly what you've told me and Lou," I said firmly. "Believe me; he won't think anything you say is ridiculous. Meanwhile, maybe we can piece this together. I'd like to ask you some questions about some of the people at the clinic. People who might have had issues with Dr. Hoffman, or the clinic, or even with you, yourself."

"As long as it doesn't involve confidential patient information," Anita said, checking in with Lou again with another glance. "I have to respect patient's privacy, of course."

"Of course." I nodded. "To start with, can you tell me what Victor was like?" I said, switching to her first person reference. "Did he have problems with anyone at the clinic?"

Anita started slowly. "Victor kept his distance from people. His manner with everyone was very remote— he was like this distant but benign king."

I wasn't so sure she was right about the "benign" part. "It must be hard to work with someone who's very remote like that. How did you handle it?" I said carefully. What I meant was, did *she* and Hoffman have any problems between them?

Anita shrugged. "Victor and I had very different ways of dealing with patients, but it didn't cause much friction between us, if that's what you mean." She pressed her fingers tightly together, so tightly that the tips started turning pink from the pressure. "I handled my patients. He handled his. We had a very professional understanding."

From what I was learning about Hoffman, and had observed for myself about Anita, they both seemed like chilly, remote beings. I flashed on an image of the two of them as Zeus and his estranged wife Hera atop Mount Olympus. Two powerful beings who were connected but profoundly detached from each other. Probably because Zeus had been spending all his time schtupping the minor goddesses.

I decided to ask Anita what she knew about Billy Hoffman. I still needed to rule him out as a suspect.

"I was wondering about this one boy I met, Billy Harris. Was he your patient, or Victor's?" I said.

"Victor's," Anita said. "And it's funny you mentioned him. Just last weekend, Victor was riding him pretty hard because he was young and doing a lot of partying, not losing enough weight. I guess he told Billy to leave the program. I spoke to Victor about it later—I thought he'd been too harsh. But by then, Billy had already moved to another program."

What Anita said confirmed what Billy had told me when I'd tracked him down at the Renaissance House diet program.

"You tried to help Billy by speaking with his parents, right?" I asked her.

"That's right." Anita looked surprised that I knew so much. "You don't think he's involved with any of this, do you?"

"So, how did you feel about Victor retiring?" I asked, ignoring her question.

"Retiring? *Hmm.*" Anita's gaze dropped away. "I don't know what you mean, exactly. . . ."

"Well, Billy said you mentioned that Victor would be retiring soon. But I guess that wasn't likely, since he was moving the clinic to a new facility." I trailed off, letting the implication linger. She had, in fact, told Billy that Victor Hoffman would be retiring soon. To my left, I sensed Lou shifting forward in his seat.

"I can't really remember what I said to Billy." Anita kept her eyes glued to the desktop. "I was just trying to encourage the boy to stick it out here on the program."

"Did you want Victor to leave?" I asked softly. Anita's memory lapse notwithstanding, I knew I'd just caught her in a blatant lie. She'd told Billy that Hoffman was leaving the clinic soon, when she knew that wasn't the case. I had to consider a possible sinister motive behind the lie. Had she *known* somehow that Victor Hoffman would be leaving the clinic—in a body bag? That would mean she was behind the murder.

"Not really." She was silent a moment. "That man founded the clinic," she continued, a bit stiltedly.

I would have loved to hook Anita up to a polygraph right now. My cousin Jenna, who was studying for her PhD in forensic psychology at Jon Jay College of Criminal Justice in New York, had once told me that when people are lying, they hesitate, shrug excessively, and use distancing language, such as referring to a colleague as "that man." Anita was hitting all the notes.

After a beat, I said, "Have you officially taken over the top position now that Victor is gone?"

"Well, yes, the president of the university is going to announce it next week," Anita said, squaring her shoulders. "But it would have happened eventually, anyway."

Would it have, though? Just before Hoffman's murder, Anita had spoken to Billy about Hoffman's "retirement," when no retirement was actually in the works. The whole thing sounded suspicious to me. Maybe she had trumped up all the so-called stalking episodes to deflect suspicion away from herself. It was something I needed to keep in mind as I pushed forward.

I paused, thinking over my next step. "I'd like to take a look at Hoffman's office, if I may," I said. "And his house."

"I heard the police are done gathering their physical evidence at Hoffman's house," Lou said to my left. "What's the status over there right now, Nita?"

"Marjory took his cat over there and has been taking care of the place, I think," Anita said. She studied her fingers, which she'd untangled from their tightly clasped position. "She's the only person who's been over there. I'll tell her to give you the key."

Marjory had the key to Hoffman's house? The more I heard about the clinic manager, the closer she moved to the top of the list of murder suspects.

"What was their relationship like? Hoffman's and Marjory's, I mean."

A longer silence, this time.

"Marjory's been here a long time," Anita finally said. "She started well before I came on board." She bit the bottom of her lip, as if weighing her words carefully. "I think Marjory might be the only person in the world Victor really trusted. I heard she used to work for him at his home before she started working at the clinic. As a housekeeper, I think?"

"And what about Paige? What can you tell me about her? Is she around, by the way?" I hadn't seen the doctor's assistant during the morning weigh-in, or when I'd arrived for my appointment. Normally, Paige was always somewhere around, working smoothly and efficiently in Anita's shadow.

"I gave her the morning off. She's been working so hard to keep things running smoothly since Victor died," Anita sighed. "I don't know what I would have done without her."

"Was she close to Hoffman?"

"Very. She was one of our dieter superstars before she joined the staff."

My eyebrows shot up. "What? You mean Paige was a dieter at the clinic?" I couldn't picture Anita's svelte assistant as a Fruiter.

"Oh yes. Here, I can show you." Opening her desk drawer, Anita rummaged around for a moment. "I know it's here somewhere." Extracting a small manila envelope, she lifted a square of yellowed cellophane tape off the back to open it. "These are Paige's 'before' and 'after' photos," she said, sliding two photos out of the envelope. She handed them to me across the desk. "We used to show them around as an inspiration for new people starting the program. Nowadays she just prefers being regarded as staff, so we don't so much."

In her "after" picture, Paige was drawn and skeletal. Her cheeks were sunken, and you could see the outline of her ribs through her white T-shirt. She was dangerously thin, anorexic, even. Then I examined Paige's "before" photo.

"Wow," I couldn't help gasping. I barely recognized Paige in this shot. She had rounded chipmunk cheeks, and her belly was grossly distended. She resembled her own fat sibling. Paige had not only been overweight—she'd been morbidly obese, at least 250 pounds.

"And after losing all that weight, she stayed on to work at the clinic?" I asked.

Anita nodded. "Paige had always wanted to work in the nutrition field, so she just stayed on. She always seemed so grateful to everyone here, especially Victor, for helping her change her life."

Why would Paige lose all that weight, but then never develop a life outside the clinic? I wondered how her history with the program colored her attitude toward the clinic, and Hoffman.

"Do you mind if I keep these pictures of Paige?" I asked, sliding them into my purse. "Can you tell me whether Hoffman had any particular favorites, anyone he was interested in romantically?"

"You mean here, at the clinic?" she said, raising

her eyebrows as if the mere question were off-putting. "No. No one."

"What about Bethany Williams?"

"Bethany?" Anita frowned. "No, I can't imagine anything between those two." Her expression telegraphed disdain and dismissal all at once. If anything *had* been going on between Bethany and Hoffman, Anita had evidently been out of the loop. "I'm not aware that he had any intimate relationships. Except I heard he'd been married once. I mean, there were always women around, but that's . . . different, you know?"

Anita's description of Hoffman's affairs sounded almost exactly like what I'd been told by Paige. Paige had described Hoffman as an "ascetic" who was surrounded by women, but never involved with them.

"What about former dieters? Or former staff?"

Anita hesitated before responding.

"Well, before I came on board there was a lawsuit filed against Victor, by someone who used to work here," she said. "I think she was the physician's assistant before Paige started. Evidently she sued Victor for sexual harassment after leaving the job."

I leaned forward in my seat. "Whatever became of the lawsuit, do you know?" I said. "Was it settled?"

Lifting her shoulders, Anita made an expression that said *Who knows?*

"He wouldn't discuss it. I don't know many details, or even what came of it, because Victor would never acknowledge that it even happened."

"I can get that information," Lou interjected. He flipped open the leather portfolio on his lap, extracted a black Montblanc pen from his shirt pocket, and scrawled some notes. "Nita, would you happen to remember the woman's name?"

"Cheryl something. Cheryl . . . *Davis*, I think?" Anita knitted her brow as she dug into her brain to retrieve the name. "No, it was Cheryl Dawson. I only know the name because I ran across it in a file one time. When I asked Victor about it, he just said, 'Oh, that stupid woman,' and made this kind of dismissive gesture." To demonstrate, she flicked her hand in the air.

The name Cheryl rang a bell. The clerk at the Vixen's Den had told me that a former employee of the clinic now worked as a bartender at the Razor's Edge. He'd said her name was Cheryl. Could it have been the former clinic employee who had sued Hoffman for sexual harassment? I made a mental note to go to the Razor's Edge, to find out what had become of "that stupid woman" and her case.

One question kept niggling—if Hoffman's murder had something to do with a sex scandal, why would that person be threatening *Anita,* now? Perhaps his murder had nothing to do with his personal life, at all. Maybe it had to do with the clinic itself.

I chewed on that thought for a moment. Hoffman had been murdered before he could finalize the sale of the property. And now Anita, who planned to continue with the property's sale, had also been threatened.

"Who on your staff knows that you're planning to move to a new facility?" I asked her.

"Just about everybody," Anita said. "It's widely known."

"Has anyone objected to the move?"

"Well, some of the grounds and housekeeping staff aren't too enthusiastic about it. Part of our budget plan for funding the new facility involves outsourcing the menial jobs. So there's a chance that a few people might not transition to the new place, or may have to take a salary cut." Anita shrugged. Evidently, the loss of "menial" jobs was beneath her consideration. "A few of the workers threatened to go out on strike."

"Whatever came of that threat, do you know?"

Another shrug. "Victor put down the strike talk with an iron fist," she sniffed. "He wouldn't tolerate worker unrest. And of course, we had the upper hand—the employees are mostly illegal, you know. The whole thing was ridiculous—Victor was prepared to send the whole lot of them back to Mexico."

"I see."

What I saw wasn't pretty, though. When faced with deportment, I wondered if the "ridiculous strike talk" had morphed into something uglier—like murder.

Chapter 20

Don't Eat to Avoid Feeling

*Why do we sometimes eat to the point of feeling sick?
For many women, it's a convenient way to avoid ex-
periencing strong emotions of any kind. There's nothing like a sugar high—followed by a nap—to zonk you
into feeling "comfortably numb," as the song goes.
As scary and uncomfortable as feelings can be, it's
much better for you to work through them. If all else
fails, consider switching from overeating to a less fat-
tening addiction, like buying stuff on the Jewelry
Channel.*

*I recommend their diamond hoops, by the way.
They look totally awesome under the studio lights.*

—From *The Little Book of Fat-busters* by Mimi Morgan

Hoffman's private office was located at the top of a
round Queen Anne–style turret—a tower, really—that
sprouted from the northwest corner of the clinic. To
get there, Lou and I followed Anita up a winding
staircase that was only a few inches wider than my
hips. I wondered how the biggest Fruiters had ever
made it up these stairs. Maybe that had been part of
Hoffman's treatment, kind of like a boot camp
challenge.

"I haven't been up here since Victor was killed,"

Anita announced when we reached a small landing at the top of the staircase. In front of us was a paneled wooden door with an old-fashioned glass knob. Presumably that was Hoffman's office.

"You mean you haven't been up here at *all*?" I said. "You didn't need anything from the office? Patient records, or his personal notes?"

Anita's expression said I'd just asked a supremely dumb question. "Our patient records are kept in the records room downstairs," she said. "I never came up here much, anyway. This was Victor's exclusive domain."

She fished a key ring from the pocket of her doctor's jacket. Rotating it a couple of times until she found the right one, she inserted the key into the lock. When the tumblers failed to turn, she frowned and jiggled the key until there was an audible click. The door swung open, releasing a whiff of ammonia-smelling air from the darkness beyond.

Anita hesitated for a beat at the threshold. Then she turned and shifted her shoulders sideways, making a sweeping wave with her hand to indicate that Lou and I should move past her into Hoffman's office. "You two go ahead. I have a patient to see right now."

I wasn't sure how to react. Anita just said she hadn't been inside Hoffman's office since his murder, and now here she was, bolting like a spooked deer at the threshold.

"Really, Nita?" said Lou, who was standing just behind me. He sounded puzzled, too.

Grimacing, Anita splayed the fingers of her right hand across her forehead. "Yes," she said. "I just can't be up here right now." Her voice sounded stressed.

Did Anita really have an appointment? I wondered. Perhaps she was feeling traumatized by Hoffman's murder and the follow-on events that had made her feel like she was the killer's next target. On the other hand, I hadn't ruled her out as a suspect, yet. It was possible that she'd fabricated her story about the threatening episodes in order to throw suspicion off herself. If that were true, her real reason for not wanting to enter Hoffman's office might be a guilty conscience.

"Okay, but I think Lou should walk you downstairs," I said firmly. Accepting for the moment that Anita was telling the truth about the events that had scared her, I didn't think it was a good idea for her to go wandering around the clinic alone right then.

Anita raised a protesting hand. "I don't need . . . ," she began.

Lou reached past me and grabbed her hand. "Overruled, Nita," he declared, pressing her fingers between his two wide palms.

Then he looked at me. "Will you be okay here by yourself? I'll come right back."

"I'll be fine," I said, waving them off.

As I watched Anita and Lou disappear down the staircase, I had to squelch the little voice reminding me that the person who had slashed up my dashboard the night before might be lurking somewhere inside the clinic. If so, it might have been a supremely stupid move to send Lou off with Anita. Right then, though, I was glad not to be distracted by their presence.

I stepped into Hoffman's office, senses on high alert. Reaching for a light switch, I had to stifle a sudden fear that a fondue fork–wielding maniac would come lunging out at me.

Hoffman's office had a domed plaster ceiling and octagonal walls. A long metal desk filled the middle of the room, with two wide-bottomed upholstered guest chairs. Behind the desk was a high-backed executive's chair where the doctor must have sat. I immediately noticed that the guest seats were oriented low to the ground, while the doctor's chair was swiveled up high for maximum height. When he met with his patients, Hoffman must have preferred the high ground.

I glanced across the doctor's desk. It was wiped clean, without a computer or scrap of paper in sight. The only visible objects were a green-domed student lamp, a leather desk blotter, and an enamel cup filled with fountain pens.

I slid open the desk's center drawer. It contained a pair of scissors, some black Sharpies, and a container of paper clips, all standard office supplies. Pulling out a file drawer to the right, I found some hanging green folders. The folders were empty except for some blank sheets of paper. Again, no files, nothing written at all. It looked as if someone had come in and whisked away all traces of the doctor's life. The faint smell of ammonia in the air seemed to confirm that someone had taken pains to clean the room thoroughly.

I sat down in the high-backed chair and swiveled back and forth a few times, thinking that sometimes it's what you *don't* find that's significant. I was concentrating so intently that I didn't hear someone quietly enter the room.

"This isn't Hoffman's office."

I nearly popped a blood vessel as a deep voice intoned those words—loudly—into my ear.

It was Lou. He'd returned from downstairs much sooner than I'd expected.

I spun around with what must have been a rattled look on my face. "What do you mean, 'This isn't Hoffman's office'?"

Lou's eyes scanned the desktop. "I mean this isn't the *way* he kept his office," he said. "Hoffman's desk was always covered with about a foot of papers, research notes—you name it. He was quite the pack rat. Plus his computer's not there. This looks way too—"

"Clean? Right. I think housekeeping has been up here already."

Housekeeping was Marjory's domain, so I'd need to ask her what became of the computer and Hoffman's personal papers.

"Where's Anita now?" I asked Lou. He must have ditched her pretty quickly to get back up here so soon.

"She's in her office with a patient," Lou replied. "Paige called—she's on her way in. She promised to stick by Anita the rest of the day. Actually, I came back just now to check on *you*." Lou held my eyes. He was now sans jacket, wearing a light blue shirt with French cuffs that were fastened together with distinguished-looking gold eagle cuff links.

"I can't stop thinking about that attack on your car," he continued. "We might have a real wacko on our hands. You could be in as much danger as Anita. Maybe even more."

When I faked a nonchalant shrug, Lou made a clucking sound of disapproval. "I want you to let me know if anything else happens," he said. "Is there anything I can do to help?"

"Actually, there is something," I said. "I need to talk to Marjory. Then can you give me a quick ride to pick up a rental car? The police impounded my car after the attack last night." Although I didn't spell it out for Lou right now, my next step would be to visit Hoffman's house. I'd already left a message for Beatty at Channel Twelve to reserve a camera crew for this afternoon.

"Absolutely," Lou said. "Let me go make a quick phone call, and I'll meet you in the parking lot, say in twenty minutes?"

After Lou went off to make his call, I wandered around the main house for a while. I checked the weigh-in area in the lobby and then the kitchen, looking for Marjory. She was nowhere to be found.

As I crossed back through the main lobby heading outside, I bumped into Paige coming the other way.

"Hi Paige," I greeted her as she paused in the small entryway just inside the clinic's front door. "Did you happen to see Marjory outside?"

"Oh, good morning, Kate." Paige glanced up at me while digging something out of her quilted silk bag, which was slung over her shoulder. She was wearing a burgundy dancer's skirt over a scoop neck pink leotard that showed off her décolletage.

Looking at Paige, I could scarcely believe that she'd once been grossly overweight. However, I'd seen her "before" pictures with my own eyes.

"Marjory's probably out back," Paige said. "Try the tool shed. Do you want me to show you where it is?" She glanced down at her watch.

"No, that's okay." It was better for me to go alone to find Marjory, anyway, so that I could ask her some questions privately. But I would have to hustle in order to meet Lou on time in the parking lot.

"By the way," I said, turning, "maybe there's something you can tell me. When I checked out Hoffman's office upstairs, it seemed like someone already cleaned it up pretty thoroughly. Do you know anything about that?"

"Well." Paige leaned against the wall of the reception area. She stared up at the ceiling as if she could see through it into Hoffman's office. "Anita asked me to collect some things we needed for the clinic. I thought that cleaning everything up made sense, so I had housekeeping go through the room."

So it had been Paige who had the doctor's office cleaned, not Marjory.

"And Hoffman's computer and personal notes and papers?" I asked. "We couldn't find them. Can you tell me what became of those?"

"The police took his computer. I put everything else into boxes and gave them to Marjory to take back to Dr. Hoffman's house. I wanted to spare Anita the pain of going through all that," Paige pronounced solemnly. Her voice had a slightly martyred undertone, as if she were Joan of Arc sparing the world from a plague of bedbugs.

"Pain? I'd kind of gotten the impression that Anita and Hoffman weren't all that close. Why would it be so painful for her?"

Paige's eyes narrowed. The expression in them had changed—there was nothing tentative about her look now. "I just thought it was for the best," she announced flatly. "Look, I know Anita asked you to help her." She leaned in toward me, her voice dropping to a confidential whisper. "We all want to know what happened to Dr. Hoffman. But really, shouldn't you leave it to the police? I mean, isn't that *their* job?"

Rather than answering Paige right away, I waited quietly to see if she would add anything else.

"You're doing *so* well on the program, Kate." Paige cocked her head and regarded me with a bright expression. But her eyes had sharpened. "Why don't you just concentrate on that success? After all, you have a *long* way to go." With a slight incline of her head, Paige shot a meaningful glance down at my hips. Then, pirouetting away, she strode across the lobby toward the back of the clinic.

A long way to go? *Well.* No doubt about it, Paige had just told me to back off, and she'd thrown in a condescending fat barb for good measure. *Nothing like a former fattie to know how to dish it out* ran through my head as I spun on my heel with an annoyed energy.

Tilting my palm vertically so that it formed a right angle with my wrist, I straight-armed my way through the front door. I felt a sympathetic jolt in my stomach

that felt like a hunger pang. *Shut up, stomach,* I repri-
manded it. *That's anger you're feeling, not hunger.* I
wouldn't let it fool me anymore.

I found Marjory planting a row of white asters on
the north side of the clinic. She was kneeling on a strip
of green foam next to a bag of potting soil, hacking at
the dirt with a three-pronged garden claw.

"Yes?" Marjory squinted up at me with an expression so neutral it bordered on hostile. "What is it?"

Ever since I'd questioned Marjory about her errands
to the Vixen's Den, she'd treated me as if I were spreading an infectious disease. It was hard to remember she'd
once acted friendly and outgoing toward me.

There appeared to be no advantage in trying to make
nice, so I got straight to the point. "Lou and I are helping Anita sort some things out about Dr. Hoffman's
estate," I said. "We need to get his key from you."

"Well, that's too bad, because I don't have the key
right now." Marjory rose stiffly to her feet, still clutching the garden claw tool in her right hand. "I left it
at the locksmith's to be duplicated."

"Really, you had to leave it at the locksmith's?
Why'd you have to duplicate it?" I asked. I suspected
that Marjory had the key, but wasn't admitting to it.

Marjory returned a stare as hard as granite. "Guess
you'll have to figure that out," she snapped. Turning
the garden claw over, she banged the flat side of it
against the side of her jeans to shake loose some dirt.
Particles of orangish-red clay fell onto the top of her
canvas sneakers.

Then she stopped banging the claw abruptly. "Did
you tell Anita about what we discussed day before
yesterday? About my doing those errands for Dr.
Hoffman at the Vixen's Den?"

"No," I said truthfully. "I haven't told anyone—but
you should tell the police about it yourself, now."

"Why should I say anything?" Marjory said in a sullen tone. "It doesn't have anything to do with Dr. Hoffman's murder. It's nobody's business."

"Even so, the police generally don't like surprises," I told her. "Trust me. You'd be better off telling them up front."

Folding her arms tightly, Marjory shook her head while closing her eyes, as if she could blink me away. Her eyelids were so translucent you could see the veins underneath the skin, like blue eyeshadow.

"Speaking of errands," I said, "I heard you were seen driving Dr. Hoffman's car last Sunday. Were you doing an errand for him that day?"

Marjory's eyes popped back open. "Who told you that?" she said.

"Can't say." I wasn't about to tell Marjory that Paige had approached me with this information as Hoffman's memorial service was winding down.

"Well, whoever told you that is a liar." Marjory's voice rose on the word "liar."

"If you say so." I shrugged. "Look, can you get that key?" I pressed. "Lou and I really need to do this for Anita. If you need me to, I can get her to come out here and speak with you about it—"

Marjory blew out a defeated-sounding sigh. "That won't be necessary," she said. "I'll get the key and leave it under the mat for you at Dr. Hoffman's house. Give me a couple of hours."

"Okay, thanks. By the way," I added, "when I get inside Dr. Hoffman's house, where can I locate all his boxes? The ones with his personal papers?"

"What personal papers?" Marjory looked confused.

"Paige said she gave you some boxes with his papers. The papers she cleared out from his office here at the clinic?"

"Oh, right."

The discombobulated look that had flitted across

Marjory's face was replaced by a thoughtful expression. I had no sense of what was behind the look, other than perhaps trying to recall where she'd put the boxes that had the papers in them.

"I'll find them," she said. "And . . . and I'll leave them in the mudroom. It's just to the left as you go in the front door."

With that, Marjory dropped abruptly to her knees. Swinging back the hand that was grasping the garden claw, she dug with renewed energy into the clay. It was a not-too-subtle signal that the conversation was over.

"One last thing, Marjory," I continued, ignoring the fact that she was ignoring me. I wasn't going to leave without trying to clarify something that Anita had told me earlier this morning. "Anita told me you spoke to Hoffman about his plan to move the clinic across town. According to Anita, some of the staff objected to the move."

Marjory stared down into the soil for a long moment, as if searching for worms. "They were afraid of losing their jobs—can you blame them?" she finally muttered.

"No, I wouldn't blame them for that," I said. "What did Hoffman say when you told him that people were worried about their jobs?"

Marjory pressed back on her ankles and looked up at me. Her eyes had taken on a desolate and careworn quality. "He said that anyone who wasn't happy could vote with their feet," she said. "I tried to protect my people, but Dr. Hoffman said it was all about survival of the fittest."

Marjory had tried to intervene on behalf of the clinic's workers and had been rebuffed. At the Hoffman Clinic, the workers were obviously regarded as expendable.

"Thanks, Marjory," I said.

Turning around, I circled back around the house toward the parking lot. Behind me, my ears picked up a thudding sound. Glancing back over my shoulder, I saw that Marjory had resumed hacking at the dirt with the claw tool.

She was gouging into the red clay earth with rhythmic, vicious strokes.

Chapter 21

Color Me Thin

*Certain colors—blue, green, and violet—are known to
suppress the appetite. Other colors—yellow, red, and
orange—stimulate the appetite. I put a blue light inside my refrigerator, which makes everything look
moldy and disgusting (even the leftover cheesecake
from Pier 4).*

—From *The Little Book of Fat-busters* by Mimi Morgan

Lou was standing next to his Lincoln with a cell phone
pressed to his ear when I located him in the parking
lot. I could tell from the license plates that the car
was a rental. Thank God, today there was no sign of
the professional driver I'd seen picking up him and
Anita from the memorial service last night. I hated
the idea of being chauffeured about like Miss Daisy.

"Okay, got it, great work," he said to the person
on the other end. "Guess what." He directed those
last two words to me, pocketing the phone while simultaneously opening the car door with his other
hand. "My staff has turned up some information about
the lawsuit Nita mentioned, the one that was filed
against Hoffman. The lawsuit was filed ten years ago
by a woman named Cheryl Dawson."

"Did they find out whatever became of Cheryl and

the case?" I asked as I sank into the deep folds of the Lincoln's passenger seat, inhaling a whiff of leathery fragrance.

"It was settled out of court, so I have to assume she collected some fairly big money," Lou said before shutting the door. He skirted around back of the car and got in behind the wheel. "This Cheryl woman was probably paid off by Hoffman or the university, or maybe even both."

Loose granite crunched under the tires as we pulled out of the parking lot and nosed onto the street.

"Did your staff find out whether Cheryl is still in town?" I asked as we made our way through a maze of residential streets, following directions I'd jotted down to the car rental agency.

Lou shook his head. "They didn't get that far, unfortunately," he said.

I thought back to my conversation about a woman named Cheryl earlier this week with the clerk at the Vixen's Den. I told Lou about the conversation.

"If it's the same Cheryl and now she's into S and M, she might have gone from sexual harassee to harasser," Lou suggested. "Maybe she went out and got herself a crop and some stilettos." He lifted his right hand from the steering wheel and mimed cracking a whip. "It's payback time, baby!" he chortled, rocking forward and back in his seat as if riding a horse.

"Or, perhaps she's on the flip side of the S and M equation, the masochistic side," I countered in a more serious tone. "If Cheryl was sexually abused by Hoffman, as the lawsuit suggests, she might still be role-playing the victim. Or as a bartender, she might simply be watching other people at the club play the victim's role."

I'd learned during a psychology course at Wellesley that it was common for victims of abuse to reenact their traumatic experience in other ways. Perhaps

Cheryl's job at the club served that purpose for her. In any case, I needed to find out whether the Cheryl who worked at the Razor's Edge was the same woman who had sued Hoffman for harassment. Since she'd won a case against Hoffman out of court, and was now working at a job deep in the underbelly of the alternative lifestyle world, Cheryl was a loose end that needed to be tied up. So to speak.

"Where you off to now?" Lou said as we pulled into the parking lot of the rental car agency, which was located in one of the strip malls that ringed the outer edge of Durham's commercial center.

"Hoffman's house. A crew is meeting me there," I said.

"I could have taken you—," Lou began.

I waved him off. "Thanks, but I need to work on the story right now, and I work better alone," I said. Much as I appreciated Lou's ride and facilitating my access with Anita, I didn't want him hovering over me.

Lou's eyes hardened. But then, just as quickly, the look vanished. Before I even had a chance to get out of the car, he'd popped around to open the door for me. Without saying another word, he gave a distracted-looking wave, got back behind the wheel, and pulled away.

Inside the rental office, a sullen clerk processed my paperwork. He slid a set of keys across the counter while pointing wordlessly to a white SUV that was parked outside the front window.

I went to the car and climbed up into the driver's seat. It felt like being perched on top of a crow's nest compared to my low slung, four-on-the-floor sports car. It felt utterly liberating to have wheels again. I'm not one of those people who could ever go without a car or use public transportation. I have a deep-rooted personal need to be independently mobile at all times.

Using my cell, I called Channel Twelve to arrange for a camera crew to meet me at Hoffman's house.

"Hey, Gallagher. What was that excitement all about last night?" Beatty demanded when he came on the line. "Heard from the night staff that your car got banged up, and the police came?"

"*Slashed* up, not banged up. And whoever did it left something behind." Quickly, I briefed Beatty on how my car's dashboard had been ripped apart while parked on the street in front of the studio the night before, and described the bouquet of lily of the valley that had been dropped onto the front seat. "The police impounded my car to collect evidence. I'm in a rental right now."

"Lily of the valley?" Beatty exclaimed. "That's what you reported was used to poison Hoffman, right? Do they think the flowers are connected to the murder? Like some kind of retaliation against you?"

"A warning is what Detective Reed suggested," I said. "And that's certainly what it felt like."

"Jesus." Beatty paused in his calculating mode. "Was there a crew around last night? You get anything we can use?"

"Of course. I took some footage myself before the police arrived. I got everything we need."

"Good girl." Beatty's voice registered approval.

I didn't mind the way he'd jumped immediately from perfunctory sympathy to considering how to use the attack on my car for the purpose of another news story. That's simply the nature of the news director beast.

"I can go over the tape with Julia later."

"Fantabulous. Well, I mean I'm sorry to hear about your car, of course. But that was a helluva job you did on that live shot last night from the memorial service."

I could hear Beatty scrabbling through some papers on his desk. "Our overnight numbers were off the charts. *Off* the charts," he said. "Everyone and their grandma in the tri-county area must have tuned to hear your follow-up last night on the eleven o'clock—we even beat the crap out of the *I Love Lucy* rerun on Channel Eighteen. That's a first for us."

"Glad to help out," I said, smiling. I asked Beatty to have the crew meet me at Hoffman's house, and then relayed the address. "I'm heading over there right now. We'll find out if there's really a sex dungeon down in his basement, like your engineer said."

"You got access to Hoffman's house?" Beatty let fly with an impressed-sounding whistle. "Gallagher, you *are* good. I don't think Silver can keep up with you—I should bring you on full-time for us."

"You'll have to make me an offer I can't refuse," I returned lightly. "By the way, what's the story with Silver today?" I hadn't seen my show horse colleague since he'd come down with chicken pox the day before.

"He's still completely covered. The man looks like a spotted skunk."

The edge of my mouth curled against the phone. "I didn't know skunks could have spots," I said.

"Well, he's putting a pox on his job right now, that's for sure."

I pulled in behind an old blue Nova that was parked catawampus across the opening to Hoffman's driveway, blocking it. The car probably belonged to Marjory, who was supposed to have left the house key for me under the doctor's mat. Perhaps she was still inside the house assembling the boxes of Hoffman's personal papers that I'd asked her to locate.

Someone had thrown a couple of white tarps over the doctor's mint green convertible, which was parked further down the driveway where it curved in front of the house. The guard and the investigators appeared long gone.

As I stepped inside the covered landing that sheltered Hoffman's front door, a brief look around turned up no sign of the mat where Marjory was supposed to have left the house key. However, the imposing wooden front door was cracked open slightly. Two pushes, one tentative and the next firm, caused it to swing wide open.

"Marjory?" Thrusting head and neck forward followed by body, I inched forward turtle-fashion, clutching my car keys in my hand.

To the left of the entry hall, a few cardboard boxes sat stacked next to a collection of dusty shoes, just inside the mudroom. There was no sign of Marjory. A gamy odor of cat suggested the presence of a litter box that needed changing.

"Marjory? It's Kate Gallagher," I repeated in a tinny-sounding voice. To my right, a staircase with a wooden balustrade angled its way up and down through the core of the house.

I heard a noise behind me. Spinning around, I saw Reggie arriving at the front door. He stepped across the threshold, an ENG camera already hoisted on one shoulder. "Hey, Kate," he greeted me. "What are we getting here?" He glanced around the entryway.

"The basement," I said, still listening for Marjory. "Let's head downstairs and get some interiors. Then you can take a few establishing shots of the outside."

"Already got those." Reggie clicked on his camera light and followed me down the staircase, clockwise.

Beneath the ground floor, the staircase terminated in a pit-type area. The pit contained only a couple of bare gray mattresses, one piled on top of the other.

While Reggie took some shots of the pit, I moved down a short corridor, stopping in front of a door that was fastened by a wrought-iron thumb latch. I fumbled for a moment with the unfamiliar latch. From the other side, I heard a faint noise. It sounded like a kitten in distress. I wondered if it might be Elfie, Hoffman's cat.

Pressing down hard on the latch with both thumbs, I felt the bar pop up with a metallic snap, and then pushed in the door.

My first impression of Hoffman's inner sanctum was blurred, quick—a flash of blue and a jumble of exposed brick walls. A white glare glanced up off the tiled floor. The light, I grasped slowly, was coming from a lamp lying on the tile, next to a small table. The lampshade had been knocked askew and lay a short distance away from its broken base, tethered to the wall by a dark cord. Somehow unbroken in the fall, the naked lightbulb remained attached to the top of the base, still glowing.

Then, time came to a full stop. I barely registered the high plantation bed that dominated the middle of the room, or the collection of riding crops that were racked on the wall like a set of pool cues. For that matter, I almost missed the empty leather bag that was hanging from the ceiling by a metal chain. The leather bag, the size and shape of a person, was suspended next to the bed like a dark, brooding chrysalis.

I barely registered all of these things, because something else had grabbed my full attention and caused my throat to constrict. Someone was sprawled across the floor, next to the broken lamp.

It was Marjory.

Marjory's neck was skewed at a ghastly angle from her head. Bright red blood had pooled just beyond her right cheek, which was squished against the floor facing me. Her translucent eyelids with the blue veins were shut. On the floor next to Marjory lay the garden claw I'd seen her with earlier today. Something fuzzy and darkly matted had tangled itself in the tips of the claw. I leaned in for a closer look, and then reeled back as a painful sensation in my throat moved down into my shoulders and down my arms. The clump was Marjory's frizzy brown hair, matted with blood and bits of pale flesh.

Someone had bashed in the back of her head with the garden claw. Her hair in back was dark and thick with blood, and still bleeding. The lower half of Marjory's body was covered with a dark blue sheet, which had evidently been yanked off the bed. After smashing her from behind, someone had carefully wrapped her up, as if tucking her in for the night.

My feet felt as if they'd turned into anchor weights. I couldn't seem to budge them from the floor.

Marjory's chest heaved and fell with a gaspy, rattling sound. I'd heard that ominous rattling noise once before in my life, when I was sent with a news crew to cover a late-night highway accident. We'd arrived before the ambulance and found the man inside the mangled driver's seat spiraling down—"crashing," as EMTs call it. The man had made that same wheezing sound.

She was pulling in and releasing her final, dying breath.

Chapter 22

Overcoming Setbacks

Everyone experiences setbacks in their weight loss journey, just like every reporter occasionally misses a story. (I once lost an anchor spot in Austin to the weathergirl, may she rot in hell.)

It's how you respond to setbacks—on the scale or in life—that makes the difference toward a successful outcome. If you have a setback, use it as a learning opportunity and stay focused on your long-term goal. Setbacks are only temporary. (For example, I went on to anchor in Boston, while Miss Weathergirl is still stuck in Austin doing cattle feed reports, haha).

—From *The Little Book of Fat-busters* by Mimi Morgan

"Oh God, no. God, no."

Dropping my keys on the floor and yelling for Reggie, I knelt over Marjory's crumpled form. Meanwhile, I kept darting terrified looks around the room to see if the attacker was still lurking. A sliding glass door along the far edge of the wall was partially pushed back. I could feel a cold draft blowing through it. That was probably the assailant's escape route.

The only sound coming from the clinic manager now was a soft gurgling noise, like a final twister of water disappearing down a drain. A last, desperate clinging to life.

"Marjory, please don't die. Don't be dying," I begged her.

"Holy shit," Reggie said as he entered the room behind me. "Who—?"

"It's Marjory Cash. The manager of the Hoffman Clinic. Call nine-one-one, and then call Beatty."

"On it," he said, setting his camera on the floor.

Freeing a corner of the bedspread that had been wrapped around her, I pressed it against the back of Marjory's head, trying to stop the bleeding. The fabric quickly turned dark.

With a final shudder, Marjory's chest stopped heaving. I pressed my palms against her chest, preparing to try CPR. I had to force myself to take it easy. Adrenaline had sent a surge of Superwoman strength into my hands. In my attempt to save Marjory, I was afraid I might actually break her ribs. After a few agonized minutes of pumping, however, the futility of the CPR became clear. Marjory was dead.

"Ambulance is on the way," Reggie said, reappearing behind me. "Should I . . . ?" His unfinished question hung in the air.

The unspoken question was whether Reggie should shoot some footage of Marjory, lying in the blood.

All I could think about was the moment when Princess Diana lay dying in that tunnel in France, and how the vulture paparazzi had taken those horrible pictures of her last moments.

I shook my head. "No way," I said. No way was I going to become a vulture.

"Good call. I'll wait for the ambulance," he said, heading back upstairs.

I dropped to the floor and sat, cross-legged, staring at Marjory's body. Then, a pulse of emotion—anger,

mostly—lifted me to my feet. Scooping up my car keys
from the floor, I looped them around my fingers like
a pair of brass knuckles.

I ran through the open door and up a set of cement
stairs, emerging into Hoffman's backyard. I was hunting for a crazy killer, and I must have been more than
a little crazed myself, right at that moment. I wasn't
thinking about the danger, or the police investigation
to come. I was thinking only about getting my hands
on whoever had done this to Marjory.

Stupid? You bet. But right at that second, I had the
strength of an Amazon. I felt I could have ripped the
assailant's face off.

But luckily for me and my surge of fool's courage,
whoever had killed Marjory was gone.

Fifteen minutes later, Hoffman's basement was
crawling with law enforcement. When word leaked out
over the police scanner that a woman had been attacked at the notorious Hoffman address, every emergency responder within radio reception had apparently
managed to find an excuse to turn up, including a
handful of firefighters who were tromping around in
heavy rubber boots. Within minutes of the first EMT's
arrival, Marjory's body had been whisked past me on
a stretcher. Even though she was clearly dead, I knew
that the final pronouncement would have to be made
by doctors at the emergency room.

Reggie was nowhere in sight. Once the ambulance
arrived, he'd returned to the news van to relay the
events to the studio.

I was leaning against the wall just outside the basement door, fielding questions from a chubby-cheeked
cop who'd been the first officer to arrive on the scene.
He had the thickest Bubba accent I'd ever heard.

"So you say you just found the woman here on the
floor. Found her—dead—an hour after you asked her

to leave a key here for you?" His tone implied disbelief.

Bubba Cop and I had gotten off to a bad start right off the bat, probably because I had to keep pausing before answering in order to decipher some of his Southern-laced words, such as "here," which he pronounced "*hee*-yah." From his tone, it was obvious he thought I'd killed Marjory, and should be carted off to jail immediately.

"When I found her she wasn't dead yet, but close," I replied. "I tried to do CPR while the cameraman called nine-one-one. And like I said, you can get more background from Detective Jonathan Reed."

"Well, until Detective Reed gets here"—Reed was pronounced *Ree*-yahd—"why don't you just come on down to the station with me?" Bubba made a move as if to grab my arm.

"That won't be necessary, Sergeant," a cool voice interjected.

I looked up to see Reed standing just beyond my interrogator's left shoulder.

"I'll take over the questioning from here," Reed said.

Bubba looked disappointed.

"Whatever you say, *Loo*-tenant." He gave me a last, scornful look before turning away.

Without saying another word, Reed put a guiding hand on my shoulder and hustled me upstairs, almost roughly. We stopped in an alcove at the top of the stairs next to the entry hall. Reed motioned me to the only seat, a wooden chair that squeaked a loud protest as I sat down.

"What the bloody hell, Kate?" His words were formatted as a question, but they came out more like an accusation. Then he took a breath and appeared to change gears. "Tell me what happened. From the beginning."

Carefully and slowly, I gave Reed a more detailed

version of what I'd told Bubba, describing how Reggie
and I had arrived within minutes of each other at
Hoffman's house, found it open, and then discovered
Marjory in the basement, dying.

"And why were you here in the first place?"

"I'm working on the story."

As if that explained everything. This would be the
logical time to tell Reed that I was also helping Lou
with his private investigation into the murder, it occurred to me. However, a certain fear—of Reed's reaction, perhaps—made me hold back.

"You've gone entirely too far this time, Kate. I'll
have to get a full statement. You'll need to come down
to the station with me now."

"Are you holding my client for probable cause, Detective?" A familiar voice broke through.

I looked up just in time to see Lou come sailing
through the front door. He stepped deftly around the
detective and dropped anchor by my side.

"Because if you're not arresting Miss Gallagher and
her crew, they'll have nothing to say right now." Lou
fished a business card from his shirt pocket and
handed it to Reed. "You can contact me at this number, and we can arrange an interview with both parties
at a later time."

"Your *client*?" Reed glanced down at the card in
his hand, and then from Lou to me. "Are you lawyering up?" He glared at me.

"Lawyering up" is what cops call it when a witness
or suspect hires a lawyer and refuses to answer questions. Lawyering up is about the worst thing you can
do, from a cop's point of view.

"Well, actually . . ."

I was too deeply shaken to formulate a coherent
reply. Marjory's murder, followed by Bubba Cop's
grilling and then Reed's, and now Lou's sudden arrival
had rendered me almost senseless. All I could feel was

Reed's white-hot glare, which made me feel like a Judas goat that had been caught herding some sheep to their doom.

"I represent the management of WDUR-TV, and by extension its employees, including contractors such as Miss Gallagher," Lou interjected smoothly. "She needs to consult with me before any police interview. It's standard protocol."

Reed's eyes took on a dangerous glint. He scanned the lawyer up and down slowly, pausing at one point to zero in on something. But he said nothing as Lou ushered me out the front door and down the driveway.

Stuck in a dreamlike state, I allowed myself to be led away from the house and its basement of horrors. I felt like a pedestrian who had just narrowly avoided being hit by a semitruck, all shocky and weak-ankled.

In the distance I heard a voice calling my name. It was Reggie. He was taking a wide shot of all the commotion going on outside Hoffman's house, including the gaggle of looky-loo neighbors standing by the curb.

"Wait here a second," I said, pushing Lou slightly away from me. I paused to run my fingers through my hair, trying to shake off the sluggishness that had overtaken me. I stepped jerkily down the street toward Reggie.

"What's the story, Reggie?"

"I uplinked the stuff we got earlier back to the control room through the satellite bird," Reggie whispered, although we were so far back from the house there was little danger of being overheard. "I think the cops will want to talk to me next."

"You're free to go for now, Reggie," I heard Lou announce behind me. "We'll set up an interview with them at a later point."

"Hey, great—thanks, man," Reggie said, giving him a thumbs-up. "Nice to have a big-gun lawyer show up right when you need 'em. Ready, Kate?" he said, looking at me.

"I need to steal Kate for a few minutes," Lou said smoothly. "But I don't think she's up to driving. Can you pick her up at the Waffle House around the corner in about twenty minutes?"

Reggie gave me a questioning look. "Kate?" he said.

I tried to open my mouth to speak, but nothing came out. It was as if there were a glitch in the satellite feed from my brain to my voice box.

"It's okay. I'll see you there," I finally said.

With Lou as my wingman, I turned and walked away from the news van.

"You're not to say anything to anyone right now, especially to the police—understand?"

Lou and I were regrouped at a Waffle House just off the interstate, beyond police officialdom's line of sight. A greasy layer of hash-brown smell surrounded us.

"I'll sort everything out with that Detective Reed later," Lou said. "You can make a formal statement when you've had a chance to recover. Legally, they can't force you to say a word. And don't worry about them charging you with anything—they're just used to bullying to get what they need. You want some coffee?"

A waitress approached our small booth. I could feel her gaze settle on me. I must've looked like I'd been pulled from a train wreck.

"No coffee, thanks." I shook my head. "Marjory was feeding Hoffman's cat," I added in a hollow voice. "Someone else will need to go get it out of there."

"I'll follow up on the cat, don't worry."

Lou's reassurance sounded like it was coming from a distant solar system. Everything felt muffled. Even the smell of hash browns barely created a blip on my radar.

Through the fog, however, something about Lou's hand resting on the table caught my eye. His left palm was wrapped in gauze. The dressing hadn't been there when he'd dropped me off at the rental car agency a couple of hours earlier. He'd also changed his shirt since the last time I'd seen him.

"What did you do to your hand?" I asked him tonelessly.

"Oh, I cut it slicing a bagel." Lou lifted the bandaged hand off the table. "That's the number one cause of emergency room visits, did you know? People cutting their hand instead of their bagel."

Lou's glib tone fell on my ears like a sour note. He'd cut his hand slicing a bagel inside his hotel room? That didn't make much sense. I stared blankly at the bandage, where some red was seeping through where it covered his palm. It reminded me of the blood I'd just seen pooling by the side of Marjory's face.

"But you didn't go to the emergency room, did you? Where *did* you go after dropping me off?" A much bleaker question suddenly fought its way to the surface of my brain. The way Lou had arrived like the cavalry and whisked me out from under Reed's questioning, it was as if he'd already known that Marjory was dead. How could he have known that? Unless . . .

"How did you find out something was going on at Hoffman's house?" I said. "That Marjory was dead?"

Lou must have realized where my thoughts were going, because he pulled in a sharp breath.

"I just went back to my hotel room to grab some papers, and then stupidly tried to use my hunting knife to slice this bagel I had there."

A *hunting knife*?

"Then . . . I guess I just wanted to see for myself

what was going on at Hoffman's house, even though you told me not to come." Lou's gold-flecked eyes held on to mine for a long moment, his hands steepled in front of him on the table. Despite the gauze wrapping, his hands looked large and powerful. "And to answer your other question, I *didn't* know what was happening when I came through the door. I simply heard you getting grilled by Reed and saw that you were in trouble. That's why people hire me—to think fast on my feet. Kate . . ."—Lou seemed to be choosing his words carefully—"you're not suspecting *me* of having anything to do with that attack on Marjory, are you?"

"No, I just—"

"Kate, I know you've been through a lot just now. But I'm on your team, remember?" Lou sounded amazingly self-controlled for someone who had just been indirectly accused of bashing a woman's head in.

"I know."

But what *did* I know, exactly? Lou had been sucking me into the murder investigation since the moment he'd dropped from the skies in his helicopter. Supposedly, his reason for pushing a private investigation was his desire to protect Anita. Who, I reminded myself, was also a potential suspect in the murder—check that—two murders, now. I'd never found out what the real connection was between Anita and Lou. The sharp surge of suspicion that had grabbed hold of me refused to let go. Up until now, I'd regarded Lou as charming, dynamic, and bigger than life—was he also a con man? Had he conned *me*?

I couldn't sit still another second. I felt jittery and anxious, like I had pepper running through my veins. I had to get out of that restaurant, to go off somewhere alone and collect my thoughts.

Ejecting myself from the booth, I balanced on still-wobbly ankles.

"They need me back at Channel Twelve right now," I said.

But Lou was too smart for that.

"Kate, let's talk," he insisted. The way he kept prefacing his sentences with my name drummed against my ears, soft and persistent.

But my feet were already moving, carrying me across the checkerboard floor and out the door, toward the parking lot, where Reggie was waiting in the news van.

Away from Lou.

I avoided returning to the Hoffman Clinic for the rest of the day. I didn't want to tell anyone there about Marjory's death—they'd find out soon enough. Plus, after discovering two murders in a row this week, I was beginning to feel a bit like the Flying Dutchman. Everywhere I went, death followed. Therefore, it seemed like a good idea to avoid civilian shores for a while.

However, journalists aren't exactly civilians in my book. So, after driving away from my tense conversation with Lou, I headed for Channel Twelve. I was determined to throw myself into the task of producing this new murder story for tonight's broadcast. At this point I welcomed any activity that would help keep at bay the sense that the world was crashing down around my head.

Beatty fell upon me the instant I set foot in the newsroom.

"Details. I want all the details." He loomed over me as he spoke. "Plus I've got you slotted for the lead, of course. Why do you smell like hash browns?" he added with a sniff.

"Let me just get the script done. Then we'll talk," I pleaded, backing away. I had just over two hours to piece together the story for the six o'clock broadcast.

But deadline pressure wasn't the real reason for my retreat. The truth was, I was only now beginning to recover a semblance of poise. Beatty's frenetic dogging was the last thing I needed.

Holing up in a production booth, I downloaded the pictures that Reggie had taken. I'd only use the exteriors of the house. Nothing at all from the inside.

Meanwhile, I confronted a lineup of monstrous thoughts. For example, would Reed actually go so far as to try to charge me in Marjory's murder? It seemed a far-fetched notion, but there'd been a dark look on his face when I'd escaped his questioning by hiding under Lou's lawyerly wing. I'd been wrong not to tell Reed right away that I was helping Lou with his private investigation into Hoffman's murder. I knew I'd have to pay for that omission in a personal way. Last night, when Reed had sat guard outside my room following our hug, I'd felt the delicate beginnings of something developing between the two of us.

"You can scratch that little fantasy off your list right now, Kate," I muttered aloud, flinching at the memory of Reed's angry look when I'd sashayed out the door with Lou. If there'd been anything there between us, it was gone now.

And what about Lou? I kept chewing over the image of that bandage on his hand, and his lame explanation of how he'd cut himself right while Marjory was being killed. That bagel-slicing story sounded like total bullshit. What the hell was he doing with a hunting knife in his room, anyway? I'm sure he came up with much better stories than that when he defended people in court.

All of these thoughts brought me to the most disturbing possibility of all—that I'd misjudged Lou entirely. That he might be a murderer.

Hold on a second. Chasing away the monsters for

the moment, I forced myself to slow down and think things through rationally.

Yes, I'd been wrong, dead wrong, for not having told Reed about Lou's sidebar investigation. The fact that I hadn't been straightforward from the start might even have been indirectly responsible for this second murder. However, it seemed unlikely that the police would actually charge me with anything. It was unlikely even though—and here a snake raised its head above the grass—I was the person who had discovered both victims' bodies.

But the prospect of arrest wasn't my worst fear right now. My worst fear was a question, actually. What if Lou really was involved in Hoffman's—and now Marjory's—murder? That would make me even more at fault for not being forthcoming with Reed.

But Lou a killer? I just couldn't picture it. Should I tell Reed about the cut on his hand, though? And about my sudden suspicions about him? As I mulled that one over, I recalled something. Just before Lou led me away from Hoffman's house, Reed had eyed the lawyer with a full body scan. The detective had paused, briefly, midway through. At the time, I'd barely registered the eye motion.

Now I realized—Reed had spotted the bandage on Lou's hand, too.

Wrestling aside this uncomfortable line of brain activity for the moment, I concentrated on finishing the immediate work at hand. *Simple steps, Kate, one foot in front of the other. Write the story, voice the audio—who, what, when, and where.*

However, right now the "who" question was looming larger than ever over my head. *Who* had killed Hoffman, and now Marjory?

And who was next in the killer's sights?

Chapter 23

Bravo to Bacchus!

A national survey once showed that moderate drinkers—especially red wine drinkers—are more likely to stay slim than nondrinkers. I would like to raise my glass to all those who participated in that survey.

—From *The Little Book of Fat-busters* by Mimi Morgan

Hours later, I was still feeling edgy and manic. The dry turkey half sandwich I'd grabbed from the studio's vending machine had long since evaporated from my fuel reserves. However, like the ballerina who couldn't untie her red dancing shoes, I couldn't seem to stop moving.

I fidgeted around the studio, trying to decide what to do next. First I watched my story about Marjory's murder run at six, and then put the finishing touches on an updated version for the late news. By the time the second story hit the air, I'd settled on my next move—to locate the Razor's Edge. I wanted to talk to Cheryl Dawson. According to my watch it was eleven-twelve p.m. Late enough on a Tuesday night for the S and M crowd to have crawled out to play.

But first I had to reclaim my wheels. I bummed a ride from the night crew to pick up the SUV, which was still parked in front of Hoffman's house. When we arrived, to my dismay the house was lit up like an airport, which meant the police were probably still collecting evidence. Holding my keys in my hand, I hurried to the car, got in, and quickly started the engine. I didn't want to linger for fear of getting embroiled in another encounter with some cop, or— worse—Reed.

Clutching a note with the Razor's Edge address scribbled on it, I cruised Durham's commercial downtown district. As I drove, one of those Southern cloudbursts opened up overhead, drenching the dark streets within a matter of minutes. For once, I was glad to be riding high in an SUV.

On the second go-round I spotted a flat bronze sculpture of a razor that hung over a recessed door on the bottom floor of an old brick tobacco warehouse, which had been converted into upscale-looking shops and offices. From its exterior, the S and M club might have been a trendy hair salon.

After parking in the lot, I paid my half-price ladies admission to a heavily tattooed woman perched on a stool inside the club's entry room. Tattoo Woman thrust a sheet in my hand as she returned my change, and then nodded me through a partition of crimson drapes behind her. I glanced down at the paper.

House Rules

No bodily fluids
No drugs
No alcohol
Watch or play—your choice
All Playroom activity is strictly voluntary

Brushing forward through the curtains, I immediately inhaled a lung-smothering dose of cigarette smoke. A long tiled bar ran along the wall to my left, lined by people dressed up in costume for an X-rated Halloween party. Only this was June.

A guy in a spiked dog collar lounged against the nearest corner of the bar, chatting up a Vampira look-alike. Slowly, I registered that there was nothing between the man's collar and his motorcycle boots. He was butt naked.

To avoid gaping at the guy, I swiveled my head to take in the rest of the crowd. Small groups of people were gathered around a red velvet couch, peering through a window that led to what must have been the "playroom." Through the window I could see a guy in a black rubber suit, holding a whip. He was flagellating a woman handcuffed to a stripper's pole. Their bored expressions made me suspect that they were hired help, putting on a show for the paying customers.

On the main floor, the men vastly outnumbered the women, who were mostly made up like Daughters of the Night. I had the sense that almost all of the women were paid to be there. Everyone—men and women alike—had metal attached to exposed body parts. Ouch.

I approached the bar, knowing I was ridiculously out of place in my prim skirt and blouse. I willed myself to become invisible to the many pairs of male eyes that were suddenly tracking me on radar. In my peripheral vision, I sensed a movement toward me from the shadows, like spiders advancing. I would need to make this quick, and then vamoose.

Easing onto a stool, I felt a sudden inspiration to gird my loins with something spirited in red, as prescribed by the tip about Bacchus. "Do you have Merlot?" I asked the woman bartender, who wore a spandex bikini top over a black leather mini. Compared to the other women in the place, her dress was relatively modest. I hoped she was Cheryl Dawson.

"Uh, no," she said, nodding at the sheet of rules I

held in my right hand, which clearly stated no alcohol. "Just fruit juice and sparkling water. Sorry."

Just as well. "Oh, right," I said. "Water, then."

"Coming right up." The woman reached overhead for a glass. Her sculptured cheekbones reminded me of Paige. Only older and taller than Paige.

"Oh, aren't you Cheryl Dawson?" I asked, accepting the glass. I tried to drop the question casually, as if suddenly recognizing a distant acquaintance.

"Yes?" The response was polite but guarded. Then she looked at me intently, and a range of expressions flitted across her face. She'd obviously recognized me. "You're . . ."

"Kate Gallagher," I said. Then waited, not adding anything else. I wanted to see how Cheryl responded next.

"I've seen you on the news. You did that murder story, right? The one about Victor Hoffman." She delivered the doctor's name flatly, without apparent emotion.

"Yeah." I nodded and took a tentative sip. I hoped they washed their glasses better than the floor, which had felt sticky on the way in. "And, actually, that's why I'm here. I'd like to ask you some questions, if you don't mind. To help me out with the story."

"Ask *me*?" Cheryl's eyebrows shot up. Her brows were about four shades lighter than her hair, which lent her face a whitewashed look. "Why?" She glanced swiftly left and right, as if checking to see whether anyone was listening to us. But the only people within earshot were Vampira and Butt Naked Guy, who were busy with their tongues down each other's throats.

"I heard you used to work at the Hoffman Clinic," I said, getting right to the point. "I thought you might be able to shed some light on whether someone might have held a grudge against Victor Hoffman."

Cheryl pursed her lips. She lifted a linen cloth off a hook and started wiping down the bar. "Come on, I'm not exactly an idiot." She made slow, careful swipes with the rag as she spoke. "You're asking about my lawsuit, aren't you?"

"Well, I know you filed a sexual harassment lawsuit against Hoffman."

"That was years ago. And I got *bupkes* for it. They gave me three weeks salary, that's all."

So Lou's theory that Cheryl had collected big bucks from Hoffman and the diet clinic appeared to be wrong.

"But did Hoffman really harass you?"

Cheryl shrugged. "I was young," she said. "Victor and I had a little thing going for a while. Then, when it ended, I was just looking for some payback, you know? I needed the money, plus I was pissed."

"I see," I said, trying not to sound judgmental that she'd filed a bogus lawsuit.

Following a short silence, Cheryl laughed sharply. "But hey, sounds like somebody else got some *real* payback," she said.

"But someone else at the clinic has been killed now—did you know that? Marjory Cash, the manager, is dead. I just reported that on the news tonight."

"No—what?" Cheryl's head rocked back as if I'd shoved her forehead with the heel of my hand. "Marjory is dead?"

"Murdered, yeah. You knew her?"

"Yes." The reply was barely audible. "Omigod. What happened?"

"She was attacked at Hoffman's house today." I saw no reason to mention that Reggie and I had discovered her there. "Can you think of any reason why Marjory would have been targeted? Any connection to Hoffman's murder? Maybe there was something going on at the clinic?"

"Hey, can we get a check sometime this century?" Butt Naked Guy snapped from down the bar.

"Keep it hanging just one more second, will ya?" Cheryl rolled her eyes at him, then looked back at me. "Look, I'm really busy right now, so . . ." She took a step back.

"Can I call you tomorrow? Or you can call me on my cell phone." I dug out my business card, then crossed out my Boston work number and scribbled my cell phone number on it. "One other thing," I said, sliding the card across the counter toward her, "I heard Hoffman came here recently with a girlfriend—Bethany Williams. Did you see them here?"

Cheryl took the card. "Maybe they came in on my off night. Glad I missed him," she said, shrugging. Then she leaned toward me. "Listen to me." She fixed on me with a steady gaze. "Hoffman always had backup girls in his stable—he spent a lot of time grooming the ones he was attracted to. He made them feel like they were special. With your gorgeous face and little snub nose, you're just his type. I'll bet he had already started grooming *you,* right?"

I glanced into the mirror behind the bar. My reflection showed high cheekbones that had gotten even more pronounced with my recent weight loss, large eyes—I guess the pieces fit together to form something that resembled classic beauty. I'd just never thought of myself that way.

I thought back to my first night at the Hoffman Clinic. Hoffman had held my wrist and complimented me. At the time, Evelyn had said that Hoffman liked me. *Liked me.* Had he been starting to groom me, as well?

"Right. That's what I thought." Cheryl turned away and focused all her attention on writing up a check for Butt Naked Guy.

Something touched me on my back. A light poke.

"Who's your master?" a truculent male voice demanded. Twisting around on the bar stool, I found myself staring into the face of a short little man. A red-bearded bantam cock of a man.

"Master?" I returned blankly. Then I remembered—I was in an S and M bar. "I don't have a master."

I slid off the stool. Standing, I towered over the man. His hair was tufted into a rooster's comb on top of his head. Lower down, something was protruding out in front of him. Something totally disgusting. It was his penis, sticking straight out from his leather chaps. The penis was hairy, purple, and fully erect.

I lurched back. The bar stool scraped as I knocked it sideways. A penis. *Ewww.* Was that what had poked me in the back?

"Are you a bottom?" Bantam Cock leaned in so close he would have been in my face, except for the fact that he rose up only to my neck. "I'm a top, myself." His eyes stayed glued on my breasts. In another second, I thought he was going to bury his nose between them.

I'd had enough.

"I don't play," I snapped, brushing past him.

"Then you wanna watch, honey?" Bantam Cock followed me as I swept through the curtains and past the tattooed woman.

As I reached the club's exit door, anxiety gripped me. What if he tried to follow me out to the car? Bantam Cock was short, but his shoulders were packed with muscles. What would I do?

As I grabbed for the exit handle, a man emerged from the corner, seemingly from nowhere. An Asian guy, with long black hair pulled back in a ponytail. He loomed large and triple-wide, like a sumo wrestler. Reaching forward smoothly with one arm, the man opened the door for me.

"Have a good night, Miss," he said politely.

The Asian guy must have been a bouncer, because behind me, Bantam Cock bounced right back inside the club. Taking his purple penis with him.

I mouthed a silent "thank you" to my sumo rescuer. Then I climbed back into the SUV, slammed the door, and clicked the autolock button, comforted by the thwacking sound of the bolts snapping shut. I took a series of shaky breaths.

Just thinking about how my blouse had been touched by that revolting penis made me want to rip it off and burn it somewhere. However, I had nothing else to put on, and driving back through town sans shirt didn't exactly seem like the brightest idea right then.

I picked up my cell phone, planning to call Brian, but it was dead. I'd left my car charger behind in the TR6, damn it to hell. Hopefully, I had remembered to pack the regular charger in my suitcase.

Driving back to the clinic, I kept glancing in the rearview mirror for any sign of someone following me. Behind me, all I could see were the reflections of the streetlights on the rain-washed street. For the moment, all was clear.

The clinic's lobby was deserted when I crossed it the next morning on my way to weigh-in. Through the dining room door, I could see a couple of dieters huddled over their half grapefruits. Two women were speaking in low, hushed tones. I didn't recognize them, but from their body language, they were probably discussing Marjory's murder. And possibly figuring out their exit strategy from the clinic, as well. Most of the dieters seemed to be missing in action, and there'd been way fewer cars parked in the lot than the day before. The clinic was starting to feel like a rudderless ghost ship.

After a subdued greeting from Paige, I weighed in.

Even though I was wearing relatively heavy jeans, I was down an amazing ten pounds in less than a week.

Paige noted the result in my chart with a fluid and slowed-down motion, as if she were writing underwater.

I wondered what had taken place at the clinic while I was gone. I'd avoided coming back all day yesterday, and so had no idea what type of announcement had been made about Marjory's death.

"I'm so sorry about Marjory," I said to Paige, trying to prompt a response.

"What? Yes," Paige said after a moment's pause. "It was unfortunate."

"Unfortunate" seemed like a detached word to use. I stared into Paige's eyes. They seemed slightly unfocused. "Are you okay?" I said.

"Actually, I don't think so," she responded. Her voice was barely audible. "It's all been too . . . much. I almost didn't come in to work this morning."

"Hey look, there's no one else in line for weigh-in right now," I said. "Let's go outside and sit down for a second."

I led Paige outside to the front porch, steering away from the side where I'd discovered Hoffman's body earlier that week. Maybe the porch wasn't the best place to talk, I thought belatedly.

"I was gone all day yesterday, so I don't really know what's been going on," I said as we sat down on a couple of rocking chairs.

Paige nodded wordlessly.

"How did they make the announcement about Marjory?"

"Anita told the staff yesterday afternoon," Paige said. "We still haven't heard exactly what happened to her. All I know is what I saw on your story on the late news. You seem to know a lot." Her tone sounded almost accusing. Paige kept her eyes glued to her hands, which were folded on her lap.

"That Marjory was killed, yes. I discovered her at Hoffman's house. She'd been attacked," I said simply.

"But why did you go over to his house in the first place? What are you *doing*?" Paige's voice rose. "You shouldn't be getting involved—I mean, look what happened to Marjory."

"What do you mean?" I asked her. "That something will happen to me, if I do?"

"Of course not." Paige buried her face in her hands. "It's just—I don't know what's happening anymore, or whom to trust."

"Has something happened that makes you mistrustful of someone in particular?"

"Well." Paige swallowed. She hesitated. "I shouldn't say anything." She glanced left and right, checking to see whether we could be overheard.

"No, what?" I urged. "It could be important. Please."

"Well." Paige swallowed again, harder this time. "I was organizing some paperwork in Anita's office yesterday. I ran across something that didn't make sense—it was about the clinic."

"What about the clinic?" I lowered my voice. Like Paige, I turned my head to see if anyone could hear our conversation. But there was no one else on the porch.

"I can tell you, but only if you promise not to tell Anita or Lou. I might be off base, and I don't want to lose my job."

The sound of Lou's name jangled up my spine.

"Okay, certainly."

"Well, I heard you talking with Anita and Lou about this the other day, so I know you know that Victor had been talking about selling the clinic property. Moving across town?"

In response to her question mark, I nodded in the affirmative.

"Well, just before he was killed, I think Dr. Hoffman changed his mind about the sale," Paige continued. "I found a notarized copy of a letter he wrote to Lou Bettinger. In the letter, Dr. Hoffman rejected his offer to buy the property."

"Rejected the offer?" I echoed. I paused to mull over the meaning of Paige's information.

According to Lou and Anita, Hoffman had *accepted* Lou's offer to buy the clinic—all that was lacking was Hoffman's signature on the contract of sale. Had they both been lying? If so, that might mean that they were working together, and together had a motive to kill Hoffman—Lou to get his hands on the clinic property, and Anita to become the new head of the clinic.

"Have you told the police about what you found?" I asked Paige, who responded with a vehement head-shake. "You should."

"What if this has nothing to do with what happened to Doctor Hoffman? I'll just get in trouble." She crossed her arms across her stomach. "And—and there's something else I found, but I'm afraid to talk about it here. Would you mind coming over to my house? If you think it's important, you can take it to the police for me. Honestly, I'm afraid to do it myself."

"Certainly," I said to her.

"Great," Paige said, looking visibly relieved. "I'll go home at my lunch break, if you can come by then. Can you make it right at twelve thirty? I have only a forty-five-minute break."

"Sure thing."

"There's a back alley behind my house—if you don't mind, park there when you come. And please don't tell anyone that you're coming. I don't want them to think I'm disloyal." Paige wrote down her address on a piece of paper she pulled from her purse and then returned inside the clinic.

My cell phone, which I'd recharged overnight, vibrated with a series of beeps to let me know I had messages. I'd missed five calls and had three voice mails waiting. The missed calls were all from my dad—he'd obviously given up on leaving messages.

The first message was from a police secretary. She said that my car was ready to be picked up at the impound lot, and that I should stop by and see Detective Reed at ten a.m. She added that I could bring a lawyer with me, if I wanted. Reed must be really livid with me if he was having an admin make his calls, I thought.

All of the other messages were from Lou. He said he had some information for me, and to call him back right away. Lou's tone was urgent. He wanted me to meet him at Anita's house as soon as possible, and left directions to her house on the message.

I'd go meet Lou, but not until I'd taken a look at whatever it was Paige had found. Because of what Paige had told me, my current of suspicion about Lou and Anita had just swollen into a raging torrent. I'd promised her not to mention anything to the police until I'd looked at the evidence myself. But as soon as I had something solid in my hand, I would go straight to Reed with it.

Meanwhile, I was way overdue to call my dad back. I'd been boycotting his calls because I was still angry about his sending Reed chasing after me the day I went to the Vixen's Den. My dad's last message had sounded almost apoplectic, however, so it was time to give in. My fingers felt heavy as I punched in my father's office number at the district headquarters.

My father picked up before the end of the first ring. "Kate."

It was a bad sign when Dad greeted me using that

tone. Normally his greeting when he recognized my number on caller ID was a chipper "Hiya Tiger."

"Now before you get started, Dad—"

"What is your situation down there right now? Are you safe?"

"Yes, of course. How did you hear about Hoffman's murder?"

"Well, obviously I didn't hear about it from my daughter, who doesn't value her own safety. I have my own sources. Have you at least gotten yourself some protection down there?"

I groaned and rolled my eyes. When most parents discuss "protection" with their children, they are delicately referring to the facts of life. My policeman father means a gun.

"Dad, you know I have a policy against carrying a firearm," I said, warming up my antigun rant.

"Well, evidently your policy is wrong headed, judging by what you've gotten yourself into," Dad snapped. "It would take just one phone call to arrange a permit for you. You're in NRA country down there, you know, not the Socialist Republic of Massachusetts."

"No, Dad. Forget it. But I've got my Swiss Army knife," I said, patting my jeans pocket.

My father let out a snort. "A pocketknife?" he said. "That's a Tinkertoy against a determined predator."

Ever since Mom died, Dad has been an incredible worrywart about me. Somehow those worries translated into his trying to teach me the art of self-protection. Growing up, he'd taken me down to the police firing range every Saturday. Over the years he'd patiently and painstakingly taught me how to hold, care for, and fire a variety of firearms. With practice I could outshoot the rookies, sometimes even the veterans. When I turned eighteen, however, I'd turned against the gun culture in a fit of adolescent rebellion.

"Remember your great-grandmother Katherine—"

"Yeah, Dad. I know," I sighed.

My great-grandmother Katherine was a legend back in the tiny Irish town of Lahinch, our family's ancestral home. The story was she'd single-handedly driven off some bandits intent on stealing the family's sheep back in the 1880s, by brandishing a pistol she drew from her fur muff. Her English percussion revolver had been passed down through the family line of female descendants, most recently to me. It was locked away in my safe deposit box at the Cambridge Savings Bank. Since Katherine's time, every Gallagher woman was expected to become a pistol-packing mama. It was an odd sort of family inheritance. The only thing I liked about the inheritance was her name.

I heard the sound of clicking on a keyboard. "Dad . . . ," I said. "What are you doing right now?"

"Looking up direct flights from Logan to Raleigh-Durham."

"You're not coming down here."

"Correct. I'm sending Brian down there. If you won't carry a gun, you need Brian."

"No, Dad. I don't want Brian to come down here. You can't order him down here to babysit your daughter. It's a conflict of interest."

"Maybe he wants to take a vacation down there."

"No one wants to vacation in Durham. The air smells like a pack of Virginia Slims."

Silence.

"Dad, you've got to let me handle this myself."

Another smattering of taps.

"Dad?"

"I expect you to be at the RDU airport tomorrow night at 11:03 p.m., because Brian will arrive on US

Airways flight 209. The Terminal A Extension. Have a good day, honey."

"Dad!"

"And lock your car doors when you're driving."

Click.

Chapter 24

Beware the Beverage Calorie

With the exception of red wine, you should eat your calories, not drink them. Studies show that people usually reduce their food intake to "compensate" for extra calories they consume from solid foods, but they don't compensate for the extra calories they get from liquids. You're better off eating a cheeseburger than drinking a triple mocha.

—From *The Little Book of Fat-busters* by Mimi Morgan

Before heading to the Durham police headquarters, I returned the SUV to the car rental agency. I got an awed look from the clerk when I told him I needed someone to drop me off at the police station. From his expression, you'd have thought I was on the lam from something scandalous, and had finally decided to turn myself in.

After being dropped off at the concrete-modern police headquarters, I found my way through a maze of yellow-lit hallways to the property claims desk. I handed my claim check to a middle-aged police woman, who handed me back the key to my impounded TR6. The key was attached to a metal ring with a red tag on it. It made me think of red-tagged homes following a natural disaster—I hoped my poor baby would be drivable, at least.

"Oh, and I got a message that you should stop by and see Detective Jonathan Reed," the desk officer said. "He's expecting you. The detective's bureau is down the hall to your right."

Inside the detective's room, I spotted Reed immediately.

"No lawyer today?" Reed greeted me stiffly, motioning me to a seat. His fabric-covered cubicle was the first of a honeycomb of eight that were jigsawed together in the middle of the room.

"Not today," I said, shaking my head. "And I want you to know something about what happened yesterday—I didn't ask Lou Bettinger to show up yesterday at Hoffman's house. He just turned up on his own."

"I figured that," he responded. His tone remained rigid. "So. Tell me about yesterday."

I recapped for Reed how I'd arranged for Marjory to leave the key to Hoffman's house under the mat the day before. "She was just supposed to drop off the key under the mat—I wasn't expecting her to still be there when I arrived. Plus, she was supposed to leave some boxes of Hoffman's papers for me to look at. I guess it was stuff the police didn't take."

"Wrong," Reed snapped. "They were boxes that the clinic hadn't turned over yet."

"So I guess you've got them now," I said quickly. Would Reed ever stop acting pissy with me? "And I should mention . . . the garden claw that was used to hit Marjory—I saw her with it earlier that morning, at the clinic. She was using it to turn some flower beds."

"Who else knew that Marjory was going to Hoffman's house yesterday morning, other than you?" Reed asked.

I thought back. "Only Lou Bettinger, I think. And through him, probably Anita Thornburg."

"Bettinger. Who turned up, without being summoned, right after the murder to whisk you out from under police questioning. With a bandaged hand."

"And he'd changed clothes, too," I blurted. Just as I'd surmised yesterday, Reed had noticed the bloody bandage on Lou's hand. "He'd changed shirts since I saw him before the murder. He told me he cut himself slicing a bagel with a hunting knife."

"And of course you believed him," Reed said, not bothering to hide the sarcasm.

"No, I didn't, really," I said, trying to avoid sounding defensive. "And there's something else. . . ." I desperately wanted to tell Reed about the letter that Paige was going to show me, in which Hoffman had apparently refused to sell the clinic to Lou. The letter would provide a motive for Lou, and for Anita, for that matter. Plus, Paige had hinted that she'd found something even more incriminating than the letter. But I'd promised her to wait until I saw her later today.

"I think I'll have something more for you soon," I said. "But I have to see someone first."

Reed rolled his eyes.

"I hope you're not going from here to see your lawyer," he said dryly. "I'd steer clear of Bettinger right now, until I can determine what he's really up to. And you should vacate the clinic, too. Just pick up what you need and clear out of there. Would you like a police escort?"

"No," I responded. "That won't be necessary."

"I think it *is* necessary, but I'll let you go." Reed stood up. "For now, that is. But I'll want to talk with you again later on today."

"Okay, you've got my cell number, I know."

"Make sure you answer this time. Don't make me keep chasing you." The hard look in his eyes had softened, ever so slightly.

I edged my reclaimed TR6 past the chain-link fence and away from the police impound lot. It was a relief to be back in the familiar driver's seat, which was so low compared to the SUV rental I'd been driving that it felt like my feet were practically running on the pavement, like the Flintmobile.

As I drove, my eyes kept straying to the gashes in the black leather dashboard. The slash marks served as a stark reminder of how frightened I'd been two nights ago, when I'd found my car gouged up in front of the Channel Twelve studios with the bouquet of lily of the valley on the front seat. Hopefully there'd be a body shop in town that could repair vintage sports cars.

The fuel gauge was dangerously close to "E," but I didn't have time to stop. Paige had said she had time only during her lunch break to show me the documents she'd discovered, so I needed to rush.

To get to Paige's place, I had to drive west through the posh neighborhood where Hoffman had lived before he was killed. The moment I crossed a set of train tracks into Paige's area, the houses shrank dramatically. On her side of the tracks, there were only cottages and modest bungalows. It looked as if the homes had once housed the servants who worked in the larger and much more luxurious dwellings east of the line.

I found the dirt alley behind the address Paige had given me, and parked next to an undeveloped lot that was completely overgrown with scraggly bamboo. As I opened the car door a chicken darted across the road, disappearing into the bamboo.

A tiny bell attached to Paige's rear gate jangled as

I opened it. I stepped through the gate into an orderly garden. Paige's backyard was subsected into a pattern of neat squares, each square planted and sectioned off with wood trim. Paige must have quite the green thumb, I thought as I passed between two shrubbery-filled squares. The only sign of unruliness was a line of climbing sweet peas that had broken out of its square and established a foothold on the rear wall of the cottage. The vine clung to the stucco, draping it with lush pink and purple blossoms that fluttered in the breeze. They reminded me of butterflies.

In response to my tap, Paige opened her back door. "Hi, Kate, thanks so much for coming," she said. "I just didn't know whom else I could ask for help." She glanced past me toward the alley with a watchful expression, as if checking to see whether I'd been followed.

"No problem. Glad to assist in any way I can."

I followed Paige into an old-fashioned kitchen. Drying herbs hung from ribbons attached to the ceiling, and candles were scattered about everywhere.

"Here, I already poured you some tea." Paige moved to the gas stove, where a stainless steel kettle was steaming. She lifted a mug that was sitting on the counter next to the stove. "I call it Christmas in a Cup," she said, smiling as she handed me the cup.

"Thanks," I said, taking a deep swallow of the tea. Vanilla and mocha . . . yum. It tasted so rich I couldn't believe there weren't any calories—there *had* to be milk in it. And lots of Splenda, too.

Paige caught my skeptical look. "Don't worry, it doesn't have any calories," she said, stretching the smile.

No calories? Christmas in a cup, indeed!

I took another sip. "This is like the White Mocha at Starbucks, my absolute favorite," I said, trying not to gulp it down it too quickly. Beneath the vanilla and

mocha, there was another taste I couldn't quite iden-
tify. But it was all manna to my starving self.

It was the first time I'd seen Paige in a sleeveless
top. As she poured water from the kettle into another
mug, I was struck by how tautly muscled her slim
arms were. Certainly she wasn't the delicate sylph I'd
assumed her to be when we'd first met.

"So what did you find that's been worrying you so
much?" I asked.

"Have a look—I put everything on the dining room
table," she said, pointing through the doorway to the
dining room. "I really want to hear what you have to
say about it."

I nodded and stepped through the doorway. As I
entered the next room, my nose caught a whiff of
something familiar. A treacly, floral fragrance.

In a glass bowl in the middle of the dining room
table, Paige had arranged a magnificent centerpiece of
lily of the valley.

The sight of the lilies sent a jolt down into my stomach, which panged back an urgent message. Something
was wrong—very wrong.

I started to turn around. Behind me I heard a
sloshing sound of water on metal.

I felt a sharp, scalding hot blow on the back of my
neck, and then . . . nothing.

My world had gone black.

Chapter 25

Watch Out for Eating Disorders

Many young women (especially those in broadcasting) go entirely too far when it comes to trying to lose weight. According to researchers, about 4 percent of college-age women suffer from bulimia (aka the Big Barf), and 1 percent from anorexia. Women are at special risk for developing eating disorders because they try to live up to the unrealistic beauty ideals they see in fashion magazines.

I think the Association of Women Broadcasters should start lobbying for more real-looking women on the air. Because the Cheesecake Factory has this Black-Out Cake I've been <u>dying</u> *to try . . .*

—From *The Little Book of Fat-busters* by Mimi Morgan

"So you're awake."

Paige's voice cut through several layers of brain fog.

Struggling back to consciousness, I forced open my eyes. I was lying sideways on the hardwood floor of the dining room. The back of my neck ached, and the ends of my hair were soaking in a puddle of water. There was a streak of bright red snaking through the water. That had to be blood—my blood.

I squinted and looked up. Paige was standing over

me, clutching the water kettle by its handle. She'd clumped me over the head with it, I realized slowly.

I tried to rub my neck with my left hand, but the hand didn't budge. I yanked it, producing a metallic rattle. That's when I saw that my left wrist was handcuffed to a cast-iron radiator attached to the wall. I was trapped.

Paige stood perfectly still, watching me with dead eyes. "I was hoping you'd stay unconscious until the Christmas rose kicked in," she said.

"Christmas rose? What is that? What the hell are you *doing,* Paige?" I said, my head pounding as if it were about to explode off my neck. But I already knew the answer. Paige had killed Hoffman, and probably Marjory, as well. And now she was after me.

Paige cocked her head. "As far as poisons go, Christmas rose is six out of six on the toxicity scale, but it takes about a half hour for it to work," she said. "You have to be patient." Her tone was detached, as if describing how dough rises.

"Poison?" I said, taking a second to digest the word. She must be talking about the tea. Like an evil Grinch, Paige had poisoned my Christmas in a Cup. As if in confirmation, my stomach let out a low, rumbling burble.

"Yes, Christmas rose—a sweet name for such a deadly flower, isn't it? I used so much vanilla and sugar that you didn't notice the taste."

Sugar? She'd said that tea didn't have any calories. The bitch had lied to me, though that was the least of my problems at the moment, I realized. I'd been lured by the witch into her house of goodies. And now I was handcuffed to it.

"What does Christmas rose do?" I said, feeling a dryness coming on in my mouth.

"First the insides of your mouth will start to blister.

Then, I'm sorry to say, will come the retching. It'll be a mess."

"You mean like the mess Hoffman made when you poisoned him?" I said, struggling to maintain a feisty tone. "You did that, didn't you?"

"Your death will be equally messy, but faster. Christmas rose is a much more efficient poison than lily of the valley."

I glared at her and released a string of expletives. Bracing my feet against the wall, I pulled on the cuffed hand, straining until my wrist practically dislocated. No result. Then I shifted around and rammed my shoulder—painfully—against the heavy, old-fashioned radiator, trying to loosen it from the wall. I might as well have tried to break down the wall itself. After a few more shoves I fell back, gasping.

Paige showed no alarm at my escape attempts. She set the kettle down carefully on the dining room table, then dropped into a chair.

"That radiator is solid iron," she said. "I made sure of that."

Squelching a rising sense of panic, I considered the handcuffs. I'd handled my dad's police regulation handcuffs as a kid, and these seemed much lighter. They were probably the adult store variety, maybe even from the Vixen's Den. Even so, it would take the Bionic Woman to break out of them.

My mind scrabbled around for something to try. Then I remembered that Brian had once told me that cheapie handcuffs could be opened by pushing up from the keyhole toward the chain with something slim and hard, like a metal nail file.

Or maybe your pocketknife, said a voice in my head. My Swiss Army knife. Did I still have it?

Pretending to struggle again with the cuffed hand, oriented my body so that my free hand was out of

Paige's line of sight, then brushed the outside of my jeans pocket. Thank goodness, the pocketknife was still there. But how to get it open and jigger the lock without Paige attacking again? I didn't think my head could survive another bash of the kettle drum.

Keep her talking until you figure it out, said the voice.

So . . . "Why all the tea party dramatics?" I asked her. "Why didn't you just poison me at the clinic without my knowing and let me die there?"

Paige shrugged. "You'd have gotten medical help," she said. "You're quite resourceful, in an annoying way."

"So you've poisoned me—like you did Hoffman—and attacked me from behind like Marjory. You killed them both, didn't you?"

Paige stared at me for a long moment.

"Miss Brainiac from Boston didn't figure it out in time," she finally said. "And now—look—it's too late for you. You have thirty minutes before the poison kicks in." She glanced at her watch.

Thirty minutes? Before I *died*? My brain tried to reject the notion of impending death. When that failed, panic staged a full-blown comeback. Just how fast-acting was this "Christmas rose," anyway—it wasn't like *cyanide,* was it?

"Hoffman must have done something terrible to you," I said, hoping empathy would prod something out of her. At the very least, I wanted to get her story before I died.

Paige blinked. "He did something more than terrible," she said, her lips tightening. "He threw me away."

"You and he were lovers?"

Paige glared at me. "Of *course* we were lovers," she said. "Victor and I had a deeply passionate relationship that lasted for ten years, ever since I started working at the clinic."

There was only one reason known to mankind for the poisonous ending of a "deeply passionate" relationship.

"He dumped you, didn't he?" I said.

Paige frowned. "For a pierced sow," she said, looking away.

Pierced sow. I knew who that had to mean. "Hoffman was leaving you for Bethany Williams?" I asked.

Nodding almost imperceptibly, Paige shifted her gaze to the bowl of lily of the valley on the table. "I was going to deal with her Sunday night, but she had that Neanderthal in there with her, Reno," she said. "Ah, the irony—Victor was leaving me for someone who was cheating on him. Not that Victor would have cared. He'd had countless other women, but with them it was just sex. Anything with open legs was good enough for Victor—and I do mean anything."

Sex with *anything*? An image of the inflatable sheepdog flitted across my brain.

I tried to picture the scenario Paige was describing. Hoffman and Paige had a relationship that had survived other affairs, but he had finally dumped her—for Bethany.

Right now, however, it was important to keep Paige talking while I figured out a way to escape—*if* I could escape. "How'd you pull it off?" I said. "Poisoning Hoffman, I mean?"

"I lured him over for one last fling. It was just like one of our games that we played all the time," she said, half closing her eyes. "When he arrived here that night, I met him naked at the door, my whole body slathered with honey. All over, even my breasts. I even put honey down *there*."

Paige ran her hand over the surface of her blouse, caressing herself. With long, sinuous strokes, she slid her fingers all the way down to her crotch to demonstrate how she'd spread honey all over her nakedness.

As she touched herself she swayed back and forth on the chair, as if in a trance.

Then her eyes snapped open. "It was poisoned honey, of course," she said in a sharp tone, breaking the spell. "I cooked it up right here in my sink, infused it with a tincture of lily of the valley.

"But it must have tasted good. Victor licked it off me like a butterscotch sundae." Paige's lips curved into a cold smile. "It took about an hour for him to begin to vomit."

I was trying to make sense of her story. "You poisoned him here, at your house? But his body was found on the clinic's porch—did you drive him back there in his car?"

"Yes. I told him I was taking him to the clinic to get help," she said. "He was a mess by then. I covered the front seat of his car with plastic so there wouldn't be any trace of vomit later."

For the first time, I noticed a sheet of plastic folded next to Paige's chair on the floor. Was that for me and my soon-to-be "mess"?

"Victor was still half alive when I got him up onto the clinic porch," Paige continued. "I had to practically drag him. Then I sat next to him and waited for him to die. It didn't take long."

"Weren't you worried about someone coming along and seeing you up there on the porch?"

Paige's lips twisted again. "I wasn't out there long," she said. "I told Victor I would call for help and waited inside the clinic. He didn't even know I was killing him. After he was dead, I went out the back way."

"But you must have returned to stick those forks through his eyes."

Paige shrugged. "Victor always appreciated black humor," she said. "He just didn't know that the final joke would be on him."

So, Paige must have been the person I'd seen driving Hoffman's car away from the clinic's parking lot, the morning I discovered his body.

As if sensing my thoughts, Paige's green eyes hardened to jade. "I've been watching you since that first morning," she said. "Wondering if you'd seen me. If you'd recognized me. You didn't, apparently, but you kept asking stupid questions anyway. By the way—you're too fat for TV."

I wondered if those would be the last words I ever heard. Talk about adding insult to injury. "And Marjory?" I said. "Did you kill her, too?"

Paige gave me a reproachful look. "Marjory was really your fault, you know," she said. "When you kept haranguing her about those missing boxes of Victor's papers, she figured out that I hadn't turned everything over to the police."

"She confronted you?"

Paige nodded. "And then I followed her over to Victor's house. I even brought along her own garden tool to use as the weapon."

"What was in those boxes? What were you holding back?"

"Victor's diary, and all the little notes I used to hide for him here and there."

Now I remembered that when I'd questioned Marjory about the missing boxes, her expression had changed—that must have been when she put two and two together about Paige.

I felt a sickening stab of pain in my stomach. Next undoubtedly would come the heaving.

I was out of options, and out of time. Reaching inside my pocket, my hand closed around the smooth casing of the pocketknife.

To hide my movements, I flinched and curled around slightly, as if gripped by stomach pains. It wasn't totally an act—my stomach was starting to shoot off Scud missiles of pain.

Slowly, I slid the Swiss Army knife from my pocket, holding the case in my cupped hand in front of my stomach. I curled my head over the hand, moaning. Then I used my teeth to pull up on the grooved edge of the blade. It swung open.

Now came the dicey part—unlocking the handcuffs.

Pretending to writhe, I pivoted around until I was facing the handcuffs, my back to Paige. Then, saying a silent prayer, I plunged the tip of the blade into the keyhole and pulled straight up toward the chain.

Nothing. It didn't work.

"What are you doing?" Paige's shrill question sliced across the air.

I glanced back to see Paige springing to her feet. She snatched up the kettle from the table.

Holding the knife close to my body, I whipped around and rose to a half stand. Then I waited.

Her face contorted in a snarl, Paige charged me like a bull rhino. She swung the kettle high, then brought it toward my head in a sweeping arc.

Just before the impact, I made a sharp fencer's lunge forward, thrusting the blade of the pocketknife straight ahead like a bayonet.

There was a fleshy *thwak* as the tip of the blade punctured the inside of Paige's wrist.

Paige let out an animal scream. Dropping the kettle, she staggered back, her wrist spurting blood. She bumped into the table, which sent the bowl of lily of the valley crashing to the floor. Flowers and broken glass washed across the wood.

I knew I'd only bought myself a few seconds. Desperately, I tried the handcuffs again. Using the pointy tip of the knife, I jiggered the keyhole. And jiggered again.

There was an audible click as the pawl inside the lock yielded.

Hooray for cheap Chinese imports, I thought, yanking my hand free.

Paige flew at me again. This time as she came, her feet slipped out from under her on the wet floor. She went down, landing on her ass in the middle of the glass splinters and flower mulch.

I pointed the knife at her. "Back off, you skinny ass bitch," I said. "You just lost your victim."

I took a couple of lurching steps. I was starting to feel dizzy. Even with the knife for protection, I knew I wasn't on safe ground yet.

Just then came the squealing sound of a vehicle— no, two vehicles—slamming on their brakes in front of the house. Then the sound of car doors opening in rapid succession.

Seconds later, I heard a staccato pounding on the front door.

Hugging my stomach with both arms, I made my way through the adjacent living room and threw open the front door.

Detective Reed was standing there. He had his gun drawn. A few feet behind Reed was another cop who held a shotgun in his hands.

Reed scanned my face. "Where's Paige Nelson?" he said. Without waiting for a reply he rushed past me, followed by the shotgun cop. They quickly spotted Paige, who was thrashing on the dining room floor.

"Police," Reed announced, aiming his gun at her. "Stand up with your hands on your head."

Paige rose to her feet. Swaying slightly, she raised her hands. Blood trickled down her arms from the cuts to her wrist and palms.

Reed motioned for the shotgun cop to take charge of Paige. Then he turned to me. "Are you all right?" he asked.

By now my gums were burning, and my stomach

had turned into a lava pit. "No, actually I don't think so," I said. "I need Poison Control. Paige spiked my tea with Christmas rose."

I took a wobbly step toward Reed, then collapsed into his arms.

Don't vomit all over his nice herringbone suit, I told myself.

Then I passed out.

Chapter 26

Shake Up Your Exercise Routine

Once your body gets used to a certain type of exercise, you need to shake things up by varying your routine. If you've been doing the treadmill every day for twenty minutes, try water walking. When you're totally bored with everything, remember that sexual activity burns roughly 150 calories per session, depending on how rough the session, if you catch my drift.

—From *The Little Book of Fat-busters* by Mimi Morgan

"So how did you discover that I was at Paige's house?"

It was a question I'd been dying to ask Detective Reed, who was sitting in a chair next to my hospital bed. He had a tape recorder in his lap and was recording my statement about my toxic encounter with Paige the day before.

"Kate, this is an official police interview," Reed said, giving me a gently reproving look. "Can you let me ask the questions for a second?"

"Okay," I said, grinning. I leaned back against the bed pillows. Next to me was a tray of bland-looking hospital food. But my stomach was feeling so delicate, even a Whoopie Pie wouldn't have tempted it at that point.

Yesterday, the emergency room doctors had washed the Christmas rose out of my system by lavaging my stomach, a truly disgusting procedure. I'd probably lost about five pounds from the whole episode; but, trust me, the Christmas in a Cup Diet will never be a best seller.

Reed clicked off his tape recorder. "I guess I can answer that question, though," he said.

The tip about Paige came from Lou Bettinger, Reed told me.

"Bettinger called me right after you left my office," he explained. "A researcher in his office turned up the fact that Paige had a history of mental problems. Evidently she once tried to poison a boyfriend who broke up with her," he continued. "The guy never pressed charges, though, so it didn't turn up on a criminal check."

So, Lou had called Reed about Paige. If it hadn't been for that call, I might never have made it out of Paige's house alive.

"I knew you had an appointment with someone, and I was afraid it might be with Paige," Reed continued. "We went to her house to check it out."

"Just before you arrived yesterday, Paige told me she killed both Hoffman and Marjory—Hoffman with poison, and Marjory with a sneak attack from behind," I said, rubbing the back of my neck.

Reed nodded. "Paige confessed to both murders after we brought both of you to the hospital last night," he said. "You stuck her pretty good with that knife, I have to say."

"And she almost stuck me in the ground," I said, wincing. "How's she doing, by the way, our little Miss Paige the Poisoner? Dying, I hope?"

Reed grinned. "She's recovering nicely in the hospital's psych ward," he said.

"Paige told me that Hoffman dumped her for Bethany Williams, and that's why she murdered him."

"Yes," Reed said. "However, Bethany doesn't

seem to be the sort of girl to let dust settle. She's moved in with Reno O'Malley, and I believe they're engaged. She seems eager to put the whole thing behind her."

"Bethany and Reno will make a charming couple," I said. "I'm sure they'll have troglodyte children."

Reed laughed. It was a nice sound to hear again.

I was still trying to piece together all the events of the last few days. "So I'm thinking that Paige was behind both of the previous vandalism attacks on me," I said. "She slashed up my car, and hung that scarecrow in my bathroom shower. Am I right?"

Reed shook his head. "The car, yes, but evidently not the scarecrow," he said. "Investigator Corley found Marjory Cash's prints all over the shower tile and the scarecrow in your bathroom."

"*Marjory's* prints? Really?"

"Yes. Before Paige killed her, I guess Marjory had her own reasons for trying to scare you off. What can you tell me about that?"

I shifted uncomfortably under Reed's steady gaze.

"I found out that Marjory ran errands for Hoffman, and they included picking up his sex play toys from the Vixen's Den," I confessed after a moment. "Marjory freaked when I asked her about it."

"Marjory knew you could put your information about her on the news," Reed said. "She probably wanted to scare you off."

"I guess Marjory caught on too late to what Paige was up to," I said. "Paige said she killed her to protect some missing boxes," I said.

"We found those boxes in Paige's closet last night," Reed said. "They contained some threatening notes she sent to Hoffman when he tried to break up with her. They also contained an impressive collection of neon-colored dildoes."

"I think I saw that collection at the Vixen's Den,"

I said, grinning. "Do you think it was Paige, then, who scared Anita Thornburg by sticking the lilies on her door? Anita thought someone might have broken into her house."

"I'd have to assume so, but because Thornburg didn't report it, we don't have any evidence connected with that," Reed said, scribbling some more notes on his pad. "I'll check it out."

"What will happen next with Paige?" I asked.

"Her case will wend its way through court," Reed said. He kept his eyes glued on his notepad. "I'd lay bets she finds a good lawyer and winds up back in the mental hospital rather than jail. Maybe she'll even hire that boyfriend of yours, Bettinger."

"He's not my boyfriend." My retort sprang out with a surprising arc of energy. "What makes you think that?"

Reed shrugged. "The way he protects you," he said. "I'd be careful of Bettinger going forward, if I were you. He seems like a guy who cuts corners to get what he wants."

"And what do you think he wants?"

"Right now, I'd say he wants *you*."

"What?" My eyes must have widened at his tone. Reed sounded almost jealous.

For the first time since I'd met him, Reed's gaze faltered. He stared at the window blinds as if trying to see through them. Then he cleared his throat.

"Until Paige's case is prosecuted, I must mind my department's p's and q's. Bother those conflict-of-interest rules," Reed said with a tight grimace. "But I'll just say this: Once that's done, I'd like to get to know you better. Would you fancy that?"

"Yes, I'd fancy that very much," I echoed, feeling a flush creep up my neck. "But won't it be months before the trial is over?" I blurted.

Reed chuckled. "Possibly, I'm afraid," he said. He reached for my hand and gave it a squeeze. Then he glanced down at the tape recorder and flinched, a startled expression on his face.

"Bloody hell. Did I turn this bloody tape off?"

"Yes, I think so," I said, laughing so hard my belly jiggled. "Ow."

"Ooh, mind your stomach, now," Reed said, shooting a concerned glance at my midsection. "You've got me right spun round, did you know that, Kate?" he added, leaning in again. "From the very first day."

"Right back at you . . . ," I said softly, and then cringed inwardly. To a Brit, that reply probably didn't even make *sense*. "I mean, me too."

But Reed seemed pleased by my incoherent reply. "Well, I have everything I need, I guess," he said, releasing my hand. "I'll have my partner get the rest of your formal statement later. I'll be back in touch with you, Miss Gallagher," he added quietly. "Sooner rather than later."

Then he was gone again.

After he left I lay back against the pillows for a long time, staring up at the hospital room's ceiling and thinking about everything Reed-related. To my total surprise, I felt a stab of frustration, mixed with uncertainty. Reed had finally let me know how he felt, but made it clear we'd have to wait before advancing our relationship further. By the time Paige's trial ended, I could be living anywhere—what were the odds that we would both be feeling the same way, six months from now? Would I be a fool to wait for him? Would I be a fool *not* to?

I sighed. Reed's vigilance about observing his department's "p's and q's" was admirable, but . . .

Obedience to the rules. It was one thing we didn't seem to have in common.

These days, apparently garden-variety poisoning doesn't require more than a brief hospital stay. So within a few hours of Reed's departure, I was released.

Brian wasn't due to arrive at the airport until later that night, and my car was still parked at Paige's house, so I called my friend Evelyn at the Renaissance House to pick me up and get me transferred to a hotel. The Hoffman Clinic was definitely out as a destination—I hoped never to lay eyes on it again, not even to pick up my things. Retrieving my car and possessions would be Brian's first mission when he arrived.

Evelyn got me settled into my hotel, which was located in the fashionable Five Points neighborhood in Durham. After about an hour of her clucking around in mother hen mode, I thanked her profusely and practically pushed her out the door.

I felt fine. So amazingly fine, in fact, that I decided to spurn the doctor's advice and check out the room service menu—surely a few teaspoons of boiled rice wouldn't hurt.

I was scanning the room service menu when I heard a knock. I opened the door to find Lou standing at the threshold. He had a gigantic bouquet of red roses in one hand, a tiny box in the other.

"Twenty-six roses for a speedy recovery," he said, handing me the flowers. "I made sure the florist didn't put anything toxic in these," he added with a grin.

"Why twenty-six?" I said, shocked to see him so unexpectedly.

"Your birthday?"

"Oh my God, right! Twenty-six. I totally forgot that today's my birthday," I cried, accepting the flowers. "Thank you, on behalf of both my stomach *and* my birthday."

"My pleasure, ma'am," Lou said in a faux Southern accent.

"How'd you know I was here?"

"I went to the hospital but you'd already escaped. Then I tracked you down via the grapevine."

"The Fruiter grapevine?"

"No, your work. Your boss Beatty has his stopwatch out and he's timing the seconds until you're back on the job."

I laughed. And after all that, I *had* to invite Lou in. So then, there he was in my room, with his flowers, his birthday gift, and his striated-gold eyes.

"Are you feeling as good as you look?" Lou said.

"I guess it depends on how good you think I look."

"Well, I'd say right now I'm looking at the most beautiful view in town," Lou said.

Not sure how to come back from that, I simply smiled.

"Open your birthday present." Lou handed me the box, which was wrapped in heavy silver paper with a cobalt blue ribbon.

"I should be giving *you* a present after what you did," I protested. "When you called Reed to tell him about Paige, you pulled my fat out of the fire. Literally. And I want to apologize for ever implying that I thought you were behind the attack on Marjory."

"Water under the bridge," Lou said lightly. "Open it."

I removed the wrapping to reveal a navy velvet box. I lifted the top, then gasped. Inside, suspended from a delicate chain, was a pendant of a white jade tiger. The tiger was exquisite, with tiny blue eyes made of lapis lazuli.

"Oh my God," I cried. "It's beautiful."

"She's almost three hundred years old, but doesn't look a day over thirty, does she?" Lou teased.

An antique like that must have cost hundreds of dollars, if not thousands.

"It looks much too expensive. I can't—," I murmured.

"Yes, you can," Lou said. Those were the same

words he'd used to get me into his helicopter the first day we met. "Only the white tigers have blue eyes, did you know that? Like you," he added. "You're an incredible woman, Kate Louise Gallagher."

I felt confused, remembering Reed's warning about Lou. But here he was, available and bearing gifts. And I had to admit, Lou was a deeply exciting man. Whenever Lou was around, I felt as if some kind of anti-gravity force was lifting me off the ground. It was a sensation I thought I could get used to.

"No, I really can't," I said decisively, handing the box back to him. "But I'll take the roses, thanks." Hugging the bouquet, I buried my nose into the flowers, avoiding his gaze. "How did you know it's my birthday?"

Lou threw back his head and laughed. "Finding out about someone's birthday is easy if you're motivated," he said. "Let's just say I'm motivated. And I'll change your mind about the tiger, you'll see. I'm mighty persuasive when I set my mind to it."

That much I already knew.

"I want you to meet somebody." Stepping out the door into the hallway, Lou bent down to pick up something beyond my line of sight. Carefully, he lifted a green, heavy plastic box with a wire mesh on one end. It was a small animal carrier.

"Meet Elfie." Lou said. Two round blue feline eyes peered out at me through the mesh. "She was Hoffman's cat."

"We've actually met once before, at the clinic," I said. "She's gorgeous."

Elfie had the coloring of a Siamese cat, but she was fluffy all over like a Persian, with four white paws and a majestic ruff.

"They tell me she's a Ragdoll," Lou said. "Elfie's a refugee right now, so I'm taking her back to Atlanta.

She's just another blue-eyed dame I've fallen for. I'll have to spoil her rotten, of course."

A pressure grew in my chest, but it wasn't a painful sensation.

It was the sensation of my heart being touched.

I felt my expression soften into something warm and receptive. Lou must have seen it, too, because next thing you knew, I was being lifted off the floor, physically. I'd never had a man do that before—hadn't even thought it possible.

"I apologize, but you're way too scrumptious. I couldn't help myself," he said, holding me gently in his arms. "Is your stomach okay?"

"Fine, thanks."

"What next?"

"Next you get a hernia and I take *you* to the hospital," I warned him.

Elfie meowed as if in agreement, which set me off into a helpless spasm of giggles.

Smiling, Lou placed me down gently on the bed. Somewhere along our trajectory I dropped about half the roses. Their petals spread out around me.

"This must look like every bride's dream of the honeymoon night," I said.

"Not a bad idea—we already share your middle name."

Before he even tried to kiss me, Lou worked his hands through my hair, around the edges of my ears, tracing his fingertips down the back of my neck. By the time he pressed against me, I was aching for the kiss. But first, I needed to know something.

"I always thought you and Anita . . ." With one hand, I pushed back against his chest. "I saw her picture on your wall that day I was in your home in Atlanta."

Lou blinked.

"I should have told you from the beginning," he groaned, slapping his forehead. "Except that Nita made me promise not to. She can't stand for anyone to know her business. Nita's my aunt Amanda's oldest daughter—she's my first cousin."

"No way."

"Yes, way."

"And you're not kissing cousins?"

"No way at all . . ." Lou, who'd been hovering over me, closed in until his lips settled softly over mine. I felt as if my body was going to burst apart before allowing it to fuse into his. Every skin cell was tingling, alive.

Lou unbuttoned my blouse, then gathered up my hair and pulled it taut as he kissed the back of my neck, a maneuver so deeply arousing that it sent a ripple of pleasure down my spine.

Oh my God, I could drink this up, I thought.

What came next was completely, totally yummy. And must have burned at *least* two hundred calories.

Chapter 27

Embrace the New You

As you lose weight, a couple of things happen. You start to shape up, so men notice you a bit more. You might also find yourself noticing them *more, now that you're redirecting some of your emotional energy away from food. Have fun with the emerging New You! Go out and buy some new—sexy—clothes. Experiment with new styles and colors. Kiss those black polyester slacks good-bye (you know the ones I'm talking about—the ones with the elastic band top).*

—From *The Little Book of Fat-busters* by Mimi Morgan

Two nights later over scallop platters at a great little Thai restaurant, I asked Brian to weigh in on my Lou-versus-Reed dilemma—should I wait to see what could happen romantically with Reed, or go with Lou?

"From what you already told me, I think you mean go *again* with Lou," Brian said with a sly grin. "Here's a bit of gay guy wisdom—when it comes to choosing between two guys, a bod in the hand is worth two in the bush."

He eyed the tiger pendant, which was now hanging around my neck. "Reed drew a line in terms of the timing between you two, so even if it's only temporary, let it go for now," he said. "For the orgasm thing alone, I vote you stick with Lou—he sounds incredible. Besides, you don't want to even think about dating a cop, not even a to-die-for Brit. Trust your buddy on this one. I've been there and back."

"You're probably right," I said, chuckling.

"Did you have any idea that Paige was behind those murders?"

"Not until I saw that bowl of lily of the valley on her dining room table," I said sheepishly. "You can't imagine a less likely looking murderer. Although, I should have been tipped off that she kept giving me information that she never took to the police."

Our impossibly slim-hipped Asian waitress came by. She set down a little plate with a couple of fortune cookies, and asked us if we cared for tea.

"Thanks, but no tea for me," I said, with a slight shudder.

"Well, thank God you're okay," Brian said after the waitress left. "Shows you that you should leave these investigations to the professionals—but you're your father's daughter, so I guess you've got it in the blood. What's the latest on the job front?"

Things were definitely looking up, I told Brian. That morning, Beatty had made me a full-time offer as a reporter. "It's an on-camera position. I guess I'm kind of taking over someone else's job."

I explained the whole history of my working with Silver to Brian. After he recovered from the chicken pox, Silver must have read the tea leaves about his future at Channel Twelve. He'd pulled up stakes and took off to a smaller station in Tennessee. "That leaves Silver's job open for me," I continued. "And I don't even need to lose weight—though I still plan to, of course."

"*Oo-la-la.* What'd I tell you? Congratulations." Brian said. "Sounds like your fortune's smiling. But just to be sure, have you checked your cookie? Yours is the one with the fold pointed toward you."

I released my fortune cookie from its crackly cellophane wrapping and broke it open.

"You are headed toward happiness, but beware the sins of the flesh," I said, reading it aloud. "Sounds like it's telling me not to eat the cookie."

"I wouldn't worry about it," Brian said, laughing. "A toast. Here's to your finally discovering your Inner Player, Katie-o."

"And we won't invite the Devil by spilling anything this time," I said, carefully clinking glasses.

"It only counts with beer," Brian assured me.

It was all good. I mean, here I was with an exciting new job, plus two men pursuing me. (Okay, one guy was on hold, and the other had already kind of caught me.)

Brian was right. Job-wise and romance-wise, my long-lost Inner Player—the New Me—was finally getting ready to step out and make whoopee. The kind that didn't involve Whoopie Pie, of course.

Glossary of Durham Dieters' Terms

Whoopie Pie: A devilishly delicious, traditional New England confection made of two chocolate cakes sandwiching a creamy center. Regional variations can include different flavors for the centers, but the classic center is made of a gooey filling that tastes like marshmallow fluff. Yum.

BSP: Born Skinny Person. Unless he or she is a member of the immediate family, a BSP is anathema to a WCP (Weight Challenged Person).

WCP: Weight Challenged Person. This is exactly what it sounds like. A category that includes most of the people in the United States.

All Gone Syndrome: A syndrome that descends on WCPs, especially when eating out, that compels them to eat everything on their plate. All Gone Syndrome is typically followed by strong bouts of Next Day Remorse.

Next Day Remorse: An emotional state that sets in following unplanned episodes of eating caused by All Gone Syndrome. (Next Day Remorse can also apply to drinking and sex.)

Snarf, Snarfing: Consuming massive quantities of trigger foods. Also called binging.

Jumbo, Overweight, Normal, Thin: The *über* categories that some dieters use to describe their clothing sizes as they lose weight (or gain). Each category spans roughly two to three clothing sizes.

Rebound weight: Weight that was recently lost through dieting, and even more recently regained by repeated episodes of All Gone Syndrome.

Plateau: An occasional, natural pause in the weight loss progress. Sometimes dieters hit a plateau even when following the diet religiously. But then sometimes they blame lack of progress on a plateau, when it's really the result of the All Gone Syndrome. Although properly a noun, dieters frequently use plateau as a verb. As in, "Dammit, I've been plateauing all week."

Gorgetown: An area jam-packed with every kind of eatery known to mankind. The most frightening section of Durham, from a dieter's point of view. To avoid temptation, some people hold their breath while passing by this strip of the 15/501.

Salt effect: A mystical belief in the power of salt to cause temporary water weight gain. When a dieter disappears into Restaurant Row and emerges three days later and twelve pounds heavier, he will be reassured by other dieters not to worry about the weight gain. "It's just salt."

Retread: A dieter who has previously lost weight on the program and returned because he regained the weight after going home.

Real world: Home, the place dieters must return to after losing their weight at the diet clinic. When dieters fail to manage the challenges of eating in the real world, they become retreads.

Trigger foods: Foods that cause us to overeat (see Snarf). The most popular trigger foods include bread, pizza, and any kind of chocolate (especially M&Ms).

About the Author

Kathryn Lilley is a former television journalist. She lives in Southern California. This is her first adult novel. Visit her on the Web at www.kathrynlilley.com.

"Live fit or die"

—Body Blast motto

Exercise can really be murder.

I learned that lesson the hard way last spring, when I signed up for a fitness boot camp in the Great Smoky Mountains. I enlisted at the boot camp—called Body Blast—to do some emergency downsizing on my butt, only to wind up sugar-crashing in the middle of a gruesome crime scene. That's when I discovered that a diva-sized derriere is a small thing compared to a broken neck. A full figure even has certain advantages, I ultimately realized—for example, a big ass can cushion your fall when somebody pushes you off a cliff.

But before I left for boot camp, I was constantly fretting about my body's proportions. See, I make my living on TV news, a job where porking up can put a pox on your career faster than you can suck down a pound of M&M's. So when I picked up a few Christmas kilos over the holidays (more than a few, actually—Santa's motto must be "The more, the merrier, ho, ho, ho"), it felt like the end of the world. My outlook turned even gloomier when my employer, the management at Channel Twelve Action! News, in Durham, North Carolina, distributed the March personality ratings. The report showed that my audience approval numbers had belly-flopped in the category of "professional image" (read: weight).

Then there were the e-mails that viewers sent in— bless their rotten little hearts—about my expanding girth. These missives contained *oh*-so-helpful advice:

To: Kate Gallagher, Investigative reporter,
        Channel 12 News
From: A concerned fan
Subject: Have you tried Curves?
Kate dear, love your work, but what's up with your weight? Your hips are looking a tad heavy these days. You don't want to end up looking like a draft horse in a field of TV thoroughbreds.

Worse—egad!—were the *phone calls* that came in to the studio:

"Please, tell Kate that she just needs to exercise twenty minutes a day, and those pounds will come right off. But wait—is she expecting? Oh my God, is Kate *pregnant*?"

After a few of these calls, management posted a "cosmetic reminder" that warned the on-air talent to "maintain a healthy BMI, or risk being suspended from the air." They might as well have scrawled my name across the top of that memo in big, fat neon letters—no one else's dress size was in the double digits.

It all seemed so unfair, because it's not like I was *obese*. But that's the pressure you get when you're five foot five, a hundred and fifty five, and you earn your dollar on the boob tube. I tried to shift the focus to my assets—wavy auburn hair and blue eyes—by telling the cameraman to shoot me only from the shoulders up, avoiding full-body stand-ups like the plague. But nothing helped. No one gave a hoot that investigative reporting is a stress-eater's nightmare, long on stakeouts and short on healthy eating opportunities. Or how hard it was to order a salad while the cameraman grabbed his super-sized fries—sometimes, I just *had* to have a Big Mac, you know? All the negative nabobing was enough to drive a girl into a round of emo-eating.

But instead of diving into comfort food, in desperation I sent an SOS to Jason Riley, an old friend who'd grown up in my hometown of South Boston. I hadn't seen Riley in years, but I knew he'd undergone a dramatic body transformation since high school. Back then, Riley had been pale and skinny-looking, but later pumped up his muscles and went on to a career as a bodybuilder—without using steroids, he claimed. From that point forward, Riley had developed an almost cultlike following as a Pied Piper of physique makeovers. In addition to a chain of gyms in the Southeast, Riley owned Body Blast, the boot camp. Fortunately for me, the camp was located in the Great Smokies, within driving distance of Durham.

Riley sounded delighted to hear from me when I called. In just one week, he assured me, I'd be able to reclaim—or at least locate—my AWOL waistline. And as it turned out, the Channel Twelve news director, Chuck Beatty, was only too happy to expense my week at boot camp under the tax category of "ratings support." Ratings support, my ass. Literally.

To get to the Great Smokies from Durham, I headed my TR6 west on the interstate for a long while, then turned south onto a winding two-lane highway that snaked through the foothills. The mountain air was noticeably nippier than in the flatlands of Durham, and grew colder with every foot of elevation.

But I didn't mind the temperature drop because it was such a sheer joy to wrap the vintage sports car's low center of gravity around the undulating turns. Just two weeks earlier, with the help of a friendly gearhead at my local Triumph car club, I'd souped up the engine's performance with triple Weber carburetors, a hot cam-shaft, and tighter shocks for suspension. The TR6 made a throaty, satisfying roar as I downshifted into the switchbacks and goosed the tachometer against the inclines of a section of road called the Dragon's Tail.

I was having so much fun flying in the car that I forgot to watch for the turnoff. Just as I decided I'd overshot and was about to turn around, I spotted an arrow-shaped wooden sign with black lettering: BODY BLAST, 2 MI.

I was expecting to find something primitive like te-pees and Tarzan ropes when I pulled into camp at two p.m., so I was pleasantly surprised to discover a collection of log-sided buildings with angled glass fronts, nestled into the slope of a rolling hill.

I unloaded my gear and was making like a Sherpa-bearer for the largest building when a red hatchback zoomed into the parking lot. It slammed to a stop with-out bothering to pull into a space. A young Latino guy with a flattop got out from behind the wheel. Flicking away a cigarette, he threw open the hatch and unloaded a pile of gear. The guy's movements were abrupt and jerky, fueled by barely suppressed fury.

A young girl emerged from the passenger side. She looked about nineteen years old, a short little thing, five foot one at most. The girl was all-over curvy—but in a bulgy way rather than sexy—with pale features and dark hair that hung limply about her shoulders. She stood quietly off to the side, fiddling with her purse.

Tossing a sleeping bag onto the pavement, the guy planted himself directly in front of the girl, arms crossed as if challenging her to speak. She continued to dig in her bag with studied indifference. After a few more seconds of the Bag Treatment, the guy wilted. He turned away and dragged tail back to the car. Then, after revving his engine a couple of times to announce that he had rediscovered his inner alpha male, he tore out of the parking lot, screeching rubber on his way.

I was actually relieved that someone in worse shape than me had turned up for boot camp—I would have hated being the fattest one.

"Need some help?" I called out to the girl, taking a step toward her. "Somehow I still have a free hand."

The girl looked slightly startled, as if she hadn't noticed me before then. "Thanks," she said, angling an oversized backpack toward me. "I'm Marnie Taylor."

I lifted the bag by one of its straps. *"Oof,"* I said, heaving it over my shoulder. "Kate Gallagher."

"Huh. You look . . ." Marnie squinted slightly, as if trying to place me.

It was a look I was familiar with from being on TV. People recognize me and think they've met me before, not making the TV connection.

"I work for Channel Twelve news in Durham," I explained.

Her eyes widened. "Oh my God, yes! I've seen you," she exclaimed.

Up close, I could see that Marnie's eyes were red. She looked as if she'd been crying. "Are you okay?" I asked.

Marnie shrugged. "I guess, yeah," she said. "My boyfriend was just having an anger management issue. *Ex*-boyfriend, I guess I should say," she added with a grimace. "We broke up last night. He insisted on driving me here, but then he acted like a total A-hole the whole way."

"I know how that is," I said, although actually I didn't. I was pretty happy with my current boyfriend, an Atlanta-based lawyer named Lou Bettinger. But Lou had just thrown me a curveball the previous weekend by unexpectedly proposing marriage. That was something else I was planning to do during my week at Body Blast—mull over his proposal.

Marnie and I staggered under our loads as we made our way up a pathway to the main building, which was perched halfway up the hill. Inside the lobby, a floor-to-ceiling window overlooked a sports field below. Beyond the field rose a panoramic mountainscape, its overlapping ridgelines swathed in the signature bluish green mist of the Great Smokies.

I looked around the lobby to see if I could spot my friend Riley anywhere, but he wasn't in sight. So Marnie and I joined a group of about eighteen men and women who were sitting on their gear piles. Their heads were bent over clipboards, pens going. Overall, it was an ultra body-conscious group. Except for one or two average-looking Joes, the men were pumped to a fare-thee-well, with an exorbitant amount of pec development going on. Several had stripped down to their wife beaters and were horsing around, flexing to show off their biceps, which shined as if they'd just rolled off a buff-and-wax line. *What do* they *need boot camp for?* I wondered. They all seemed to know each other, too—maybe they were Riley's bodybuilding groupies. Most of the women looked like the yoga bunnies who always claimed the front row of my weekly Flow class. My usual spot in that class was in the rear, where I'd cower and hope that the teacher wouldn't criticize my Awkward Chair Pose.

Oh shit, I thought. I'd hoped that a few more exercise novices would show up. But except for Marnie, this was looking like a very tough crowd.

A tall, Nordic-looking blonde who introduced herself as Erica handed me a board and a stack of forms.

"Liability releases," she announced briskly.

I glanced down. Across the top sheet was a message: *Attention NOBIT (Novice Boot in Training): Press hard. You are making three copies.*

The forms were our promise not to sue Body Blast in the event we met injury or—*yikes!*—even *death* during the boot camp, followed by an entire paragraph of all the ways you could eat the dirt, including falling, being crushed, drowning, and heat stroke. For the first time, I started to feel anxious. What exactly had I gotten myself into?

Erica stepped to the center of the group and announced that our first activity at Body Blast would be the Eval Course.

"Our drill instructors will be evaluating you closely during the obstacle course," she announced. "And I have to warn you, some of you may not make it into the Regular Basic Training program." She swivelled her head, sizing up the assembled recruits. Her radar sweep stopped on the pudgiest blip, which was Marnie.

"As you know from your intake agreement, if you can't make it through the Eval Course, you'll be reassigned to Remedial Basic," Erica said, keeping her eyes on Marnie.

"Reminds me of the army—I had to go through basic training twice," a guy to my left muttered to no one in particular.

When Erica approached to collect our paperwork, Marnie opened her purse and started fishing for her ID.

Erica's eyes snapped on something inside her bag. "What's that?" she said. "Is that *chocolate*?"

Her face reddening, Marnie extracted a Snickers bar.

Erica snatched up the candy. Dangling the bar from two fingers like a wad of slimy hair she'd plucked from a drain, she turned to face the other campers. "I'm sorry, but we have to ask you all to turn over anything with sugar or caffeine now," she said, raising her voice. "Only *clean* foods are allowed at Body Blast. There should have been a sheet in your enrollment package explaining that," she added, lobbing a glance over her shoulder at Marnie. "Any of you NOBITs have anything else you need to turn over?"

A cowed silence gripped the room. Marnie turtled her neck into her shoulders, as if trying not to take up less space.

"I have some breath mints. You need those?" I piped up. Okay, it was a lame attempt at humor, but I was gratified to hear a chuckle bounce around the room.

The skin around Erica's eyes tightened. "If they're sugar free, you can keep those," she snapped, then swivelled on her heel and left the lobby.

Some drill instructors—aka DIs—wearing camouflage uniforms assumed control of the group at that point. Led by a gung ho young woman named Hillary, the DIs herded us in the direction of our rooms, which were spread out in a series of bungalows clustered around the main building.

Marnie and I got assigned as roommates and "body buddies," which meant that we were supposed to look out for each other during the fitness trials ahead. Our ground-floor room was a Spartan little rectangle that had twin beds covered by coarse navy blankets. Through a small window I could see a couple of Carolina hemlocks—conifer trees that released a tangerine scent when you crushed their needles underfoot—standing at attention like sentries.

"Oh, goodie, I'm glad we'll be body buddies." Marnie gave me a shy smile as we dumped our loads on the floor. "I get the feeling I'm going to really *need* a buddy to make it through this thing alive."